Heart of the Rose

A Modern
Old-Fashioned
Love Story

Alene Roberts

Published and Distributed by:

Granite Publishing and Distribution, LLC
868 North 1430 West
Orem, Utah 84057
(801) 229-9023 • Toll Free (800) 574-5779
Fax (801) 229-1924

Cover Art by Jennett Chandler
Cover Design by Tammie Ingram
Page Layout and Design by Myrna M. Varga, The Office Connection, Inc.

ISBN: 1-930980-86-8
Printed in the United States of America

First Printing August 2002
10 9 8 7 6 5 4 3 2 1

If you like *Heart Of The Rose*, you will enjoy these other romantic books by Alene Roberts:

Fragrance of Lilacs

A Rescued Heart

A Butterfly in Winter

It's Bliss

Pipit's Song

Acknowledgments

Gratefully I thank Deseret News for carrying the column *Confidentially Yours by Mary Marker.* Mary Marker was the pseudonym for Ramona Cannon, wife of Joseph J. Cannon, one of the former publishers of the Deseret News. The column ran five days a week from 1947 to 1974.

One of her columns is included in this book, and was the pivotal moral around which I wove this story.

My father, A. Jay Redd, cut the column from the pages of the Deseret News and gave it to me between my freshman and sophomore years at BYU. Its message so affected me that I applied its principles to my life from then on. I have saved the article and it has been passed down to my daughters and my granddaughters.

A thank you goes to Jim Cole in the Deseret News library for his patience in answering my questions, and in sharing with me the fascinating history behind the column. At one time he served as a copy courier, going to Ramona Cannon's apartment, picking up the column and taking it back to the newspaper for publication.

A thank you, also, to Linda Woodard at the Deseret News who gave me other pertinent information.

Dedication

To my granddaughter Leah, who took
Mary Marker's advice to heart and
didn't accept her first kiss until she
was twenty-one

Prologue

Peter Holmes entered his office in a state of near shock.

This ludicrous experiment—the challenge he had accepted—had boomeranged! And he had only himself to blame.

"Why," he asked himself aloud, casting his eyes upward, "did I ever think this idiotic scheme was going to work?" His mind was in turmoil. *All these wasted days—my miserable attempts to win—had accomplished what? Nothing! Nothing but the dreaded ordeal facing me tonight. If only …*

His desk piled high with letters to be answered, memos awaiting attention, and calls to be returned did little to lessen his agitation. Most importantly, he had to go over a stack of papers from his marketing team and make out an agenda for their next meeting. They needed to put the finishing touches on the winter promotions and get started on the spring promos.

The computer screen was at hand, ready for him to peruse the stats from last winter, and study the projections for this year. Everything looked like business as usual. The same. But would *he* ever be the same again? It felt like someone had struck him in the solar plexus, knocking the breath right out of him. The impossible had happened!

Peter Holmes paced his office. He felt trapped. What were all those things he had learned growing up? *A man's word is his bond; a man of honor keeps his word.* As a young boy, he learned and embraced these principles taught to him by his father, who was his ideal. Now, he wanted to ignore them. But favorite phrases bombarded his mind: *Do as you would be done by, On my honor ... and Man's word of honor is God in man.* He stopped in mid-stride. What was he thinking? Of course he had to go through with it. He had to do what he *said* he would do!

Engrossed in his misery, Peter blocked out the recurring ring of the intercom on his desk.

Beatrice, his secretary, frowned when he didn't answer. She got up from her desk and stepped to his closed door. As she listened to the movement inside, she stared with unfocused eyes at the brass plate: PETER HOLMES VICE PRESIDENT. *Why didn't he answer?* Hesitantly, she knocked. No answer. She knocked louder.

"Yes!"

Beatrice, surprised at the unusual impatience in his voice, opened the door timidly.

"Mr. Holmes, your father wants to see you in his office."

He ran a hand through his hair and sighed heavily. "Tell him I'll be right there."

Chapter One

Seven Days Earlier:

Droplets of sweat rolled down Peter Holmes' back and chest as he moved rapidly behind the mower. If it hadn't been for the sweat dripping onto his swim trunks, they would already be drying in the blistering August heat of the Arizona sun. His blond hair crimped into tight curls from the moisture.

Three more lengths of the yard, and Peter would take another dip in the pool. As he passed the kitchen window he saw his mother watching him with one of those *looks.* In Peter's mind, she might as well have hoisted the danger flag warning him of rough weather ahead. What was bothering her was bothering him too! He had just turned twenty-nine, and was still not married.

At the office he was the executive vice-president with the responsibilities and power that title gave him. His father, the chairman of the board, treated him with respect and viewed him as a valuable member of the team. But here at home, he was just his father's son, and at times felt like what he was, the youngest of four children. He could remedy that, of course, by getting a place of his own. So—why hadn't he?

Later in the shower he asked himself that question again, mainly because his father had been hinting about him moving out. *The last thing I want to do is live alone,* he thought. He loved this big old house, with its expansive yard, citrus trees, and swimming pool. But more than that, he enjoyed the companionship of his mother and father and his sisters and their families when they came to town. They had all been close growing up. He smiled as he recalled several times turning down an activity with his friends as a teen because he was having so much fun playing a game with his parents and sisters.

He was a family man—without a family of his own! And it was eating him up. Until he found a wife, what sense was there living alone in an apartment? He did his best not to be a burden on his parents. Though his father could well afford to get the yard care done and the pool cleaned, Peter did it for them. He also helped his mother as much as he could. *And besides that,* he assured himself, *I do my own laundry and ironing!*

His parents' motives for wanting him to have his own apartment were obvious. He was sure they didn't realize that his desire to be married far outweighed their concern! He hadn't wanted to worry them by telling them just how discouraged he was about the situation.

A confrontation was coming. He felt it. His thoughts had been on how to handle it, if and when it came. After much thought, he had come up with an idea—a crazy idea, but nevertheless, one that might buy him a little time.

ON THIS SAME day, while driving home from a meeting, Peter Edwin

Holmes Senior made a decision. He had been putting it off, but today he realized he couldn't procrastinate any longer. He could see the signals of another major crusade on the part of his wife, Gladys, to get Peter married—a crusade he knew wouldn't work. She was marshaling the forces and bringing up the heavy artillery ready to launch a full-fledged campaign, and frankly, it was wearing him out!

Turning into the driveway of his home, he parked in one of the garages around back. As he stepped into the hallway that led to the kitchen, Gladys met him.

"Edwin, we need to talk."

"Yes we do, Gladdie," he said leaning down and giving her a kiss. "Let's go into my study."

Ed followed his wife to the study, closed the door and sat down on the small leather couch beside her.

"You first, Gladdie," he said, knowing she would travel the same path they had been over and over ever since Peter's twenty-ninth birthday. He had wanted to do something drastic to wake Peter up. She had agreed in principle only, for she had told him more than once that his method of solving the problem was too severe. However, her determined expression this afternoon gave him hope that maybe she might, this time, approve his decision.

PETER BOUNDED DOWN the stairs dressed for the singles ward soccer practice only to find his parents standing there waiting for him. *Uh-oh*, he thought. *Here it comes!*

"Peter," his dad began, "we need to talk to you."

"Okay," he responded with a grin. "I have soccer practice, then I have to come home, change and run over and say good-bye to Harriet. I'll be free after that."

"No, not tonight. Now."

"But, Dad, since it's so hot, soccer practice is short in the summer. The guys need me there on time."

"They'll just have to do without you for a while."

The smile left Peter's face. "All right, Dad." He followed them into the family room.

Sitting on one of the overstuffed chairs, he faced his parents. "Okay, Dad, shoot."

"Peter, it has become very apparent to your mother and me that you've quit trying to find a wife."

Peter rested his elbows on his knees, placed his chin upon the back of his cupped hands, and stared at the floor, silent.

"What have you got to say, Peter?"

"Not a thing, Dad," he said, his eyes still on the floor.

"I take it you don't want to get married?"

Peter slowly raised his head and looked directly at his father. "You know I want to."

"For nine months now, you could have fooled your mother and me."

"Frankly, I'm baffled about the whole thing," he muttered. "I want a wife like my sisters. I've prayed, fasted, dated, and haven't found a girl who even comes close."

"Peter, you've dated some very nice girls, so I wouldn't say that," his mother stated.

"You're right, Mom, I guess I have. Apparently I can't see the forest for the trees. It's just that when I find a neat girl, I don't feel the attraction I should, or her goals and mine don't lead in the same direction."

"So you're giving up, is that it?"

"I guess that's about the size of it, Dad," Peter admitted.

"Your father," his mother interjected, "has been telling me that we've made it too pleasant and comfortable here for you, but I didn't want to believe him. I do now."

"So," his father finished, "start looking for an apartment."

"Come on, Dad," he entreated, a smile hovering about his lips, "I'm not a teenager who might straighten up with a little discipline."

"No, you're not. You are a twenty-nine-year-old vice-president of four department stores who can afford to *buy himself a house.*"

"But, I don't want to buy a home, I want my ..." He stopped himself.

"Go on, Peter, you want what?"

"My wife to help me choose it," he finished, grinning. "You caught me."

"There! You haven't given up hope, Peter," his father stated triumphantly. "You've just quit doing *your* part."

Peter looked at his watch. "Can I go now?"

"No, we're not through."

"But Dad ..."

"Look for an apartment, Peter. I want you out of this comfortable situation in one month."

A half-smile surfaced on Peter's face. "You're not serious."

"Dead serious."

Peter looked at his mother for help and saw that *look* he had seen earlier and realized she was just as determined as his father. "All right, Dad, I'll start trying to find someone to date, but I would like to stay here."

"No, Peter."

"I can't believe this. You're really going to do it? You're going to kick your only son out onto the street?" He laughed.

His parents couldn't help but laugh with him. Peter's infectious laugh made others follow suit even if they didn't know the joke. Here he was again—laughing at his situation. Few outside the family understood Peter's sense of humor, his ability to *laugh at himself.* Gladys' mind flitted back briefly to the time when his seminary teacher told her and Ed about a time Peter stood up to answer a question. He made a mistake and started to laugh, which came out sounding strangely like a burp. This made Peter laugh harder. When he had begun to gain control, one of his friends piped up, "Hey, Pete, you're the only one laughing." This started Peter's amusement all over again. Gladys couldn't help but look from son to father. Edwin was tall and blond with gray at the temples. His green eyes seemed to twinkle with a perpetual smile. The slightly upturned corners of his mouth suggested his *own* ability to laugh at himself. *Was it any wonder that Peter acquired the sense of humor he had,* she thought.

Quickly erasing his levity, Ed said, "Peter, we're serious."

Peter believed him. Deciding it was time to run *the idea* by them, he replied, "All right, I'll show you how serious I can be about searching for a wife."

"Okay, show me," his dad stated skeptically.

"You know our pet peeve in the stores, Dad?"

"I have a lot of them, Peter. Just which one did you have in mind?"

"You know, the one I was going to do a marketing plan around."

"Oh, yes."

"Wait a minute," his mother interrupted. "Why don't one of you explain what this is all about."

"Remember, Gladdie, how I've talked about people dropping clothes, knocking them off the table or hangers, or seeing something on the floor and never having the courtesy or consideration to pick it up?"

"I certainly do. You've complained about it often enough."

"Well, as you know, women seem to be the worst offenders. Peter came up with the idea of giving a gift certificate to the first woman we or the clerks saw picking something up, especially picking up something she *hadn't* dropped herself. Peter suggested that when that rare customer showed up, not only would we give her a gift certificate, but if the customer is willing, we'd pay her $100 for a photo shoot of us giving her the certificate, then use it as a newspaper advertisement for the store."

"Sounds good," Gladys said. "Why haven't you done it?"

Ed scratched his head. "I guess other matters needed our attention more, other advertising, so we never got around to it. Peter is always coming up with so many marketing ideas, I can't keep up with them."

"But Peter," Gladys questioned impatiently, "what does this have to do with you doing your part about getting married?"

"Patience, Mom, I'll get to that. I'll make a deal with you, Dad. I'll take some time off and personally watch for that woman who picks something up, but I'll only look for a *young* woman. If she's married, I'll continue looking until I find one that isn't. Not only will I give her a gift certificate, I'll take her out to dinner. And, of course, the other part of the deal is I won't have to move out into an apartment."

"You can't be serious, Peter!" exclaimed his mother.

His father thought about it a moment, then threw back his head and laughed. Gladys frowned at her husband, totally baffled at his reaction to Peter's outlandish idea.

Edwin gazed thoughtfully at his son. Suddenly, with great gusto, he exclaimed, "All right! I challenge you, Peter, to find that young woman who is thoughtful and considerate enough to pick up something *someone else* has knocked off or dropped, and who is also around your age and not married."

"I accept the challenge!" exclaimed Peter with equal gusto.

Gladys stood up, aghast. "You both call that looking for a wife?"

Her husband winked at her. "It's a start, Gladdie."

"Yeah, Mom, it's a start," Peter repeated, grinning.

Gladys, her fists on her hips, glared at both men. "I give up! I give up on both of you."

Chapter Two

After swimming a few lengths of the pool, Gladys rested on a lounge chair by the pool, enjoying the warmth of the sun. Her husband was still doing his laps. Though the Phoenix summers were hot, sunshine always lifted her spirits, and they certainly needed lifting now.

She shouldn't have been surprised at what happened with Peter and his father. From the time Peter turned fifteen, they had enjoyed challenging each other. When a challenge was offered by one to the other, it was always accepted, whether it was a contest of how many baskets they could make, how many laps they could swim in a certain amount of time, or by what percentage they could increase the sales at the stores. She had always smiled at it because they enjoyed each other, but she wasn't smiling now!

She was totally aggravated at Edwin. He had worked on her for several months to kick Peter out, and when she finally agreed, did he follow up on it? No! He fell for Peter's outlandish idea—the most unbelievable challenge yet. Or was it Ed's challenge to Peter? Yes.

It was Ed's challenge. She was so shocked over the whole episode, she was amazed she could even remember.

Beneath her almost closed eyelids, she watched Ed climb out of the pool and breathlessly plunk his tall, physically fit, fifty-eight-year-old body down on a lounge chair beside her. Noticing his wary glance, she was sure he was hoping she had cooled down. Simmering, she watched him close his eyes and relax in the warm sun.

Then she exploded. "That is absolutely the most ridiculous challenge you two have ever gotten into!"

"I know," he mumbled, a nervous smile tugging at his lips.

Swinging her legs over the side, she sat upright. "Edwin! It's nothing to smile about."

"Gladdie," he said, turning his face toward her, but not moving from his supine position, "I understand why you're upset, but at least it will get Peter off his duff and make him start looking."

"You realize don't you, Ed, if by some miracle he happens to see a woman stop and pick up something someone else has dropped, it would be an even greater miracle if she were near his age and single?"

"Yes."

"And—if that set of miracles happens, we can be almost 100 percent certain she won't be a member of the Church."

"I know."

"And she'll get her heart broken. You know that every girl who even sees Peter gets a crush on him. It isn't fair, Edwin."

"I know."

"Stop saying, 'I know!'"

He sat up and faced her. "But, Gladdie, I know all this. Don't you think all that went through my mind the minute he proposed that far-fetched idea?"

"It did? Then why did you go along with it?"

"I really don't know. All I know is I felt I should. It was just a feeling."

This stopped Gladys. She had always trusted her husband's *feelings*. After a long pause, she replied, "All right, Edwin. I don't understand it, but I'll support you, reluctant as that support is."

"Thanks, sweetheart." He reached over and took her hand, noticing as he always did how attractive she still was. Her hair was beginning to dry into its natural loose curls. Dark curly lashes framed her hazel eyes, contrasting attractively with her blonde hair. Prominent lines fanned out from the corner of her eyes because of her deep and ready laugh. She worked hard at keeping herself trim and fit by swimming vigorously every day.

"I'm feeling hot again," Gladys said. "Let's take another dip."

"Okay, I'll race you to the end and back."

She smiled. "I'll take that challenge."

As usual, he beat her by half a pool length. They climbed out and sat down, feeling relaxed.

"Why should I be surprised at this crazy turn of events, Ed?" Gladys said, breathing hard. "The trials we've had with Peter were all a little on the ridiculous side."

Ed chuckled. "They were for a fact, especially the one when he was sixteen."

WHEN PETER ARRIVED at the playing field for the practice, several of his teammates ran over to him. "You're late, Pete," one of them said. "Did you forget we're having a game this afternoon?"

"I thought that was next week."

"What's up, Pete? You never forget. Get over there quick. We've been waiting for you. We have some stiff competition tonight."

As he walked to the bench, he noted the small set of bleachers was filled with girls around twenty-one to thirty ready to cheer for their respective ward soccer team. He grinned at them and waved. A dozen hands went up and waved, all except one in the middle who glowered at him.

"Hey, Maribell, how about a smile at least!" Peter yelled.

Maribell Gunther turned her face away scornfully.

Nicole Neely, a girl from the other singles ward sitting next to Maribell, was surprised at this reaction to the most attractive guy out there. She had noticed him the minute he walked onto the playing field. Now, on closer view, she was intrigued by his wide, charismatic smile, his handsome tan face, and curly blonde hair, the color of corn silk. He was tall and had the broadest shoulders a guy his height could possibly have! *What a cool guy,* she thought.

Turning to Maribell, she asked, "You know him?"

"Yes."

"How about introducing him to me."

"Hmph! You don't want to know *him*," Maribell announced with disgust.

"Why not?" Nicole's face fell. "Is he engaged or something?"

"Far from it. He's twenty-nine years old, rich, and still not married!"

Nicole, who was twenty-seven herself, remarked, "Sounds good to me. What's his name?"

"Peter Holmes. I've known him for years. They used to call him 'Casanova Pete.' That might give you an idea what he's like. He's the 'love 'em and leave 'em' type of guy."

Nicole studied Maribell Gunther's sloppy shirt and jeans, her straggly hair, and raised a brow. "Did you date him?"

"No. I wouldn't date him if he asked me." She rolled her eyes. "With his reputation."

"Tell me about it," Nicole asked, thoroughly intrigued.

Leaning over eagerly, Maribell swiped a strand of hair behind her ear. "When Peter turned sixteen, did he date? No! But he went around the ward and stake kissing every girl he could. Just wanted free kisses without spending a dime on them."

Nicole laughed. "How did he manage that?"

"He'd take a girl outside in the parking lot at a dance or outside on the lawn at a party. You name it."

"The girls could have refused, couldn't they? He didn't force them, did he?"

"Oh, that's what's so disgusting. He didn't have to do a thing. The girls practically threw themselves at him. After he kissed them once, he *never* asked them for a date. Like I said, he'd 'love 'em and leave 'em!' In fact, an informal club was even formed, a club called: 'Girls Who Have Been Kissed By Peter Holmes.'"

Nicole laughed again.

"It's not funny, Nicole. Several of the braver members of this growing club went to see Peter's bishop to complain. The Bishop called his parents in and talked to them. From what I heard, they had no idea Peter was doing that because he wasn't even dating."

Nicole could hardly keep her eyes off the subject of the conversation. "Did that stop the kissing?"

"I asked him point blank if he'd stopped kissing all the girls. Now listen to this. He grinned and said, 'Yeah, but I sure had a great time while it lasted.'"

Smiling, Nicole said, "He didn't sound very repentant did he? Has he been a better boy since?"

"No!"

Shocked, Nicole replied, "You don't mean it. Surely he doesn't still go around kissing the girls?"

"No, but I think he's dated every girl in every stake!"

"You're exaggerating, Maribell."

"Well, not much. He dates them a couple of times and drops them."

"I can't see what's wrong with that. At least he's *dating*. So many guys have become so complacent, they sit back like a potentate waiting for their subjects to bow to their almighty masculine charm."

Maribell thought about this a moment, not exactly sure what Nicole meant. "Huh?"

"What I mean, Maribell, is they just sit back waiting for the girls to make the moves, basking in their freedom from responsibility and commitment."

"You're right! Most of the guys are so lazy." She paused. "Come to think about it, Peter Holmes hasn't dated at all for quite a few months."

"How come you know so much about him, Maribell?"

"Oh, Peter and I have kind of a love-hate relationship I guess. I ask him about everything, and he grins and tells me what he wants me to know, then I find out the rest from other sources."

"Sounds to me like you have a crush on him."

"A crush!" she almost shrieked. Heads turned in her direction. Embarrassed, Maribell lowered her voice. "I most certainly do not have a crush on Peter Holmes. Why, do you know what he's been doing lately?"

Nicole shook her head, eager to hear. Though the game had begun, the conversation was much more interesting.

"He'll go up to a girl and ask if they'd like to see such and such a movie. They *always* say yes because they're all dying to go out with him, all except me, of course. When they say yes, he says, 'It's on at such and such a theater. Go see it.'"

"Why in the world does he do that?"

"That's what I'd like to know!"

Maribell had finally run out of tidbits about Peter Holmes, so Nicole turned her attention to the man himself, who was aggressively engaged in a hotly contested match.

The game was a close one. Peter's face, flushed from the summer heat and the fire of competition, would have turned a deeper red if he could have heard the gossip about his sullied reputation at sixteen. The last part of the conversation would have only brought a sardonic smile and a shrug of the shoulders.

AFTER ARRIVING HOME and taking a quick shower, Peter left for Harriet's. On his way, he realized how much he was going to miss her while she was in California trying to peddle her CD. Though he felt her voice was good enough to hit the professional market, he didn't feel she would have the success she was hoping for. "The competition out there in the music world is just too cutthroat," he muttered to himself, wishing it were otherwise for her sake.

He thought about Harrie, as he affectionately called her, and their unique relationship. They had been friends for years. Two years ago, they began dating. Harriet was overweight and extremely casual in her dress, but she was a pretty girl with a great personality, and a lot of spirituality. He had felt himself drawn to her. They had almost fallen for each other, but both of them, for some reason, didn't feel it was right. After a lot of soul searching and prayer on both their parts, they reluctantly quit dating, but remained close friends.

Harriet lived with her grandmother, who had raised her. Her grandfather had died five years before, leaving her grandmother well off. Peter drove into the circular driveway of Camille Flower's nice middle-class home and parked in front. He stepped up on the porch and rang the bell. Harriet opened the door, grinned and gave Peter a quick sisterly hug, after which she led him into the parlor, as she called it. They sat on the couch together.

"So, Harrie, are you all packed and ready to leave tomorrow?" he asked, eyeing her usual attire, an oversized T-shirt over jeans. Her long dark hair was pulled back into a ponytail with loose strands escaping here and there.

"Yes. And I'm so excited, Peter. But nervous, too."

"How long will you be gone? I'll miss you."

"I'll miss you too, Peter. I'll probably be gone at least six months or more."

"Let me know when you're going to return, will you?"

"I will. Be good while I'm gone, Peter and quit alienating all the girls in the ward, will you?"

"Me?" he asked in mock surprise. "Alienate the girls? Impossible."

Harriet laughed and shook her head. Sobering up, she said, "You know, Peter, I don't think it's a good idea to do that movie thing you do."

"What movie thing?" he asked with exaggerated innocence.

She cocked her head and rolled her eyes in exasperation. "Peter!"

"But Harrie, I've already hurt a few girls. I don't want to do that anymore. If I find out our values aren't the same before I take her out, I won't have to drop her, so to speak, and hurt her feelings. Besides, Harrie, I ask them in a joking manner if they would like to see a certain movie. I'm not always sure they take me seriously."

"Oh, Peter. Yes, everyone knows you're a joker, and you give them that charming, mischievous smile of yours while you're asking, but nevertheless, you're such a neat guy they can't help but get their hopes up and say they'd like to see the movie. Then you lower the boom, and their hopes are dashed."

"But Harrie ..."

"I'm not through, Peter. I'm sure that some of those girls you've asked in this way got so flustered that the heartthrob of the ward, Peter Holmes, might be asking them for a date, they hardly *heard* the name of the movie."

"I hadn't thought of that, but ..."

"I'm not through yet."

"Whew! I see you want to set me straight before you leave. Well, go ahead."

"Peter, why don't you get to know the girl a little, get to be friends, then you'll find out her goals and values, and ..."

"That's a great idea, but time is running out on me. I'm twenty-nine! I don't have time to develop friendships first."

Harriet let out a sigh of resignation. "I understand your feeling of urgency, Peter. On the other hand, even if you were to develop a friendship with a girl first, she'd just get a crush on you like I did."

Peter smiled affectionately at her. He took hold of her hand. "Why couldn't you be the girl for me, Harrie? You're a hard act to follow."

"Thanks, Peter. You're a hard act to follow, too. Why do you think I'm not having any success yet?"

"But you will, Harrie. I know it. Back to my bumbling efforts to find a girl to date. You know I'm also trying to get over to the girls, in a subtle way, that they shouldn't go see those kinds of movies. They should think more of themselves."

"I know, Peter. But I think it might be a little too subtle."

"If I were a female, I'd preach to them, but guys don't do that, so what am I to do?"

"I don't know, Peter. I have my own set of problems. Frankly, I'm disgusted over most of the guys in the singles wards! Many of them won't date like they should, and there are so many lovely girls who should be married by now."

"You certainly get your share of dates, Harrie, even though, you turn most of them down."

"I know, Peter. I want the other girls to have opportunities to date."

"I do too, Harrie."

"Lately, you could have fooled me. You haven't dated for a while."

"My parents feel the same way, apparently. They're about to kick me out of the house. They think they're making it so comfortable for me, I've quit trying to find a wife."

"So what are you going to do about it, Peter?"

"Well, I've got something going with my dad that will give me a little time to find a girl to date. Maybe I'll find someone to take *your* place, Harrie, sweetheart."

Immediately, Harriet's rich singing voice belted out, "*I only want a buddy, not a sweetheart …*"

Peter laughed. This had become their usual greeting and parting. It was a song that was popular many years ago before they were born. "In that case, Harrie, good luck peddling your CD, and come home soon."

Chapter Three

Monday morning, in the corporate offices of Holmes Department Stores, Peter met with the president, Bob Spears, and the chairman of the board—his father. The three of them discussed business, profits and losses, projections for the coming year, employees and advancements, and the agenda for the coming sales and marketing meeting.

Afterward, as they left the conference room, Edwin said, "Peter, come into my office. We have something to discuss."

Peter followed his father, his eyes briefly rolling upward, certain he knew what the discussion would be about. He was hoping to put off the dreaded task for a while. His desk, as usual, was piled high with work and demanding schedules.

"Have a seat, Peter," his father said, sitting and rocking back in his chair. "I take it you have a plan on how you're going to go about winning our little contest?"

"Sort of. I thought I'd start with the Phoenix store on Central since it's the closest."

"When are you starting?"

"I have a lot to do so I uh ... thought I'd start in a few days, a week maybe."

"Hmm." Edwin rocked forward in his seat and leaned toward his son. "I would suggest you start today if you're going to find 'that needle in the haystack.'"

"But, Dad, I have things piled up on my desk waiting to get done."

"This wasn't my idea, Peter. How you get it all done is your problem."

Peter's jaw worked back and forth. He could see he wasn't going to get away with putting it off as he had planned, but he gave it one more shot. "I'm not dressed for it. I plan to wear jeans and dark glasses so the clerks won't recognize me."

"Good idea. Go home, put them on, and get started."

Peter blew out a heavy breath and threw up his hands. "Okay. I guess I'll have to work late in order to get everything done." His tone pleaded for sympathy.

"Whatever you have to do, do it," his father replied grinning. "And good luck."

"Thanks a lot, Dad," Peter mumbled as he got up.

AFTER GOING HOME and changing to jeans, Peter drove to the North Central store knowing what was ahead of him—pure boredom. He knew it was a useless exercise watching for that improbable young woman, but it was buying him time until he could at least find someone he *wanted* to date.

A day never goes by that I don't pray to find a wife, he thought.

But I know I've stopped doing my part. I'm stumped. I don't know how to try anymore. "I've tried everything!" he muttered aloud, attempting to reassure himself. "I've met and dated every girl in the stake and many in the other stakes! Or at least it *feels* like it."

Arriving at the store, he parked and walked briskly into the main entrance of Holmes Department Store in jeans, sunglasses, and a visor cap. Just inside, Peter stopped and admired his handiwork. He had suggested to his father, soon after he started working for him, that the high-ticket items, jewelry and perfume, should be displayed in the front in an inviting way. To the right a beautifully decorated alcove housed the expensive jewelry, diamonds, opals, rubies, etc. Cushioned seats, curving to follow the line of the low counters, drew the customers who wanted to look and contemplate the purchase of engagement rings, wedding bands, and other special items. Soft music played while the customers sipped fruit drinks from delicate glasses. At night, a burglar-proof gate slid across the alcove. This section competed admirably with jewelry stores throughout the area and brought high profits to the company.

Behind the perfume counter in the center, the clerks were trained to give special service to those women who were wanting to buy perfume but were undecided over which fragrance they liked. The clerk would dab the customer's chosen perfumes on small individual blotters with the names of the fragrances on them. Each blotter was slipped into a small plastic envelope. Then they were all placed in a floral-designed envelope embossed with the store name. The customer could then take it home and, in turn, rub a fragrance on her wrist, deciding at her leisure which of the scents she favored. This also had been Peter's idea. In his mind, unique service was a top priority in the marketing field.

The store was buzzing with activity. Holmes' stores were noted for their good sales. At present, they were in the midst of their

August sale, 40 to 75 percent off the last of the summer clothes, making more room for the new fall line. His father, a great merchandiser, outsold most of his competitors, in spite of the fact that while the clothing was always fashionable and up-to-date, none of it was extreme.

Peter went to the gift section first. He decided he would saunter around sale goods and pretend he was a customer. Already, several women were going through the items. One knocked off a gift, but immediately picked it up. Peter smiled. *That was easy,* he thought. He wished that this had been the challenge, but he was the one who had made the qualification more difficult.

After an hour of watching women look through things, or rather, 'plow' through them, leaving them in haphazard piles, his patience was getting thin. He was itching to go straighten up the tables and pick things up himself. To keep from acting on this impulse, he went up to the department that carried women's better dresses.

The minute he arrived there, he cringed as he saw a middle-aged, athletic looking woman step on a dress that had fallen off the hanger. Immediately, he went over, crouched down and tried to pick it up, not realizing that his visor had brushed the woman's leg as he tried to extricate the dress.

"Excuse me, ma'am, could you please ..." A sudden thud on top of his head caused him to tumble to the floor. He looked up dazed.

"How dare you, young man! Clerk! Clerk!" she shrieked.

Without thinking, Peter leaped to his feet and ran in and out of the racks of dresses and down the aisle. Suddenly, he felt a powerful force hit him in the back and down he went. The next thing he knew, he was being handcuffed and pulled roughly to his feet. Half doubled over, gasping for the breath that had been knocked out of him, he heard a familiar voice.

"All right, mister, we're going to the back room and ..."

Peter's head shot up. He found himself gazing eyeball to eyeball into the wide face of Marv, the store's huge security officer.

Marv blinked several times, not believing his eyes. "Mr. Holmes?"

"That was some tackle, Marv," Peter grunted. "I may never be the same again."

"What uh ... were you doing, Mr. Holmes? The clerk said you or a man dressed like you was down on the floor rubbing a woman's leg."

A crowd was beginning to gather around them. Peter, realizing his dark glasses had fallen off, frantically searched the floor. Locating the glasses, he whispered to Marv, "Grab those glasses and let's get out of here and into the employees lounge." They pushed through the curious onlookers, who had witnessed the altercation, and walked rapidly away.

Several women in the group shook their heads sadly as the officer escorted the handsome, supposed shoplifter around the corner.

When they entered the lounge, Peter was relieved to see it empty. He turned to Marv, shaking his head. "You are some security officer. Where in the heck did you come from anyway?"

"Oh, I was around. I try to do my job well." He smiled proudly.

"You sure did it well today. Too well!"

Marv stared at him slightly puzzled.

"Hey, Marv, don't just stand there, unlock these cuffs!"

He grinned. "Are you sure you weren't rubbin' that woman's leg?"

"Uncuff me," Peter growled, "or I'll have you permanently stationed by ladies lingerie."

"Okay," Marv said, shaking with silent laughter as he unlocked the cuffs. "So why the hat and dark glasses? And why were you down on all fours? You takin' a survey or somethin'?" he asked with a teasing grin.

Peter rubbed his wrists, and glared at him. "Yeah, I'm takin' a survey or somethin'. That woman was tromping on a dress! All I can tell you, Marv, is that I made a deal with my father."

"Let's see if I've got things straight. You made a deal with your father to see how many ladies' legs you can rub in a day?" he asked, chuckling at his own question.

A smile twitched at Peter's lips. "I warn you, Marv, mum's the word. Got it?"

"Got it."

"See you later," Peter said, leaving the lounge. Grimly, he headed toward ladies lingerie. This time he watched from a distance, neither getting near the horde nor trying to salvage merchandise. After an hour of total boredom, he left.

While driving back to the administrative offices, Peter considered this contest, wondering if he had been a little hasty. Surely his father wouldn't expect him to waste two or three hours *every day* as he had this morning! Upon arriving, he went directly to his father's office.

"Well," his father grinned, "back so soon?"

"Soon? It felt like a week!"

"How did it go?"

"It went well, except for being bashed on the head by a purse belonging to an NFL fullback while I was trying to rescue a dress she was trampling on. Apparently my hat touched her leg. Then she started screaming to the clerk for help. I got up and ran. Next thing

I knew I was tackled from behind and found myself on the floor being handcuffed by Marv."

Ed Holmes blinked a couple of times then broke into laughter. He stopped only long enough to ask, "That really happened?"

"It did," Peter replied, trying hard to keep a straight face.

His father laughed so long, Peter gave up and started to walk out.

"Hold on, son," his father gulped. "where are you going?"

"To work, Dad. My desk is piled high. Besides, I'm allergic to mobs, especially female ones."

"Go watch for a morning at the west side Phoenix store tomorrow," his dad suggested. "The next day go to the Scottsdale store, and the day after that the Mesa store, or start over again."

"Every day? For a whole morning? You can't be serious, Dad."

"I'm very serious. How can you find that young woman unless you really work at it?"

Whoa! Peter thought. *I was so sure Dad wouldn't want the marketing to suffer because of this lamebrain idea!* "Dad, I was intending to drop into one of the stores only now and then." *About once a week for an hour, maybe,* he added to himself.

"Only now and then? If we're also going to use this as a marketing stratagem, let's get on with it."

"But, Dad, as I said, my desk is piled high with work."

"Go to the stores at night, then. I'm sure you'll see more young women at that time since most of them work."

"I can't go at night. All this week I have church obligations."

"Well then, I guess you'll have to continue to watch during the day. You might delegate some of your work to Dan; he wants to move up."

"Dad, I'll go crazy if I have to spend most of a morning at each of the stores during this sale. Maybe later."

"Maybe later?" Ed Holmes' smile vanished. "This was your idea, Peter, not mine. How can you find that young woman if you just glance in once in a while?"

"Uh ... frankly, I really don't expect to find her if I spend all day every day for a year." At this admission, he noticed his father's face assume an unyielding expression.

"Oh? Then why did you suggest this?"

"Well, I guess it was wishful thinking. I've always wanted to reward a courteous customer," he added honestly.

"A sale is a great time to watch, Peter, because of the number of women who shop. I feel Plan A should be that you watch every morning during this sale. If you don't see the young lady, we'll talk again. Maybe you can implement Plan B—dropping in at the stores and watching for an hour or two at each store once a week for about a month."

Peter panicked. "But, Dad, the sale continues for several more weeks." He paused, opened his mouth to say something, then changed his mind. "All right, Dad. I'll go to each of the stores every morning this week and *waste* my time." With that, he turned and strode out of the office, shaking his head, feeling as though he had been outmaneuvered somehow.

Ed leaned back in his chair and smiled. He, too, knew it was a waste of time. The odds against Peter finding just the one he was looking for were far too high. It was going to be awkward for Peter to do this, but he had been slipping into a far too comfortable rut, enjoying the comforts of home and not dating. Ed hoped that it would spur him on to seriously look again in the *right* direction. Ed's first reaction to Peter's proposal had been to dismiss it. Then he had a distinct impression he should accept it.

The marketing would suffer, he knew. But it was worth it. Peter's marketing had already added substantially to the business of the four stores. Leaning back in his chair, Ed remembered when Peter, at thirteen, had asked if he could work in the store closest to home. He had put him to work in the back rooms unpacking merchandise, cleaning up afterward, and breaking down boxes. Since Peter had proved to be a good worker, he let him take inventory and run errands. When his son turned sixteen, he allowed him to begin clerking.

Peter had continued to work hard and save enough to keep himself on a mission and pay for most of his college. He worked part time while he went to school year-round, graduating in business administration at twenty-three. When he had gotten a masters in marketing, he came to work for him at the age of twenty-five.

An uneasy thought struck Ed. What if, by some wild fluke of chance, Peter did see a young woman doing that courteous thing—a woman near his age and unmarried? The chance of all three coming together was one in a million, but what *if* it happened? Ed blew out a gust of air. If it did, he could see real complications—the kind Gladys mentioned—the girl getting a crush on Peter and getting hurt. He reminded himself again that he felt he should challenge Peter. His wife had always trusted his feelings. He hoped his impression was right this time, because he would be in the doghouse big time with Gladys if it wasn't.

Chapter Four

After getting to the office at 7:00 Tuesday morning, Peter worked until 9:30, then reluctantly left for the west side Phoenix store on Bethany Home Road. He was feeling quite disgusted with himself for suggesting this stupid idea! In the first place, the whole plan was to have bought him time! He had figured that if he personally watched for that illusive, courteous, young customer for about an hour at one store once a week, this would give him *weeks* to find a girl to date. But the way his dad had maneuvered him into doing it, it wouldn't buy him a nickel's worth of time!

Peter had never reneged on a challenge, nor had his dad. But he was sorely tempted to do that very thing now. His dad was right. It was obvious he was more apt to see who he was looking for during a sale, simply because of the number of women shopping. *But if by some fluke I do stumble upon her any time soon, where does that leave me? Nowhere! The pressure to date—just to be dating—will be on again.*

At the moment, the only thing that lifted his spirits was the cloudy sky with its promise of a long overdue rain, which he hoped would help alleviate the oppressive August heat.

He was dressed as he was yesterday, except for the hat. He had chosen to wear a canvas hat since the one yesterday precipitated a near disaster. The store opened at 9:00, and the parking lot was already filling up when he arrived at 9:50. Entering, he walked quickly through the store and ended up at the women's purses and wallets. He pretended to browse and, just as he did so, he saw a purse on the floor. Almost immediately, an attractive young woman appeared. She noticed the purse, picked it up and placed it back on its hook.

In spite of his attitude, Peter was impressed. He stepped over to her. "Ma'am?" She looked up at him startled. "That was nice of you to pick up that purse and replace it."

"Anyone would have done that," she said, dismissing him to look through the purses.

"Ma'am, because you did that ..."

"I'm sorry, but I'm in a hurry. I'd rather not stop for a discussion."

Frustrated, Peter tried again. "Because of your courtesy, ma'am, Holmes Department Stores would like to present you with a gift certificate."

She stopped in mid-movement and scrutinized the canvas hat, the dark glasses and jeans. What she saw clearly didn't resemble a bona fide employee of any store, let alone Holmes. "Look, mister, I don't know what you're up to, but ..."

"Ma'am," he interrupted, clearing his throat, uneasy over her perusal of his attire, "I know I'm not dressed like it today, but I'm a representative of Holmes Department Stores and I'm happy to inform you that you've won a gift certificate, and uh … one other thing."

"And what is that other thing?" she asked suspiciously.

"Dinner at a nice restaurant."

"Oh? Another gift certificate for that too, I suppose?" she asked, her expression still distrustful.

"Not exactly." Peter was beginning to feel like a fool. "It would be a dinner date with me." Unnerved by her sudden expression of anger, he quickly added, "but only if …"

Before he could finish, she grabbed the purse she had hung up, and forcefully shoved it into his stomach, letting it drop at his feet. "You pick it up. I don't appreciate you trying to pick *me* up. I'm married!" She turned and walked away in a huff.

"B–but, ma'am," he called after her, "I didn't see a wedding ring!" She was out of sight before he could utter another word. He rubbed his stomach, irritation mushrooming in him like a fast-growing abscess. He stared at the purse still on the floor. *Obviously*, he thought, *I'm not going about this right. How in the heck was I supposed to know she was married!*

Before he could pick up the purse, a solidly built young woman appeared before him, eyeing him accusingly.

"Well, what're you going to do about the purse at your feet? Step on it?"

Taken by surprise, he stared at her a moment, then bent down to pick up the purse. At the same time, the woman decided to pick it up herself. Their heads collided. Since the greater force was on her side, he was bowled over, landing on his backside. His mouth opened in shock. He watched her grab the purse, indignantly hang it up and continue to shop for one, ignoring him.

He stood up and backed away, not daring to approach her with the reward she had earned. Though she wasn't wearing a wedding ring, he didn't want to take the chance of getting slammed again, especially by this young lady.

Retreating quickly to women's casual wear, Peter's mind reeled with the amazing odds that he had seen two courteous women in a row, and within twenty minutes! He smiled at a sudden thought. *Courteous?*

His surveillance continued in women's casual wear, women's sports wear, better dresses and lingerie. He spent the last twenty minutes in men's shirts. Nothing happened, just the typical pandemonium generated by Holmes' great sales.

At 12:00 noon, he went into Holmes' Tea Room and morosely swallowed down a sandwich before leaving for the office. When he stepped outside, he noticed that the fickle clouds had disappeared, leaving only the bright hot sun against a canvas of blue sky.

As he drove, it occurred to him that he obviously hadn't given this project enough thought. In fact, he admitted to himself, he hadn't given it *any*. Half-heartedly, he tried to think of an approach that would work. *Frankly, at the moment I don't care whether I succeed or not!* However, if he were to protect himself against the possibility of bodily harm, he would need to plan a little better. He decided he might look more like a representative of the store if he wore a suit and tie. But there was a problem. His blond curly hair was a dead giveaway to the clerks who knew him. The last thing he wanted was more complications. *I know, I'll borrow Dad's nice dress hat, and continue to wear dark glasses until I actually approach a woman.*

Work was piling up on him, but regardless, he had to return to the dreaded task tomorrow morning. Maybe it would be easier to move out into his own apartment!

In no mood to talk to his father, Peter went straight to his own office and dove into work. It wasn't long, however, before his father walked in.

"How did it go this morning, Peter?"

"You don't want to know, Dad." He grimaced. "Uh ... let me put it this way. If I had been in my right mind I wouldn't have gone."

Ed exhaled in relief. His uneasiness that Peter might actually find who he was looking for left. He smiled. "In that case, son, it probably can't get any worse tomorrow."

WEDNESDAY MORNING AT 10:00, Peter, dressed like an executive with his dad's fine woven straw hat covering his head, entered the Scottsdale store. His attitude toward the situation he had gotten himself into hadn't improved, but there was a new dimension to it this morning. Still restive over having to let things slide at the office for something that seemed so unproductive, and still disgruntled over his dad's suggestion to carry it on for the duration of the sale, it nevertheless had begun to arouse his determination. If he could actually discover that courteous young lady, undeniably, it would be an excellent marketing ploy. And this always excited him.

Slipping on his dark glasses, Peter's long strides took him to men's casual wear. He parked himself in an unobtrusive spot and watched women and a few men plow through the shirts leaving them unfolded in heaps. However, he noted with smug pride that men were less guilty of 'plowing.' Tired of viewing the pillage, he rounded the bend to men's suits. As in the other department, both men and women were looking through them. Still no luck. He left shortly and strode quickly to women's casual wear.

While pretending to look for something, he was unaware of the glances from both young and middle-aged women. A shrill, small voice squealed, "Mama, look!" The little girl was pointing a finger at Peter. "There's a movie star!" Her mother gawked at Peter, wondering if he really was.

Peter smiled uneasily, shaking his head at the child's mother. Quickly leaving that rack, he went two racks over, bumping into a young, stylishly dressed woman.

"Oh, excuse me," he said hurriedly and moved to the next rack.

She moved with him. "Are you looking for something for your wife?" Peter shook his head.

"Your girl friend?"

Peter shook his head, still trying to look preoccupied.

"Whatever you're looking for, maybe I can help," she said, smiling and rubbing her shoulder against his arm.

"No thanks," he said, backing away. Before he could turn and run, she was in his space, her body only inches from his. Alarmed, he stuttered, "M–ma'am, as I said, I don't need any help."

The woman, ignoring his protest, gave him a provocative smile and moved with him as he continued to back away until he bumped into a circular rack full of jeans. Having no room to move, he almost tipped the rack over. In desperation, he turned and grabbed a huge armload of jeans off the rack, whirled around and shoved them into the woman's arms, almost knocking her over. "Why don't you keep yourself busy trying these on," he suggested with a mirthless smile. Sidling out of his precarious spot, he quickly headed for the entrance. As he exited the store, he wondered what the woman was thinking. Maybe by now, she was looking for someone in a white coat to carry him off!

After this unnerving experience, he made a decision. Even though he always got fired up when his father challenged him, and as determined as he felt this morning, he, nevertheless, decided he was only going to carry on this farce, win or lose, for a couple of days. Then let the consequences come!

That night, his mother's curiosity finally got the best of her. "So, how are you doing in your search for the courteous female customer, Peter?"

"I think one might say … I'm batting zero, Mom," he answered, then muttered an excuse to go upstairs.

THURSDAY, PETER AGAIN took up his grim and lonely vigil at the Bethany Home Road store. He wore a suit and dark glasses, but this time he wore something of his own to cover his hair, a French beret cap.

Entering the store, he was unaware of the admiring stares from women who happened to be looking in his direction. Going straight to the escalator, he rode it up to the second floor and meandered around women's better clothing, pretending to look while watching women ransack through the dresses.

A high-class matronly clerk eyed him suspiciously. *There's something familiar about him,* she thought. *Was he one of those men they'd been warned about in a staff meeting?* It was obvious to her that buying clothes was not the thing uppermost in his mind! Deciding on a course of action, she intercepted him. "May I help you, sir?"

"No thank you," he replied, still preoccupied, "I'm just looking."

That voice was familiar. Now where had she heard it? She studied him more closely. "Oh! Mr Holmes?" she asked tentatively.

Through the dark glasses, Peter looked at the clerk. He would have to run into Ethyl, a clerk who had been with the store ten years! "Uh, hello, Ethyl. How are you?"

"I'm very well, thank you." She smiled broadly. "I might say, you look rather nifty today. Is there anything I can help you with?"

"Thanks, Ethyl. I was just admiring the ... uh dresses," he finished lamely.

"Are you looking for a dress for your mother?"

"No, I was just passing time. I was expecting to see someone up here. I mean I was hoping to meet someone. I'm not sure which department. I guess I'll go down to women's shoes. Maybe that's where I'll find her. Nice to see you, Ethyl." He walked away quickly and went down the escalator.

Soon after he left, a young woman came rushing breathlessly up to Ethyl. "Did you see a tall handsome man wearing dark glasses and a hat up here?"

"I certainly did, miss. He went down to women's shoes looking for you."

"Thank you! And your name?"

"Ethyl."

"Ethyl, you've been very helpful."

Ethyl frowned as she watched the young woman step rapidly to the escalator. The movement of her hips from side to side, drew her attention to the skin-tight pants. *Doesn't seem like Mr. Holmes' type,* she thought.

When Peter arrived at women's shoes, he knew he wasn't in the right department. As far as he knew, women didn't usually drop shoes like they did clothing. He had just started for the aisle when a young woman accosted him.

"There you are!"

"What?"

"Ethyl said you were looking for me." She smiled up at him in a coquettish manner.

"Ethyl? Uh, I'm sorry, miss, I'm not the one you're looking for."

"Oh yes you are. I saw you from a distance when you walked into the store, and I knew you were exactly the man I've been looking for. I certainly don't see a wedding band." Sidling closer to him, she added, "But then, a lot of married men don't wear wedding bands, do they?"

Peter couldn't have described her face if he had to because his attention was drawn elsewhere—to her low cut blouse. "No, I guess they don't," he muttered nervously. "I'm sorry, but I have to go." He turned and walked quickly down the aisle. Glancing back, he saw her following him.

He didn't dare run. Ray, the formidable security guard of this store didn't have the sense of humor Marv did. Turning a bend, he ducked behind a clothes rack and peeked around it. Just his luck. He had ditched an aggressive female yesterday only to bump into another one today! The overbearing young woman stopped, looked around searching for him. As soon as she turned her face, he dashed for the escalator, taking three steps at a time, almost toppling a man in front of him.

"Sorry, sir," he said in passing. Striding over to Ethyl's department, he frantically looked for her. She was just coming from the women's dressing room when she saw him.

"Oh, Mr. Holmes, did the young lady find you?"

"She did, Ethyl. Hide me somewhere, quick!"

Alarmed, she was about to ask why, then thought better of it. "Come with me," she stated authoritatively. She marched him into the ladies' dressing room, opening a door to a cubicle. The department was so crowded, no one noticed. "Sit down so the ladies won't see you and I'll be back to check on you," she whispered, then promptly closed the door.

As she exited, she spied the same young woman looking around. *Could she be the one Mr. Holmes was running from?*

Her question was soon answered when the young woman came over to her. "I'm sorry, Ethyl, I'm still trying to find the gentleman you said was looking for me."

"You didn't meet up?"

"Yes, we did, but we got separated somehow."

Ethyl studied the young woman. *One could say she had a pretty face*, she thought, *but still she didn't seem to be Mr. Holmes' type.* Her suspicions easily aroused, she asked rather bluntly, "Miss, I'm well acquainted with the gentleman. How did you meet him?"

"Oh, I don't know him, but I soon intend to remedy that. My horoscope said I would meet a tall handsome man today. The minute I saw him I knew he was the one."

"Miss, you're going about it all wrong. Men don't like aggressive women."

The girl smiled knowingly. "Yes they do."

"Young lady, I think you've been watching too much television or seeing too many movies. If I were the man you're looking for, I'd be out of the store by now."

"Oh! Maybe he has left the store." With that, she ran over to the escalator and went down.

"My, my!" Ethyl muttered. She squeezed through crowds of women to the dressing room. Just as she entered, a woman screamed. "There's a man in here! I saw his shoes when I bent down to pick something up."

A woman on the other side of Peter screamed. "I see his shoes, too. Clerk!" she yelled.

"I'm here," Ethyl spoke up. "It's all right. He's works for the store."

"A detective?" a fearful voice came from another stall.

"I'm coming out now," Peter stated gruffly, "so everyone cover up."

Peter opened the door, sweat dripping down his face. He hesitated. Ethyl motioned for him to come out. He followed her out quickly and as far away from the crowd as was possible.

"Thanks, Ethyl. When was your last raise?"

She smiled. "Last week. Am I due for another one?"

"You are. I'll see to it." He looked around nervously. "Have you seen a ..."

"Yes. I've seen the young lady. I told her you probably left the store. You better watch the parking lot when you leave. Her horoscope might have told her to wait around."

Peter looked at her blankly. "What? Uh ... yes, I will, Ethyl. Thanks again. Be watching for that raise."

By the time Peter had furtively reached the car, he wondered if he was in any condition to go to the office. He was as wet with perspiration as if he'd played a furious game of soccer in the hot sun. He needed a shower badly. Nevertheless, he went back to the office, hoping to avoid his father at all costs, and wondering if he could stand one more day of this absurd game. All the way back, he ruminated on his bad luck. He had never had these kinds of experiences before when visiting the stores, but then he hadn't stood around and watched the women.

Chapter Five

Friday, shaking in his boots, Peter glumly haunted the North Central store where he had first started. Back to jeans, canvas hat and dark glasses, he went to women's casual clothes and did his best not to be noticed.

The sale was still on, but the women seemed to be coming and going in a more orderly fashion. He leaned against a pillar and watched for some time. However, standing wasn't easy for Peter's long legs. Giving in, he sat down on one of the comfortable chairs placed on each side of a dressing room entrance, and pretended to be waiting for a female member of his family to try on clothes. He had talked his father into purchasing two chairs for each dressing room. For the department that carried the more costly clothing, he had even talked him into purchasing a small couch, and a magazine table so the husbands and fathers could read while waiting for the fashion show. Holmes Department Stores were now noted for comfort as well as good service.

Time passed as women came in and out of the dressing room to show their family members the clothes and to look into the three-way mirror. Peter ignored them, focusing his attention on the women who were pulling blouses, skirts and slacks off the racks, looking at them, and shoving them back. Several women, he noticed, just flung the clothes across the rack, and, of course, several things fell to the floor.

Hearing a voice in his ear, he looked up. Leaning over him in a menacing fashion was a prim stick of a woman.

"Look, mister. You have hogged that seat long enough! What have you been doing? Leering at us?"

Peter shot to his feet. "I assure you, ma'am, I wasn't leering."

"Oh yes you were!" another woman agreed. "You were ogling through those dark glasses. Every time I've come out of the dressing room, you've given me the once over."

Out of nowhere, Marv suddenly appeared. Addressing the woman who had just spoken, he asked, "What's the problem, ma'am?"

"*I* had you called, officer," the prim stick of a woman interrupted, "because this man here has been sitting on that chair for an hour, leering at us as we come out of the dressing room."

Marv's eyes followed her pointing finger, locking on the nervous Peter a few feet away. He blinked a couple of times, swallowing his surprise. "Okay, mister, come with me." Marv grabbed Peter's arm and they walked quickly away from the irate women.

As soon as Marv led him down another aisle, Peter said in a condescending tone, "All right, Marv, you've done your duty, you can let go of me now."

"Sure, Mr. Holmes, sure," Marv said, grinning. "First you're rubbing legs and now you're ogling?" Marv let out a belly laugh. Peter glared at him. "Okay, okay, I'm goin', but I'll be watching you.

After all, I'm being paid to watch for guys like you." He strode down the aisle laughing.

Peter grimaced. Marv was getting on his nerves! He ambled down an aisle just about to give up on the whole thing once and for all, when he saw a young woman with a shapely figure in front of him. Actually guilty of ogling this time, he followed her. She stopped suddenly, and walked over to a table of folded men's shirts where one had fallen into a crumpled heap on the floor.

The miracle happened. She picked up the shirt and folded it neatly, put it back, then turned down another aisle. He was totally amazed. Though having seen only the back view of the young lady, he had carefully checked her left hand. It didn't have a wedding ring. So far so good. She also didn't have a large purse with which to hit him. Things were looking up.

He followed her. This time he was going to be smart. He pulled off his dark glasses, stuck them in his pocket and yanked off his canvas hat. Quickly running his hand through his crumpled, unruly hair, he called to her. "Ma'am!"

She kept walking. "Ma'am!"

Still no response. He decided to wait until she stopped, which she did at the jewelry counter. Peter was about to say something when she sauntered off toward a display of women's scarves.

Speaking louder this time, he said, "Ma'am?"

She turned toward him. "Yes?"

The sudden breath he sucked in felt as though someone had thrown him a punch. The shock was so great, he felt tremors of it coursing its way down his spine. He had never seen such a—a homely girl in his whole life!

"Yes?" she asked again, a little impatient.

"Uh, ma'am, uh," he floundered, "I'm an executive of Holmes Department Stores," he finished in a rush, "and ..."

"And I'm Marilyn Monroe," she interrupted, resuming her inspection of the scarves.

Peter's impulse was to turn on his heel and get out of there as fast as he could, but his integrity held him fast. That darn integrity! Pushing back the impulse to run, he gulped in a breath of air. "But," he insisted, "you've won a gift certificate, ma'am."

"And you've won a kick in the shins if you don't leave me alone."

"But, miss, you *have* won a certificate," he protested, then cringing inwardly, he forged on, "as well as a dinner date with ... uh me." It came out clumsily.

She stopped inspecting the scarves and really looked at him for the first time. "Well, if you aren't heaven's gift to women," she stated with sarcasm. "But you're only a nuisance to me. Now leave me alone."

"Miss," he insisted, "when you picked up that ..."

The young woman turned abruptly, and walked over to the first counter she could find and said something to the clerk behind it.

Peter, thoroughly frustrated, stood for a few moments arguing with himself, then with relief decided to give up, telling himself that he had done his best. He started to walk away when a big hand firmly grabbed his shoulder. Turning, he looked into Marv's grinning face.

"Is this the man the clerk said was bothering you, ma'am?" Marv asked, looking at the young woman for the first time. Unable to hide his shock with the finesse that Peter had, Marv's eyes widened, staring in disbelief at the indignant and weird-looking young woman. "Is ... uh, this the man?" he stammered.

"Yes!"

Marv snorted, trying to hold back his laughter. "You can really pick 'em," he muttered in Peter's ear. "Okay, come with me, mister," Marv said once more, thoroughly enjoying the situation.

"Marv! Tell this woman who I am."

Marv's thick brows shot up in surprise. "You really want me to?" he asked starting to chuckle.

"Yes!"

"Miss, this is the man who was just sitting next to the lady's dressing room, ogling all the ladies as they came out."

Peter gaped at Marv in shock. Soon, he too was struggling to keep from laughing while at the same time trying to mouth a reprimand to the irksome Marv.

"Then arrest him officer," the incensed young woman demanded.

"I can't. He's my boss."

"Yes, I am, and I'm about to fire him," Peter stated, breaking into laughter.

The young woman first looked shocked, then confused.

"Tell her who I am, Marv, or I *will* fire you!" Peter demanded, trying to keep a straight face.

"Miss," Marv began, still chuckling, "this off-beat guy here is Peter Holmes, the Vice President of Holmes Department Stores."

"He is?" Her large blue eyes widened in total surprise. "Well, he doesn't look it!"

"You may go, Marv. You've done enough for one day."

"Yes, Mr. Holmes. I'll be on hand for the next lady who finds herself in distress on your account."

"Marv, you're fir..."

"I'm outa here!" he exclaimed, grinning from ear to ear, his palms outward as he backed away. "Honest!"

Peter glared at him, trying not to laugh. Turning back to the puzzled young woman he said, "Will you take me seriously, now, miss?" he asked, still struggling to control his laughter and *act* serious.

"Maybe, maybe not," she replied, a spark of amusement in her eyes.

Peter, taking in a deep breath to summon courage, managed to say, "Uh, we have an advertising campaign in mind. I'm vice-president of marketing, and I've been concerned at how discourteous women are, in general, in handling our merchandise. They knock things off, drop things and so on. We decided that when I saw a woman pick something up that she herself had not dropped, we would give her a $25 gift certificate. We *were* planning to have a photograph taken of us giving her the certificate and use it as an ad." He emphasized the 'were' hoping she would not consider herself photogenic. "And ..." he stopped, wrestling with himself again, "we decided that if she were unmarried, I'd take her to dinner at one of the finest restaurants in Phoenix."

Her brows rose imperiously. "You think that would be a reward for a single girl? The dinner date, that is?"

Peter was taken back. "Well, I ..."

"I assure you it isn't a reward for me. As I said, you may be heaven's gift to most women, but not to me."

Though feeling great relief at her refusal, he responded testily. "I didn't say I was, miss. Since you feel that way, may we offer you just the gift certificate then?"

"When did I earn it?"

"When you picked up that shirt off the floor, folded it nicely and put it back."

"Oh."

"I can't tell you how rare that is. Now, may we give you the certificate?"

She smiled for the first time. "You may."

Peter noted that her smile might have been nice had it not looked so stiff, giving it an odd, unnatural look. "Please come with me to the accounting office and I'll give it to you." He led her down the aisle smiling to himself. *Now*, he thought, *this whole asinine thing will be over and I can, in all good conscience, tell my father I've done what I said I'd do.*

When they arrived, he offered her a seat, and went in. Soon, he came back out looking disconcerted. "I'm sorry, miss, they've just run out of gift certificates. I've told them to order some from another store. In fact, I'll have them send it to my office, and I'll deliver it to you personally," he stated magnanimously.

"In that case," the young woman said, "you might as well take me out to that nice restaurant for dinner."

Oh no! he thought, almost choking. He coughed. "Uh, yes … fine." Strange, but, again, he thought he saw amusement in her eyes. Why? Surely, she didn't get very many dates—if any at all. Noting that not only was she homely, but she was a little abnormal looking. "Let me think, would tonight be all right with you?" he asked, hoping like everything that it wasn't.

"It is. What time will you pick me up, Mr. Holmes?"

He let out a silent breath of misery. "About 6:30?"

"All right. What should I wear?"

"A nice dress would be fine. By the way, what is your name?"

"Melba Beasley."

The name fits her! he thought. He pulled a pad and pen out of the pocket of his knit shirt. "Will you please write down your phone number and address?"

All the way back to the office, Peter couldn't believe that *the* courteous customer had revealed herself so soon! And he couldn't believe the poor girl was so homely! He had studied her as she wrote down her address and phone number. Her forehead was more like a ledge and her brows were wisps of straggly hair. The end of her nose was bulbous with wide flanges for nostrils. *I wonder if she has ever considered plastic surgery?*

What was just as bad as her misshapen forehead and nose was the thick base of makeup she spread all over her face, with a dab of blush on each cheek. Her shoulder length brown hair, slightly curled under, was dull and lifeless looking.

What a nightmare he had gotten himself into by suggesting this crazy experiment—and for what?

Chapter Six

Peter entered his office in a state of near shock. His desk was just as he left it, piled high with an accumulation of things that needed immediate attention. Everything looked like business as usual. The same. But would *he* ever be the same again? The ludicrous experiment—*the challenge* he accepted had boomeranged! It felt like someone had struck him in the solar plexus, knocking the breath right out of him. The improbable had happened!

He couldn't focus on work. His attention was elsewhere—the upcoming dinner date with Miss Melba Beasley. Several times he went to the phone to cancel it. But each time, his sense of honor warred with his desperate desire to chuck the whole absurd idea and go ahead and move out into an apartment. *It was only one evening,* he reminded himself. Still, he wondered if he could endure even that after what he had gone through these last five harrowing days.

His pacing was interrupted by his secretary giving him the message that his father wanted to see him.

Peter slouched into his father's office and plunked himself down on a chair in front of the desk.

Ed looked up, prepared to launch into a question about a marketing account when Peter's expression stopped him. "Why the face, Peter?"

"I just came from the North Central store," he mumbled.

Ed smiled. "You ready to holler 'uncle'?"

"It's too late. I found her."

Ed Holmes held his breath. He almost didn't dare ask. "Tell me about her."

Peter told him of seeing her pick up a shirt, fold it and put it back.

"And?"

Peter blurted out the whole story. His father laughed unmercifully at his run-in with Marv again, but was stunned into silence when Peter described the young woman's looks, then told him of their dinner date at 6:30.

Ed's heart sank. Visions of Gladys came into his mind. He hoped fervently that this hapless young lady wouldn't allow herself any false hopes. At last, he asked, "Where are you taking her?"

"The Terrace Dining Room on Camelback Road."

PETER ALLOWED HIS father to tell the story to his mother while he showered and dressed in his best suit and tie. Ducking out of the house quickly to avoid his mother's questions, he drove to Camelback then turned East, glad that Miss Beasley's apartment, just off Camelback, was on the way to the restaurant. Turning south on 40th Street, he drove a short distance and turned into the parking lot of the Sun Ridge Apartments. Finally, locating the apartment, which was on the first floor, he reluctantly got out, walked slowly to the door, and rang the bell.

The door opened and there stood Melba Beasley, dressed in what she probably considered her best. The large colored flowers on the filmy shift contrasted horribly with her pale face caked with makeup.

"Hello, Mr. Holmes," she said, without expression.

However, Peter noted that her eyes were bright with excitement … or something. He stared at her transfixed, unable to even say hello.

"Mr. Holmes? Mr. Holmes?"

"Oh, hello, Miss Beasley."

"Would you come in while I put the finishing touches on my makeup?"

"Oh … sure," he said, gingerly stepping in.

Melba went out of the room, and Peter wondered how she could possibly put on more makeup!

Soon, she came out with a garish dab of red on her cheeks. Peter gulped silently.

"I'm ready," she said brightly.

Peter forced himself to smile. "Good, let's go."

On the way, Peter couldn't think of a thing to say after he looked over at her and noticed that her profile was even worse than the front view. *Was she in an accident, he wondered, or dropped on her head? Poor girl. However… she didn't act like anything was wrong. Amazing.*

"So how long have you worked for Holmes Department Stores, Mr. Holmes?"

Why hadn't he noticed the nasal twang in her voice before? Probably because he had been so shocked by her odd face. "Since I was thirteen. My father inherited the first Holmes Department Store from his father, and he eventually built three more. I began earning money breaking down boxes, taking trash out, running errands. I went on up through the ranks, so to speak."

"Did you go to college?" Melba asked.

"Yes."

"This is very strange," she said.

"What is?"

"I can understand a gift certificate—but a dinner date with *you*? Do you think going out to dinner with you is a reward for some girl?"

Stupefied, Peter thought, *Who does she think she is? Miss America?*

"Uh … this is a private thing between my father and me. I'd rather not explain it, if you don't mind."

"Since I'm the recipient of such a reward, I think you owe it to me to answer the question. Do you think going out to dinner with you is a *reward* for a girl?"

Peter felt irritated. "Hardly," he answered honestly.

"Then why did you and your father add a dinner date with *you* to the package?"

"Miss Beasley, that is none of your business."

"It most certainly is my business, Mr. Holmes."

Peter pulled off the road into the vacant parking lot of a business closed for the evening.

"Miss Beasley, do you want to go to dinner with me?"

"I don't know you. How could I know that? I do want to go to dinner with an escort since I'm new in town and I don't know the nice places to eat. You happen to be only an escort who was vouched for by a Holmes Department Store security officer."

Never in his life had Peter Holmes been treated in such a cavalier manner by a female. And to be treated so by one with such oddities made it even more unnerving.

They sat in silence for a few moments. Staring morosely through the windshield, Peter finally asked, "Do you want me to escort you to dinner even though I refuse to answer your question?"

"Of course."

Disconcerted that the answer was yes instead of no, Peter swallowed hard, took a deep breath, left the parking lot, and drove on toward the restaurant.

He pulled into the driveway of The Terrace Dining Room. A young valet opened Miss Beasley's door. Not able to hide his shock over her appearance, he gasped audibly.

The hostess, more mature, hid her shock well and seated them. After they ordered, Peter still didn't feel inclined to talk to her, but forced himself to anyway.

"You said you were new here. Where did you move from?"

"California."

"What prompted you to move to Phoenix?"

"Personal circumstances."

"Are you working?"

"Not yet, I'm looking for a job."

"What do you do … or what is your specialty?"

"I have several," she answered evasively.

"Do you like Phoenix, Miss Beasley?"

"I like it very much. Do you?"

"I was raised here. Unlike my mother, I've learned to like it so well, I even like the dust storms."

And so it went, both straining at small talk, but the expression in her eyes gave him the impression he was doing most of the straining.

The waiter brought the appetizers, a specialty of the house. Peter had ordered a plate to share. Melba reached for one and knocked her glass of water over covering them with water.

"Oh! I'm so sorry."

"Don't worry about it; I'll order another one."

Later, after the main meal was served, Melba commented on how good the food was while picking up her glass of water to take a drink, but began pouring a split second before it reached her mouth, spilling water down her front.

"Oh my!" she exclaimed, grabbing a napkin and wiping herself off.

Peter stared at her. If her face flushed with embarrassment, one couldn't tell through all that makeup. Along with everything else, she was a klutz too!

They were finishing dessert when Melba exclaimed, "They have a dance floor here! How nice."

Peter didn't respond. He had forgotten about the dance floor. Panicky, he noticed that Melba looked to be about five foot six inches. Though he was six feet, it was possible she could and would initiate a cheek to cheek. No way was he going to dance with her and get smudged with makeup!

Peter stared at the table as if in deep thought and noticed something for the first time, freckles on her hands and arms. "You have freckles on your arms," he blurted out.

Startled, she looked at her arms. "Uh, yes, I do."

"Do you have freckles on your face?"

She studied him a moment as if trying to decide how to answer him. "Why do you want to know?" she asked.

"If you do, I can't see them."

Thoughtful a moment, she replied, "I don't like the freckles on my face so I cover them up."

"Oh, but I like freckles. You shouldn't cover them up with all that makeup." Immediately, he flushed at his bluntness.

Did he see amusement in her eyes again, he wondered? He wasn't sure, but he had an inkling she might be a very contradictory person.

"Well," he said, as they both finished the dessert, "I have a lot of work to catch up on tomorrow, so we better call it a night."

"We aren't even going to dance once?"

"No, Miss Beasley, I'm just your escort, remember?"

They drove home in silence. Exhausted, Peter was reluctant to talk, so the conversation ground to a halt.

On Miss Beasley's doorstep, Peter wondered what to do next; she seemed to be waiting expectantly. Surely, she didn't expect a goodnight kiss!

"Mr. Holmes, aren't you going to give it to me?"

"What?" he blurted out in alarm.

"My $25 gift certificate."

"Oh." He expelled a breath of relief. "Oh! I forgot to bring it!" *Where's my head?* "I'll bring it to you. May I have your phone number again?"

Melba pulled a small card and pen from her purse, wrote it down and handed to him. "I thank Holmes Department Store for the nice dinner."

"You're welcome, Miss Beasley. I'll pass your thanks on to my father. I'll call you about the gift certificate. Good night."

As Peter drove home, he berated himself. He knew why he had forgotten, of course. He was so unsettled that Melba Beasley had changed her mind and decided to accept the dinner offer, he couldn't think of anything else. If he hadn't forgotten, this crazy episode would all be over!

He drove his car into one of the garages. With halting steps he walked to the back porch and entered the family room. Gladys and Ed, who were both reading, looked up.

"You're home early, Peter," his mother said, trying to hide her anxiousness. "How did it go?"

"It was grueling," he mumbled.

"Surely it couldn't have been that bad, Peter," his mother stated, trying to read his expression.

"I would like you to meet her and see for yourself," he said, sinking into a chair and leaning back in exhaustion. "Even the valet was so shocked when he saw her appearance, he couldn't hide it."

"Well, I guess it's over with, huh?" his father asked.

He sat upright. "I'm afraid not, I forgot to get the gift certificate. I was so anxious to leave her doorstep, I blurted out that I would bring it to her. I could have mailed it to her!"

"What's the problem, son? Take it to her and say thank you, it was nice to meet you, and leave."

"Yeah, I guess you're right, Dad."

"Wait a minute, you two," Gladys said, "I thought this was an advertising scheme. You were going to take a picture of you handing the young woman the gift certificate and use it as an advertisement for the stores."

"Did you tell her that, Peter?" his dad asked.

"Uh–oh, I did! But I said we *were* going to as if we had changed our minds."

"Nevertheless, you have to do it, Peter," his mother stated emphatically.

"But I don't think she's expecting it because I used the past tense, Mom."

"Do you know that for sure, Peter?"

"No."

"I'm afraid I agree with your mother, Peter. You'd better arrange to hand her the gift certificate in front of a camera for the ad."

"But, Dad, I doubt if she feels photogenic."

His dad gave him one of those silent looks that usually galvanized Peter into action. He groaned. "All right, Dad, I'll arrange it."

Ed, feeling a little uneasy, asked, "Did she ... uh come on to you?"

"No. I would say just the opposite."

His mother's brow rose in surprise, a smile teasing her lips. "That's a first. You know, all your life, Peter, from sixteen on, girls have spoiled you."

"Well," he began, a grim smile on his face, "Miss Melba Beasley put me in my place."

"Go on," his mother insisted.

"I think she said something like, 'Why a dinner date with you?

Do you think you're heaven's gift to women or something?'"

His parents were so surprised, they simply stared at him, both their mouths slightly ajar. Then they broke into laughter.

Their laughter went on so long, Peter complained, "Okay … okay! Enough is enough," he said, grinning. "I didn't ask to be born a gift to women—I can't help it."

"Yeah, we know," his father said, smiling, "but I think I like this Melba Beasley."

"I think I do, too," his mother agreed.

"All right, Dad, you can call the photographer, and both of you may have the privilege of handing her the certificate."

"I'll be there," his mother said, "but this is just between you and your father."

"Okay, Dad, you can have *your* picture taken with the young lady you like so much."

"No sir! This was your marketing idea; you took the challenge, Peter. You're the man of the hour."

Chapter Seven

All day Monday, Peter buried himself in work, hoping this business of Melba Beasley would all go away, but no such luck. His father stepped into his office at 5:00 PM.

"When are you going to coordinate with the photographer and Miss Beasley?"

"You know, Dad, seriously, Miss Beasley may not want her picture taken. She didn't say so at the time, but maybe she won't."

"When you tell her we intend to pay her $100 for it, she may. Why don't you ask her?"

"Dad, why don't we just mail her the certificate and let it go at that?"

"I lean that way, Peter, but you heard your mother. She was upset over the whole idea in the first place, and she's insisting we finish the project as we said we would. Besides that, you don't want to offend Miss Beasley."

Peter groaned. "All right, I'll call Miss Beasley and ask her if she'd be willing to do this. If she is, I'll call the photographer and set it up."

As soon as his father left, Peter reluctantly picked up the phone and called the young woman in question.

"Hello?" The voice was pleasant, not nasal.

"Hello, this is Peter Holmes. May I speak to Miss Melba Beasley?"

There was a moment of silence, after which the voice said, "Just one moment please."

"Hello?" came the nasal twang.

"Miss Beasley?"

"Yes, Mr. Holmes."

"I'm sorry if I'm disturbing you. Do you have company?"

"She's a friend of mine. You aren't disturbing me."

Peter explained the reason for his call. "Would you be willing to do this, Miss Beasley? Of course, in addition to the gift certificate, we would pay you a hundred dollars for your time."

"When will it be?"

"Wednesday if I can arrange everything. I'll let you know tomorrow morning."

"All right, I'll do it. Where will it be?"

"Here at the offices of Holmes Department Stores." With great reluctance he gave her the address.

THE PHOTOGRAPHER HAD chosen Ed's plush office to take the picture, not because of its large burgundy leather chairs or the huge glossy mahogany desk, but because of the wall of enlarged pictures of the first Holmes Department Store and the picture of the man who owned it, Ed's father. He had set up his equipment to take the picture with the participants slightly to the side in order to get some Phoenix nostalgia in. Ed was pleased with the idea, but Peter cringed.

True to her word, Peter's mother arrived promptly at 10:00 AM. "Where's Miss Beasley?" she asked.

"She should be here any moment, Mom," Peter stated flatly.

Shortly, Ed's secretary peered in, the whites of her eyes showing. "Mr. Holmes, a ... a Miss Beasley is here."

"Send her in."

Though forewarned by Peter, Ed and Gladys were only partly prepared for the young woman who walked into the office. By his expression the photographer revealed that he hadn't been prepared at all.

Peter greeted the object of their jolted senses and led her over to meet them. "Miss Beasley, I would like you to meet Tom Edmund, our photographer, and my parents, Mr. and Mrs. Holmes. Tom, Mom and Dad, this is Miss Melba Beasley."

Tom nodded wordlessly, but his mother spoke with graciousness. "How do you do, Miss Beasley. We're glad to meet such a considerate and thoughtful customer of the Holmes Department Stores."

"Yes," his father agreed, "we're glad to meet you."

Peter noticed Miss Beasley's surprise and uneasiness over the presence of his parents. Nevertheless, she greeted them as pleasantly as was possible with her adenoidal voice.

The picture was taken with Peter Holmes handing the certificate to Miss Beasley while Ed Holmes stood by his side, smiling.

When all the shots were taken, Peter said, "If you'll excuse us,

Mom and Dad, I'll take Miss Beasley into my office and write her a check."

"It was nice to meet you, Mr. and Mrs. Holmes," Melba Beasley replied.

Peter led her to his office. "Please have a seat, Miss Beasley."

"Thank you," she said, seating herself.

Peter wrote the check, picked up the gift certificate, and stood up smiling. "We appreciate you as a customer, Miss Beasley, and we appreciate your time here today," he said, feeling relaxed and relieved that this would be the end of it. He had just started to step around the corner of the desk, when Melba stood up.

"Thank you, Mr. Holmes," she said, stepping quickly over to him to take the check and gift certificate. But just as she reached for them, she stumbled over the leg of the desk, propelling her toward him. Peter caught her as she fell forward.

"Oh my! I'm so clumsy sometimes. I'm sorry," she said. Looking up at him, she was startled at the horrified expression on his face.

"Miss Beasley! Your … your nose! Half your nose is gone!"

Her hand flew to her face. "Oh!" Horrified herself, her eyes slid down, locking on the lapel of his suit. Gasping, she whirled around and ran out of the office.

Peter, still in shock, looked down at his suit and saw a flesh colored blob stuck to his lapel. It was part of her nose! He couldn't move. All he could do was stare at it, aghast.

Ed and Gladys entered Peter's office. "I see she's gone," his father said.

Gladys was the first to notice her son's state. "What's wrong, Peter?"

Speechless, he held up his lapel with one hand and pointed with the other.

"What's that?" his father asked.

He finally found his voice. "I think it's part of, uh—part of Miss Beasley's nose!"

"What!" they exclaimed simultaneously.

"She stumbled over the corner leg of the desk, and I caught her." He grimaced. "She left part of her—nose."

Ed and Gladys stared at the small clump on his coat, dumbfounded, silent.

Gladys stepped over to Peter and studied it carefully. "Why that's nose putty used for makeup in plays."

"Makeup for plays?" Peter asked. "Then ... then her homely, weird face was a fake?"

"It looks like it," his mother said. "But why would she do that?"

"Yeah, why? She came into the store like that, Mom. She went to dinner with me like that—and even allowed this picture to be taken!"

"And look, she dropped both the check and gift certificate," Ed said picking them up from the floor.

In an outburst of panic, Peter exclaimed, "Oh no! I have a feeling that this whole crazy thing is never going to end. Me and my ideas."

"Well, son, you'll just have to take these to her after work tonight."

"Maybe you'll find out what she really looks like, Peter, and why she disguised herself," his mother said smiling. "I'll be on the edge of my seat waiting to hear about it." Taking her husband's hand, they left Peter's office.

"She's probably wanted by the FBI," Peter mumbled to himself, grabbing a tissue and pulling off the nose putty then wiping the residue off the best he could. Throwing it into the waste basket, he sat down and moaned. "Why is it that females *always* cause me trouble?"

Wanting to get it over with as quickly as possible, Peter left the office at 3:00 PM and drove directly to Miss Beasley's apartment. He walked to her door and rang the bell.

A middle-aged woman answered it. "Yes?"

"Is Miss Beasley at home?"

"No one lives here by that name."

Peter was confused. "But I picked her up here last Friday night."

"Oh. She must have been the last tenant. I moved in yesterday."

Peter asked her where the office was. Thanking her, he walked back to his car, and drove over where she had directed him. He parked and went in.

A tired, pasty-faced man looked up from his desk. "May I help you?"

"Yes. You had a Melba Beasley renting apartment 116, and I found she has moved out. Did she leave a forwarding address?"

"I'll have to look at my records. Just a minute. You see," he said opening a file drawer and withdrawing a folder, "they come and go rapidly because our apartments are furnished and are rented by the day, the week or month."

"Oh. But surely you would remember her. She was very odd looking, brown hair, large nose, protruding forehead."

The man scratched his head. "I would remember someone like that. If Melba Beasley looked like you described, I would have noticed. Here it is. We did have a Melba Beasley in apartment 116. She's moved out."

"Did she leave a forwarding address?"

"No, she didn't."

"Do you remember anything about her?"

"As I said, so many people come and go here. Let me think. I may be wrong, but I think she had bright red hair and otherwise somewhat nondescript."

"Could you be thinking of someone else?"

"I could be. No. I remember now. Miss Beasley came in and complained about a water faucet leaking. Yes. As I said, she had red hair and ... well, all I can say is she wasn't memorable."

"Did she have a lot of makeup on?"

He thought a moment. "I believe she did now that you mention it."

"Here's my card. If you hear where she moved, would you call me?"

"I'm sure I won't, but if I do, I'll call you."

"Thank you for your time," Peter said as he walked out of the office.

Placing himself behind the wheel of his car, his thoughts were racing. *Maybe she really was hiding from the police. I'll wonder forever why she disguised herself—and what she really looked like! And, unless she contacts us, we'll never be able to pay her and give her the gift certificate.* "Me and my big-mouth advertising ideas!" he exclaimed under his breath.

He drove back to the corporate office and went straight to see his father. After Peter had related the latest information about the infamous Miss Melba Beasley, they sat in silence for a few moments, and together, they wondered if the name, that fit the disguise so well, was an alias.

LIFE, FOR PETER, settled down to the old conflict—needing to date—but not finding anyone he *wanted* to take out. Regardless, Peter knew that he would have to date at least twice a month to satisfy his parents, to show them he was trying. The alternative would be moving to a lonely apartment.

Though consumed with curiosity over Melba Beasley, he threw himself into work, soccer, and church, managing to squeeze in a date now and then. He also managed to attend the stake and regional singles activities to look over the crop of young ladies.

Ed and Gladys were feeling more hopeful for their son. Both felt that their edict and the incident of Miss Melba Beasley had spurred Peter to at least make motions toward finding a wife, halfhearted as they were.

Chapter Eight

March 17, seven and a half months later:

When Peter parked behind the garage of his house, the delicious smell of orange blossoms tingled his nose, evoking emotions which always came with spring—a fresh beginning and renewed hope. He sighed, realizing that this year it also brought a sense of loneliness, an acute loneliness that ate at his insides. He would be an old man before he even had children!

Several years ago, he silently nicknamed this time of year in Phoenix, the "mating season" because it always increased his urge to find that elusive and special girl. He even prayed more fervently this time of year to be guided to her.

It was Friday, and he was going to attend a stake singles dance. In four and a half months, he would turn thirty and be booted out of the singles ward, but until then, he planned to continue attending. He usually went to the dances begrudgingly, but tonight, he actually looked forward to it.

"It's the orange blossoms," he muttered as he entered the kitchen.

"Hello, Peter," his mother said, smiling. "What about the orange blossoms?"

"They smell great."

PETER DROVE TO the stake center with the windows down, taking in as much of the fragrant evening as he could. Pulling into the parking lot, he looked around. The dance started at 8:00. It was only 8:20, and the lot was already full. *Yes, it's the mating season in Arizona,* he thought.

When he stepped into the building, he saw a couple of girls from his ward.

"Hi," he greeted, smiling.

They refused to speak. They turned to each other, snubbing him. Peter didn't blame them. They were two of the girls he had used his *technique* on, trying to discern their standards before dating them. He had given Harriet's advice a lot of thought, but the thought of dating a girl and finding that her values and goals weren't compatible with his, then hurting her by not asking her out again, made him feel rotten. He was sick of the whole dating scene!

The music sounded good, less loud, as he walked into the cultural hall. The dance was casual, so he came in beige cotton pants and a light green knit shirt, one that his mother said "enhanced his sage green eyes." Ordinarily, he wouldn't pay attention to that, but on this spring night it seemed important.

He always started dancing with girls in his ward. Even the ones who were upset at him or wouldn't speak to him accepted, for which he was grateful. The DJ was playing fun music tonight, music that made it possible for a couple to be inventive. He realized he was having a great time for a change, certain it was due to his better frame of mind.

He returned his partner to her seat and thanked her. He meandered around looking for another one, when he heard a commotion. A few yards in front of him, a group of both young men and young women encircled someone. All the faces he could see were animated and excited. Whoever was in the middle, he mused, must be an interesting person.

Stepping over to the crowd, he tried to see who was causing all the excitement. Tall guys, his height and taller, kept getting in front of him, but he managed to get a glimpse of the back view of a young woman with the prettiest sunshine-blonde hair he had ever seen. He finally gave up getting any further view of her and sat down on a seat nearby waiting for the crowd to disperse.

The girls in the group left one by one, and soon there were only guys standing around her like bees buzzing around a flower. Soon, one of the men led her out to the dance floor.

Peter angled his head trying to see her, but the man moved her away so quickly he still didn't get a good look. He waited for him to bring her back after the dance. The group of young men also waited. Soon realizing that the man who spirited her away was not coming back, the men went their separate ways, and Peter asked another girl to dance, then another. As he danced around the floor, he would now and then get a glimpse of the newcomer's sunny golden hair.

When the refreshment table was ready, Peter headed for a drink of punch. He picked up a cup and drank it. When he lowered the cup, there was the young woman with the sunshine-blonde hair standing in front of the refreshment table staring at him.

She smiled. "Hello," she said in a pleasant husky voice.

"Hello," he said, reaching back clumsily to place the empty cup on the table without taking his eyes off her. Never in all his life had he seen such a beautiful face! Her smile was an open smile that spread across her face. She literally glowed. Her eyes crinkled at the corners, sparkling with an inner happiness.

He was just about to introduce himself when a man walked up and spoke to her. "You promised me this dance."

Barely aware of anyone or anything, Peter held out his hand to her, his mouth open, ready to speak volumes of poetic phrases when she turned and bestowed that enchanting smile upon another man! Off they went, leaving Peter in a state of suspended animation.

Frantically, he watched the dancing crowd, but couldn't see her. Slowly, he circled the whole cultural hall trying to catch a glimpse of her. Finally at 11:00 PM, he gave up, certain that some enterprising man had whisked her away from the dance so he could have her to himself. He felt bitterly disappointed.

Chapter Nine

Before church Sunday morning and after church all afternoon, Ed and Gladys noticed a change in Peter. Neither could quite describe it. "Though he's preoccupied, there's an excitement in him we haven't seen for a long time," Gladys told Ed.

Ed agreed and finally asked Peter, "What's on your mind, son?"

Shrugging his shoulders, Peter kind of grunted, his usual way of saying he didn't want to talk about it. He didn't want to tell his parents anything until he had something of substance to tell.

At church, he had asked a few guys if they knew who the new girl was at the stake dance the night before. A couple of them hadn't gone to the dance. Another one had said he didn't see a new girl. Finally, one had looked at him in surprise. "You mean you don't know who she is?"

"No."

"Did you get a good look at her?"

"I did."

"Hey, Pete, you're not up on things, are you?" He walked away laughing.

Peter found another guy who had seen her at the dance.

"Are you kidding, Pete? You really don't know?"

"No!"

"Well, do you think I'd give you—the 'Don Juan' of the whole region—her name then? No way."

By this time, Peter was so frustrated and desperate, he asked several girls. Each one said almost the same thing. "You don't know who she is? Are you living in another world, Peter?"

"I guess I am, so tell me."

"Why should we add to our competition?"

"Competition? I thought you couldn't stand me. Half the time you won't speak to me."

"You know why, don't you?"

At that point, words were useless.

He was determined to find the girl! Driving home from church, he silently asked himself, *When I do, am I going to test her as I have other girls?* His first inclination was not to—for fear of what he would find out. Did he have the *courage* not to take her out if she didn't pass muster?

PETER BEGAN ATTENDING sacrament meetings at other wards when possible, as well as his own, sitting at the back watching for the golden-haired girl who had so mysteriously disappeared. He even attended dances at the other stakes and still saw no sign of her.

A month later, while walking in the hall of his own ward, he almost ran into her. He was so stunned at his good luck, he was mute.

"Hi," she said, smiling, breaking the ice.

"Hi! Do you go to the singles ward?"

"No, I go to the family ward that meets just before the singles ward."

"Why haven't I seen you then?"

"I guess it's because I've been out of town."

"May I ask you what your name is? I've been looking all over for you since I saw you at the stake dance a month ago."

"You have?" she asked, surprised, continuing down the hall.

"Yes. My name is Peter Holmes and yours?" he asked, walking along with her.

"Jenny McDuffy."

The name fits her adorable face, he mused. He followed her out to her car.

"Miss McDuffy," he began.

"Call me Jenny."

"Thank you, Jenny. Would you like to …" He stopped. Could he go through with it—ask her to go to a movie he personally would not see? Swallowing hard, he mustered up courage to give her the *test*. "Would you like to see the movie, *Flowers for Amy?"* he asked, mentioning the name of an R–rated movie he had seen advertised.

Her shoulders sagged; her brows contorted, and she looked as if she were going to cry. "I most certainly would not!" She opened her car door, got in and slammed it shut.

Peter tried to talk to her through the closed window, but she backed out too quickly, leaving him bewildered and a little chagrined.

"Oh great! That backfired," he mumbled. *Why did she react that way? Why was she on the verge of tears?* He hoped she was offended—that would mean she didn't go to that kind of movie. This thought lifted his spirits. At least he could now go to her ward clerk and get her address and phone number.

He found the ward clerk's office locked, so he waited outside her bishop's office until he opened the door.

"Bishop Thompson, could I ask a favor of you?"

"Certainly, Peter."

"Could you give me Jenny McDuffy's phone number and address?"

"I'm sorry, Peter, but she has asked me not to give it out."

Peter's mouth dropped open. "Why?"

"I think you need to ask *her* the next time you see her."

"But that's another whole week, Bishop."

"I'm sorry, Peter. You aren't the first young man who's asked for that information."

"That figures," he said, nodding. "Thanks anyway."

THE NEXT WEEK dragged for Peter in spite of his busy schedule and the exciting things happening at work. The March sale had cleared out more of the winter merchandise than they had projected and the spring promotions had been highly successful. These kinds of successes were heady and usually galvanized him into an effort to top himself in the coming season. But Jenny McDuffy kept coming into his mind. Thoughts of her brought him both pleasure and uneasiness, diverting his mind away from the thing he loved doing. This had never happened to him before.

Peter decided to attend Jenny's ward sacrament meeting in hopes that he could see her and explain. When Sunday arrived, Peter was in the foyer of the ward building five minutes early. He stepped into the chapel and looked for Jenny. He spied her golden hair near the front. Quickly stepping down the aisle, he was relieved to see that a couple of seats next to her were vacant. He slid in and sat beside her. She looked over at him startled, then moved away from him as far as she could. He slid over next to her.

Compressing her lips, she folded her arms tightly across her waist. He studied her body language and then her beautiful profile. Her hair was pulled up into an attractive loose, golden coil, held up by a translucent clip.

Jenny, feeling his eyes on her, turned and glared at him, only to receive a charming, roguish grin. Resisting it, she turned away.

At the end of the meeting, Jenny scooted away from Peter to the aisle. He followed. Once out in the hall, he took hold of her arm.

"Please, Jenny, let me explain something."

"I have to go to class."

"Do you teach?"

"No."

"Would you please give me a few minutes outside?"

She sighed in resignation. "All right, but just a few. I want to get to my Sunday School class."

Peter led her outside onto the lawn, stopping under the shade of a ornamental orange tree. "Jenny, I ... uh, don't know quite how to say this, but straight out. I test girls before I take them out. It saves a lot of problems and hurt feelings later on. I didn't want to, but I was only testing you when I asked you if you wanted to see that movie. You see, I didn't know you ..." his voice trailed off.

"I don't like the sound of that, Mr. Holmes. What do you mean you were only testing me?"

Peter heaved a sigh, reluctant to continue, his courage weakening. "Well, I'm not proud of it. Maybe you'd better ask one of the girls in the singles ward. They would be more than glad to tell you. They're all upset at me."

Jenny McDuffy's curiosity was aroused. "This sounds interesting, but I think I'd like to hear it from you, Peter, not them."

"All right. I ask a girl if they would like to see such and such a movie, a movie I wouldn't go see. Disappointingly, they all say yes for some reason. You are the only one who's turned me down. Anyway, after they say yes, I say, 'Well, go see it then, it's on at such and such a theater.'"

Edgy, Peter watched Jenny's reaction. First, there was total surprise on her face, then a smile teased her lips. "You don't!"

"I do."

"That isn't nice."

"I know."

"What if I had said I would like to see that movie?"

Peter's brows furrowed, thinking. *What if there was another reason she didn't want to see the movie other than the content of it?* "Before I answer, Jenny, may I ask you why you became upset when I asked you if you would like to go to the movie?"

"I'd rather not answer that. Now as you were about to say?"

"It would take more courage to say the same thing to you, but—I guess I would."

"Hmm, is that right? Well, I need to go to class," she said, sidestepping away.

"Jenny, may I have a date?"

She stopped. “I don’t think ...”

”Have you always lived in Phoenix?” he asked quickly, before she could turn him down.

“No. I’m new here.”

“Then may I have a date to show you the Arizona desert, scorpions and all?”

Peter noticed her expressive blue eyes light up, but in spite of her apparent eagerness, she seemed to be struggling over the answer. At last, she said, “I would like that.”

“Great!” A smile of relief spread across his face. “I went to your bishop to get your address and phone number, and he wouldn’t give it to me. He said you asked him not to give it out.”

“You’re one determined man, Peter Holmes.”

“Why did you ask the bishop not to give out your address and phone number?”

“You really don’t know, do you?”

“No, I don’t.”

She smiled. “Let me meet you some place, Peter.”

“Why, Jenny? The mystery surrounding you is driving me crazy. I saw an animated crowd around you at the dance, and I couldn’t figure out why. All I could see was the most beautiful sunshine-blonde head of hair I’ve ever seen. It wasn’t long before someone whisked you off before I could get a good look at you. I danced with every girl who would dance with me and still I could only catch a glimpse of your hair.”

Before he could go on, Jenny said, “That doesn’t impress me, Peter. The girls I’ve met tell me that the guys in the singles ward go for anyone new—and apparently I’m just someone new.”

Peter was speechless for a moment. “I’m afraid the girls are right, but not in this instance. When I saw you there at the refreshment table and you smiled, I thought it was the most beautiful smile I had ever seen. You ... you literally glowed. Before I could even introduce myself, you were whisked away. I walked all around the dance floor and didn't even catch a glimpse of you. I was sure some lucky guy had taken you away from the dance. I felt as bereft as the prince in Cinderella when the clock struck twelve, but you didn't even leave a glass slipper so I could trace you."

Totally charmed, Jenny McDuffy laughed.

Peter had never heard a laugh like hers. It ended in a delightful lilt. "So, Miss Jenny McDuffy, will you give me your phone number and address?"

"No."

He blinked in surprise."Why?"

"Maybe I'll tell you later."

"Jenny, I went around church that Sunday after the dance asking girls and guys who you were and why everyone was crowding around you. You know what they said?"

"Tell me," she said, curiosity lighting her eyes.

"Well, the gist of it was: 'You really don't know? You must be living in another world.' My curiosity is about to eat me up, Jenny."

She gave him a small mysterious smile. Her eyes twinkling, the smile widened into one that lit up her whole face. "Maybe I'll tell you sometime. Can we meet someplace?"

"I give up. All right, let's meet at my place. It will give my poor parents hope. You see, they're afraid I'll never leave home."

"You still live at home?" she asked, surprised.

"Yeah, I like the company of my parents."

"A mama's boy?" she teased.

"Hardly, Mom's trying to kick me out."

Jenny laughed. "All right. Give me your address." She pulled out a small notebook and a pen from her purse and handed it to him.

"Can we make it tomorrow night?" he asked as he wrote down his address.

Jenny hesitated. "All right. Why don't I make a picnic lunch to share with the scorpions?"

Peter's eyes lit up. "Great! How about 3:30 in the afternoon before rush hour starts? Or do you work?"

"No." She paused. "I'm between jobs." She looked at her watch. "Oh, I have to go, I've already missed half of the class. See you tomorrow."

Peter watched her move gracefully toward the door and enter, once more very aware of her shapely figure.

Chapter Ten

Peter, in jeans and a blue polo knit, began pacing the floor at 3:15 Monday afternoon. His mother smiled. *A good sign,* she thought. She had never seen Peter this anxious over a date. And what luck, the girl was meeting him here! It was a rare opportunity to meet one of Peter's dates.

The doorbell rang at 3:35. Peter ran into the front room and opened it. He stared at the vision before him. The sun behind Jenny's head created an aura of light around her blonde, shoulder length hair, matching the radiant smile that lit her face.

"Are you real, Jenny?" Peter asked. "Are you sure you aren't a sunbeam that floated down from that big orb behind you?"

Jenny laughed, the lilt more musical. "Are you going to invite me in?"

"I'll say! Come in and meet my mother." Peter took her arm and led her into the kitchen.

"Mom, I'd like you to meet Jenny McDuffy. Jenny, my mother."

They smiled and greeted each other. "Won't you sit down a minute, Jenny?"

Jenny looked up at Peter questioningly.

"Mom, I think we'd better get out on the highway before rush hour."

"All right, another time. Go on, you two, and have a good time."

"Thank you, we will," Jenny replied smiling.

Gladys stood at the front window and watched them transfer a picnic basket and a water jug from Jenny's small car to Peter's SUV. *What a delightful young woman*, she thought. Dare she hope she was the kind of a girl Peter was looking for, praying for? The kind he deserved?

WHILE DRIVING ALONG Apache Boulevard, Peter asked Jenny questions, hoping she would accidently drop a little here and there about herself that might reveal something of the mystery that surrounded her. She answered in generalities, not offering more than he asked, then turned the questions to him.

Arriving at Apache Junction, he headed north on State Route 88. Five miles further, they reached the Lost Dutchman State Park. Jenny gasped when she saw several giant fortresses reaching toward the blue cloudless sky. The irregular rocks of dark brown with highlights of golden chestnut rose up out of the ground as if guarding their army of saguaros.

"Those are the Superstition Mountains, Jenny," Peter explained. "Have you heard the story of the lost Dutchman Mine?"

"No. It sounds fascinating."

"I'll have to tell you about it sometime. This park is named after that." Peter pulled off onto a small dirt road that ended after a short distance. He stopped the car and turned off the ignition. "Well, here we are, Jenny, the best place in the world, the Arizona desert." He opened his door and went around and opened Jenny's.

Jenny stepped out and looked around. "This is beautiful, Peter. Everything is so green."

"It is in the spring. In the hot summer when water is scarce, some bushes, such as the brittle brush, shed all or part of their foliage and enter a state of dormancy. So does that ironwood tree over there," he said pointing. "During that time, their water use is drastically reduced and, to the uninitiated, they may appear dead. When the winter rains come, they return to life and produce new leaves."

"That's interesting, Peter. I'm such a city girl, I haven't ventured anywhere except to the beach. My family never introduced us to nature, only city life and the beach, and I've kept myself so busy, I've haven't done it on my own."

"I'd be glad to introduce you to it on a regular basis," he said, grinning. Before she could respond, he said, "Excuse me, Jenny while I get the picnic table out of the trunk."

"The picnic table?" she asked in surprise, following him. She watched him retrieve a rectangular object with a handle.

Shutting the trunk, he grinned. "You bet, a portable picnic table. Our family loves picnics in the desert, but since we like to get out like this where there are no people, we bring our own tables. My sisters and their husbands each own one also. We just have to be sure we pick up all our trash and take it home. Hmm ... let's see, where shall we set this up?"

"Over there, Peter, by that large bush with the pretty yellow flowers."

"That's a creosote bush."

Jenny followed Peter over to the bush and watched him open up the small picnic table, locking the seats into place. She was very aware of his muscular, tan arms and his attractive strong looking hands. He turned and grinned—that mischievous looking grin that almost made her laugh when she first saw it.

"Let's go get that picnic basket and the water jug," he said, acting as excited as a little boy.

The first thing Jenny did was pull out a blue and white checkered tablecloth from the basket and spread it over the small table.

"Mm, nice," Peter said.

"Thank you," she responded, placing the basket back on the table. "Before we eat, Peter, could we walk around a little and enjoy the desert?"

"We sure can," he stated exuberantly, reaching for her hand. A thrill went clear through him as their hands touched. He noted that her slim hand was strong, gripping his with firmness. Wondering if Jenny had felt the same as he had when their hands touched, he glanced at her and found her looking at him, her cheeks flushed. She looked away quickly, studying her surroundings.

They sauntered around the speared-leaf yuccas, stepped over small barrel cactus and around a tall ironwood tree while Peter explained the names of each plant and tree.

"Oh Peter, look at those beautiful rose-colored wild flowers," she exclaimed.

"They're called desert globemallow. April's a great month to see desert wild flowers in bloom."

"I didn't realize how beautiful a desert could be. And look, over there are some pretty little white flowers," she said, pointing.

"Those are blackfoot daisies."

"Well, if you aren't a walking fount of information, Peter Holmes."

"I like the desert, so I've made a study of it."

It was a little after 5:00 and the sun's warmth had turned soft and mellow. Suddenly overhead, they heard a breathy whistle from the rush of air over a pair of wings. Jenny looked up in time to see the span of the bird's two-toned wings and its naked red head as it rocked side to side in flight.

"Is that a buzzard?"

"No. It's a turkey vulture. Spring is its breeding time."

As they walked around, Jenny began asking the names of different flora, deciding she would also like to learn about them since she was going to live in Arizona. After a while, she said, "I haven't seen one scorpion, Peter."

"And I hope we don't," he said.

"Oh!" she squealed, "there's a strange-looking lizard." Pulling her hand free, she crept closer to get a good look at it. Its long tail scattered fine gravel as it slipped underneath a bush.

"That was a tiger whiptail lizard."

She looked up at him, her blue eyes full of admiration. "I'm impressed with your knowledge, Peter."

Peter's heart swelled, almost choking him. "Thanks. I ... uh, was hoping I wasn't overdoing it. Though I will admit I *was* trying to make points with you." The desire to take Jenny into his arms and kiss her right that very moment was so overwhelming it took all the willpower he could muster to resist.

Jenny seemed to sense what was in his mind. She turned and

quickly wound her way back to the picnic table where she began taking the food out of the basket.

Peter felt his face flush at being so transparent. He would have to be careful with this young woman. She wasn't like any girl he'd known or dated, and he wanted to play his cards just right.

When he reached the table, he found two white plastic plates with a bunch of green grapes on each, several slices of bread from a baguette, a large slice of Brie cheese and some chicken wings.

"Man, that looks good!"

"I hope you like Brie cheese, Peter. I brought some butter to spread on the bread in case you don't."

"I love it, Jenny."

After Peter said the blessing on the food, he threw a couple of grapes into his mouth. "Mmm, I've never tasted such crisp, sweet grapes."

"I found a specialty grocery store that carries these as well as the spicy chicken wings."

"You'll have to show me where it is. I'll need to know when I'm kicked out of the house and have to find my own apartment," he said, grinning.

"You're joking, of course."

"I wish I were. Mom and Dad think I've quit looking for a wife because they make it too comfortable for me at home."

"*Have* you quit looking for a wife?"

"Not really. It's just that I've been a little dis ..." He stopped and turned silent.

"How old are you, Peter?"

"I'm twenty-nine."

"It seems a shame that a man your age, who is a vice-president of four department stores, is single when there are so many available young women who need husbands."

"Yeah, I know. How old are you, Jenny?"

"Twenty-eight."

"It seems a shame that a beautiful girl of your age is single when there is an eager twenty-nine-year-old bachelor like me wanting to get married," he said with all seriousness.

"When you've had all you want to eat, Peter," she said, quickly changing the subject, "there's apple pie for dessert." She went to reach into the basket and knocked over her glass of water.

"Oops!" she said, grabbing some napkins and soaking it up.

"I'm glad you did that, not me," he stated, "I goof up enough."

She shook her head. "I'm such a klutz sometimes."

When they were through eating, Jenny pulled out the pie and a couple of small plates and forks.

"Did you make this, Jenny?"

"Yes. I thought I ought to add something homemade to the picnic," she said, cutting him a piece.

Peter took a bite, then another. "This is good!"

"Thank you, Peter."

Jenny finished her piece of pie, while Peter was finishing his second. She looked around, noticing how the twilight sun had transformed the desert. "It looks like a fairyland, doesn't it Peter?"

Peter admired her while she admired the desert. The twilight on her pale yellow cotton blouse and her ethereal hair made her look like *she* had come from some mystic far away fairyland.

"Peter?"

"Oh. Yes, it does," he said, jerking himself back to reality. His brows drew together as he studied the air. "It also looks like a dust storm is brewing. We better fold up and get into the car."

Jenny stood up and took a step, catching her toe on the protruding metal leg of the table, propelling her forward. Peter grabbed her before she could right herself.

"Oh my! I'm sorry."

"I don't mind—if you'll let me catch you," he said, laughing, still holding her.

"Thank you," she said breathlessly, pulling away.

Peter carried the basket and thermos jug to the car while he mused over the feeling of deja vu that came over him when he caught Jenny. He was still trying to remember, when he returned to fold the table.

Jenny was already fiddling with it, trying to figure out how to fold it up. Amused, he watched her. As she peered under the table, he couldn't help noticing again her nice figure in the smooth fitting, faded jeans. He watched her trying to maneuver the mechanism. Suddenly, he noticed something he hadn't before—the freckles on her hands and arms. Freckles! She also had freckles on her face. *No! It couldn't be,* he thought. He must be wrong. Shaking his head, he pushed the unsettling suspicion out of his mind.

"Here, Jenny, let me show you."

She watched him. "Oh. That's simple. Still, I don't think I could have figured it out if I'd tried all evening."

After placing the table in the trunk, Peter opened the passenger door for Jenny. The unsettling thought came back and continued to bother him. He walked around to his side and got behind the wheel. Peter was glad Jenny was silent. It would be difficult to keep up a conversation with the kind of speculation that was going around in his head.

At last, he realized the only thing he could do was face it head on. Melba Beasley had *freckles* on her hands and arms and said she had freckles under all that makeup. Surely Jenny wasn't the kind of girl to masquerade like that! But then another fact hit him. Jenny had mentioned that he was vice-president of Holmes Department Stores. He certainly hadn't given her that information. Melba Beasley, on the other hand, had been informed of that by Marv. And another thing—Melba Beasley was also a klutz! And she also used the same expression as Jenny, 'Oh my.'

Peter didn't want it to be true, but he had to know.

By the time they reached his house, it was turning dark. Pulling into his driveway he parked next to Jenny's car. He opened the door for her and retrieved the picnic basket and thermos jug. Jenny unlocked her trunk and Peter placed them in.

Jenny had sensed the change in Peter immediately, and his silence on the way home validated it, therefore, when he invited her in, she refused, telling him she needed to get home. *He accepted my refusal far too easily,* she thought. Especially since he had worked so hard to find her and get a date with her—and after he had treated her so wonderfully on the picnic!

Stiffly, she thanked him. He thanked her as well, opened the car door, and they said good night.

The minute she drove off, Peter got into his car and followed her. When he caught up, he followed at a reasonable distance. The purpose of this maneuver was to find out where she lived and end this mystery once and for all!

Arriving at an expensive-looking condominium complex near 24th Street and Indian School Road, Jenny turned in and drove around a corner and into a front-facing garage of one of the units. Peter stopped where his car couldn't be seen and waited for Jenny's garage door to open and close behind her. Parking a few yards away, he got out and walked to her front porch and rang the bell.

The front light went on, and the door opened.

"Peter! You followed me!"

"Yes. I did," he stated without apology.

"You had no right to do that."

His manner pensive, he asked, "Could I come in and talk to you for a few minutes?"

Uneasy over Peter's mood, she replied, "I'd rather you wouldn't, Peter."

"Why?" he demanded.

"I'd just rather you wouldn't."

"Will you step out on the porch a minute then?"

She hesitated, then stepped out, closing the door behind her.

"Where are you from, Jenny?"

"Why?"

"Tell me, Jenny."

"California."

Peter scrutinized her for a moment, then stated suspiciously, "Melba Beasley was from there also."

A long silence followed. When she spoke, her voice was almost inaudible. "Who's Melba Beasley?"

Peter could tell by the expression on her face that he had hit pay dirt. "Don't deceive me anymore, Jenny," he said, feeling miserable.

"All right. I was Melba Beasley. And I didn't deceive you!"

"What do you call it then?"

"I didn't know I was going to run into *you* that day in the department store, so how can you say I was deceiving you?"

"You were deceiving everyone you came in contact with, and I was one of them."

"So—what are you going to do about it, Mr. Holmes?" she asked defiantly.

Suddenly, Peter turned angry. He pulled her roughly to him and bent down to kiss her. She struggled, pulling away far enough to plant a fist squarely into his stomach. Peter grunted, grabbing his midsection in pain.

"What right do you have to kiss me, Peter Holmes?"

"I've earned something for all the trouble you've put me through," he said through clenched teeth.

"You've earned nothing! Good night." She turned and opened the door, shutting it quickly and locking it.

Peter stood there on the porch, feeling the pain in his stomach—and in his heart. He turned and slowly walked back to his car. As he drove toward home, he worked up anger again. "To heck with it all! I should have known that Jenny McDuffy was too good to be true! She's no different than all the other girls who have disappointed me. No, she's worse. No other girl has *deceived* me."

By the time he reached home, however, the anger had dissipated, leaving him feeling altogether miserable again.

Chapter Eleven

Tuesday evening Peter paced the floor in his bedroom. He could hardly keep his mind on work throughout the day for thinking of Jenny, and the still unsolved mystery surrounding her. Who was she that everyone in the ward knew her? Why would she masquerade in that awful disguise?

No matter how he tried to hide his misery from his parents, he could tell that they knew something was wrong. He didn't want to tell them anything just yet. *Maybe*, he thought, *I should go ahead and move out and save them from worrying about me!*

After work, Peter had gone over to Jenny's apartment and rung her bell, not knowing what he was going to say except to plead with her to talk with him. Either she wasn't home or she refused to answer. He had called information for her phone number and found that it was unlisted.

Who could he ask to get it for him and help him solve the mystery surrounding her? Harrie! Of course! Why hadn't he thought of Harriet before now? Probably because she had been out of town for months. But, if he remembered correctly, she was due back last night. He picked up the phone and rang her number, hoping.

"Hello," Harriet Flower answered.

"Hey, Harrie, sweetheart!" he exclaimed in relief.

Immediately, her full, rich singing voice belted out, *"I only want a buddy, not a sweetheart ..."*

Peter laughed. "Harrie, I need a buddy, too. Am I glad you're back in town. I desperately need some help."

"Come on over and tell me about it."

"I was hoping you'd say that. Thanks! I'll be right over."

Driving over, Peter was anxious to hear what kind of luck Harriet had peddling her CD. He still had mixed feelings about her getting into that business.

Arriving at the Flower residence, Peter parked, got out, walked briskly to the porch and rang the bell. Harriet opened the door.

"Peter!" she exclaimed throwing her arms around him. "It's so good to see you."

"It's even better to see you, Harrie," he said, giving her a big hug.

When they entered the parlor to talk, Peter's brows shot up. "Hey! Let me look at you, Harrie." Harriet whirled around for him. He could hardly believe his eyes. She had lost a lot of weight; her figure was slim and attractive. Her dark brown hair was cut shoulder-length and was shiny and slightly curled. Gone were the jeans and sloppy over-blouses she used to wear. She had on a faded jean skirt and a red knit tee. And she was actually wearing some makeup—just enough to enhance her beautiful cocoa brown eyes.

"Wow! You look great."

"Thanks, Peter," she said, pleased with his reaction. "I finally decided to follow the advice of Brigham Young."

"Oh? What was that?"

"I stayed with my aunt Marnie while I was in California, and she showed me this quote and suggested I even memorize it. She said that if I intended to try cutting a record, I'd better quit looking like a slob."

"Tell me the quote, Harrie."

"Okay, here goes: '*Let the sisters take care of themselves, and make themselves beautiful, and if any of you are so superstitious and ignorant as to say that this is pride, I can say that you are also ignorant as to the excellency of the heavens, and of the beauty which dwells in the society of the Gods. Were you to see an angel, you would see a beautiful and lovely creature. Make yourselves like angels in goodness and beauty.*'"

"I remember that now. I wish you could influence your friends in the singles ward. It seems a lot of them are, uh … becoming more and more casual in their dress, in fact, in their whole appearance."

"That's a nice way to say they're turning into unfeminine slobs like I was."

Peter smiled. "You've met my sisters. As I've already told you, they're the yardsticks by which I measure other girls."

"I know, and I can see why. If Aunt Marnie could meet them, she would be pleased over the way they keep themselves and, I'm happy to say, she's pleased with me—now. And, Peter, I feel much better about myself. I'm happier."

Peter smiled at his friend. "I'm glad, Harrie. Did you have any luck peddling your CD?"

"No. There's so much competition out there. I'm afraid it's a business where you have to know someone who knows someone."

"You have the voice that will sell if you find the right person to contact. However, you know how I feel about you getting into the recording business."

"I know, but since I'm twenty-seven and Mr. Right hasn't come along, I have to support myself somehow. Now, back to you, Peter. What's up?"

Peter started at the beginning with his parents telling him to move out, then related the challenge between himself and his father. He told every detail of his adventures at the department stores knowing Harriet would enjoy it. And enjoy it she did. She almost fell off the sofa laughing, and her reaction to Melba Beasley was what he needed. At the time it happened, his sense of humor had fled him, so looking at it from Harrie's perspective, he was able to see how humorous it really was. When he ended with the mystery woman, Jenny McDuffy alias Melba Beasley, and how he couldn't find out her phone number or why everyone knew her but him, Harriet was totally intrigued. Peter continued the story to the end.

"But, Peter, you know you deserved the punch in the stomach, don't you?"

He turned glum. "I don't know, but ..."

"Peter?"

"Okay, I deserved it. Are you going to help me solve the mystery surrounding Jenny McDuffy?"

She grinned. "This is what I call a *juicy* mystery, Peter. Maybe I'll change from a singing career to detective work. What do you want me to do, Chief?"

Peter chuckled. "I knew you'd cheer me up, Harrie. The first thing I want you to do is go to her ward Sunday and make a point of meeting her and, as soon as you can, get to know her. Then report back to me, Detective Flower," he said in mock seriousness.

"Right, Chief. Good plan."

He grinned, but a frown soon eclipsed it. "You know, I don't think I can wait until Sunday."

"All right, let's implement another plan. How about I knock on her door and say, 'I'm Detective Flower, Miss …'"

"Sur–r–re."

"Or, I can call her ward Relief Society president and ask if there are any single girls in her Relief Society. If she answers yes, I'll ask their names."

"Oh, and …"

"Don't interrupt, just listen. If she names a few I'll ask for their phone numbers. I'll find out her phone number one way or another."

Peter grinned. "I'll bet you will. Thanks, buddy!" He got up and sat down at her grandmother's old upright piano and began playing Harriet's theme song. She always had him accompany her when she sang. She joined in. *"I only want a buddy, not a sweetheart …"*

JENNY MCDUFFY LOOKED around the nice, but small condominium that housed her new furniture. She loved decorating it in her favorite colors, pale yellow, light tan, with accents of blue, from Dresden to robin's-egg blue. The entertainment center was antique white with blue and yellow tole painting on the doors. The small magazine table in front of the couch was an old basket chest. The couch, a light tan, was piled high with soft pillows of different textures and shades of the blue accents. A pale yellow overstuffed chair hugged the front window.

It was her first home, or the first place that felt like home since moving out of her parents' home in California. She curled up in the big plush chair and looked out at the palm tree in front. The husks of its trunk and the lower palms were lit up by lamplight, leaving the upper palms silhouetted against the sky. It reminded her of California, making her feel even more homesick. She missed her parents and her brother terribly. Nevertheless, she was glad she had moved to another state. It was too depressing to live in the same city as her parents, knowing that if she visited them they would only greet her with coldness and anger.

A tear rolled down her cheek. She wiped it away with her fingers, soon realizing that the tear didn't come from homesickness, but from the rift between her and Peter Holmes. Never in her life had she met a man who had such a zest for life and whose boyish smile charmed her—making her want to both laugh and sigh at the same time.

Her face felt hot with embarrassment that Peter had discovered she was Melba Beasley. *Why?* she asked herself. *I knew it was a possibility that someone would discover my disguise, so why the embarrassment?* The answer was obvious. *She* wanted to be the one to tell Peter about it herself—when the time was right. However, she had wanted it to be in the future sometime, because telling him *why* she disguised herself would be more than embarrassing. What she already knew of Peter, it could be devastating. Would he ever want to have anything to do with her when he found out the reason?

In Jenny's mind, there was no question that she *needed* to disguise herself, and the natural way for her was with makeup. Since high school she'd had a talent with makeup for school plays, but to the dismay of her parents she had carried it further. In spite of her distress, she smiled as she recalled the time she had suggested to several of her friends that they make themselves up in comical ways and go out in public just for a lark. They had a great time shocking strangers. They did it several more times, but it ended abruptly when the school principal heard about it and called them and their parents into his office. He gave her and her friends a severe reprimand. Jenny got an additional one from her parents. Though unable to work up a feeling of contriteness, she and her friends promised never do it again and offered to pay for the use of the school makeup.

"And there *was* a reason for the *grotesque* disguise I was wearing out in public the day Peter first saw me," she reminded herself aloud. Thinking about that day almost eight months ago, she laughed. She was amazed at how well Peter hid his shock when she turned her face toward him for the first time. She had noticed right away how handsome he was, and immediately this caused her to react with the usual chip on the shoulder—the one she had developed while working at her job in California. When he had told her about the gift certificate and a dinner date with him, she had forgotten her hideous disguise and treated him like she had all the self-centered men she had encountered at work. She chuckled.

When he had taken her out to dinner, she felt as stiff as a board trying to remember her nasal twang and trying to smile through the layers of veneer. She was impressed at what a good sport he had been through it all. But, the big question she had asked herself more than once was—why in the world did she agree to go to dinner with him while in that terrible disguise? There was only one answer she could come up with. Though skeptical of him, she was also intrigued and wanted to get to know him—so much so, she even agreed to get her picture taken while accepting the certificate!

The shock at seeing his parents there made her extra nervous about the whole thing. Her face turned hot again as she remembered stumbling and falling against Peter, knocking off part of her nose! Luckily, she had moved out of that apartment before it happened! She would have been too embarrassed to face him after that catastrophe.

What tipped Peter off that I was Melba Beasley anyway? she wondered miserably. She had been so angry last night over the incident on the doorstep, she hadn't thought it over carefully, and today, in order to take her mind off of it, she had gone on a shopping spree for knickknacks to decorate the condo. However, tonight, it was all she could think about. *What tipped Peter off?* she asked herself again. Probably her clumsiness! But it had to be more than that. "I know. My freckles!" He had made reference to them that night in the restaurant.

One thing she knew for certain, one day Peter would find out who she really was, and she was terribly afraid of what he would think of her. *But why do I care anyway?* He had no right to try to kiss her like that! She got up and stormed back and forth as the embers of indignation and anger again heated up inside her.

She picked up a pillow and threw it across the room. "Ooh! How dare he treat me like that!" Grabbing another pillow, she pounded it with her fist. "He's no different than any other man—no different than all the men I've had to contend with at work in California!" Angry tears flowed like a geyser.

When her tears dried up, Jenny realized that the anger stemmed mainly from crushing disappointment. She had never felt so attracted to a man. And never in her life had she *expected* so much from one as she had from Peter Holmes, first, because he was a member of the Church and secondly, because he had exhibited such high values. Even before he had said a word, his twinkling green eyes radiated a deep spirituality.

Blinking back another flood of tears she headed for the bedroom, remembering when the first important turning point in her life had taken place. It was when she was in high school and Grandma McDuffy had given her that special article. It was then that her goals and ideals rose. Trying to *achieve* those goals and *live up* to those ideals generated lofty expectations of herself and of all the young men she dated.

And Peter Holmes had disappointed her terribly—more than anyone ever had. Her chest heaved as she determinedly refused to let one more tear fall because of him.

"As far as I'm concerned, he's history!"

Chapter Twelve

Thursday night, Harriet Flower, with Jenny McDuffy's phone number in hand, sat down to call her. Amazingly, it had worked out as she had hoped. She had called the Relief Society president of Jenny's family ward and asked if there were any single girls who attended Relief Society. The president told Harriet the only single member of Relief Society at that time was a girl named Jenny McDuffy. Harriet then asked her if by chance she could sing. The president told her she just recently learned that she could. *It was almost too good to be true!* The Relief Society president had given her Jenny's number with the promise that Harriet wouldn't give it to anyone else. This piqued Harriet's curiosity even more. She could hardly wait to meet this mystery girl!

Immediately, she had called the teacher of the upcoming lesson in her own Relief Society and asked if she and Jenny could sing a duet that would go along with the theme of the lesson. Not only did the teacher agree to this, but thanked her profusely.

Now she had a good reason for calling Jenny. She dialed and

waited. A pleasant voice answered.

"Hello, may I speak to Jenny McDuffy?"

There was a short silence. "I'm Jenny, who's calling please?"

"My name is Harriet Flower. I called your Relief Society president and asked her if she knew anyone about my age who could sing a duet with me for my Relief Society next Sunday. She gave me your name and phone number, making me promise not to give it to anyone else. Will you be able to do it?"

Jenny's heart sank. She wanted to stay in the background a while longer in the meetings. If she got up in front to sing there would be a few gasps from those who recognized her. *Oh well*, she thought, *I'll just have to live with it, and hope it will eventually all die down*.

"All right, I'll sing with you, Harriet."

"Good! Where shall we meet? My piano needs tuning, and I don't know when there will be a free room at church."

"I have a piano," Jenny said. "Would you like to come over here?"

Harriet couldn't have been more pleased. "That would be great. Where do you live?"

Jenny gave her the address.

"Thank you. Are you free right now?"

"Yes. Come on over."

Jenny hung up the phone, happy that she was having company. She was lonely.

AT 9:50, PETER RECEIVED a call from Harriet. He told his parents

he would take the call in his room. Excited, he asked, "Did you find out anything?"

"I sure did."

"Tell me!"

"I can't."

"Not you, too!"

"I can tell you one thing, Peter. She and I are singing a duet in the singles ward Relief Society this Sunday."

"She sings?"

"She does and she sings beautifully."

"Can I come to Relief Society, Harrie?" he asked wistfully.

Harriet laughed. "You can stand outside the door and listen. We're singing just before the lesson. Maybe you can open the door and sneak a peek."

"Please, Harrie, tell me about her."

"I can't. For one thing, I don't know everything about her yet, just a little, and I promised her I wouldn't tell anyone even that much."

"I give up! I'm going to go pound on her door and …"

"Peter! Be patient. I'll try to find a way to tell you without breaking my promise."

Peter calmed down. "I guess if anyone can do it, you can, Harrie sweetheart."

She burst into song. *"I only want a buddy, not a sweetheart …"*

No matter how often they had this little interchange, it always made Peter chuckle. "See you Sunday." He hung up the phone feeling a little more hopeful. Immediately, he ran downstairs to the front room, sat down at the piano and began brushing up on his skills. *Who knows,* he thought, *maybe I can come up with a way to accompany Jenny.*

Gladys and Ed, were in the family room when they heard the music. They looked at each other questioningly.

"Peter hasn't touched the piano for almost a year, Gladdie."

"I know, and that isn't like Peter. As cheerful as he always is, no one but us would know he hasn't been happy." Gladys' mind went back to the day Peter was born. After three girls, to her, he was a miracle. As his silk curls turned into the color of flax, and as his mellow and happy disposition became apparent, she thought of him as her "golden boy." Early on, his smile innocently suggested mischief, teasing or not, and one couldn't help but smile when he smiled, laugh when he did. She sighed. "I do wish he would take out that Jenny McDuffy again, but when I ask about her he clams right up. I would like you to meet her, Ed."

"I want to, but the couple of times I've mentioned her to him, he's changed the subject."

Chapter Thirteen

Sunday morning, just after Relief Society began, Peter hung around in the hall outside the door listening. He was missing the first part of his priesthood meeting to do this, so he hoped they would get to the duet soon.

At last he heard the piano play an introduction and then he heard two beautiful voices. He opened the door ever so slightly. Jenny and Harriet were standing in front of the window. The sun shone on Jenny's golden hair, giving her that familiar halo of light. Peter was certain he'd never seen anyone who looked more like an angel.

"Well! What are you gawking at, Peter?"

Startled, Peter turned and saw Maribell Gunther standing beside him, waiting to enter the room. He quickly shut the door. "Oh … uh, I was listening to Harriet sing for a moment." He stepped back, and with a flourish, motioned her toward the door. "Don't let me keep you, Maribell."

Maribell opened the door slightly, looked in, then shut it. Her eyes narrowed with suspicion. "Oh, yes. You were listening to Harriet, were you? Do you think I'm dumb or something, Peter? You were gawking at the *new* girl in the stake, just like all the other guys in this ward. There are lots of neat girls in the ward, but the minute a new one comes, all of you ignore the rest of us—and I, for one, am getting sick of it!" With an imperious air, she opened the door and went in.

"Whew!" Peter exclaimed under his breath. He headed toward priesthood meeting, thinking. Maribell was one of the girls in the singles ward who would do well to take some advice from Harrie on grooming. She had a pretty face, but in his mind, the way she kept herself reflected how she felt about herself. "It's a darn shame," he muttered.

"You talking to yourself now, Peter?" smirked Muriel Martin, who was also late for Relief Society.

He slowed down. "Yeah. I have to. None of *you* will talk to me."

She gave him a snide smile in passing. "And why do think that is, Peter Holmes?"

Peter shrugged his shoulders innocently and walked on.

When priesthood meeting ended, Peter looked for Harriet, but apparently she and Jenny had left quickly. Disappointed, he left for home.

During Sunday dinner and the clean up, Ed and Gladys tried to engage their son in conversation, but he seemed far away in thought.

PETER PACED HIS room Sunday evening. He had called Harriet three times, but she wasn't home.

Suddenly the phone rang. He grabbed it. "Hello?"

"Hi, Peter," came Harriet's welcome voice through the phone.

"Harrie! I've called you three times."

"I just walked in. I've been over at Jenny's place."

"Oh?" His face lit up with eagerness. "And ...?"

"Peter, as I told you, I promised her I ..."

"I know. I know, but you said ..."

"Peter! Let me get a word in edgewise, will you?"

"Okay, go on."

"All I can say, without breaking my promise, is go rent a video. It's a popular movie called, *Flowers for Amy.* It has just been made into a video."

"Great Scott, Harrie, that's an R–rated movie."

"I'm not through, Peter."

"Go on," he urged impatiently.

"Go rent it and you and your parents watch it together."

"What? They'll never hear of it. Why?"

"That's all I have to say, Peter. Bye."

The phone went dead, and the dial tone soon buzzed in his ear. He quickly dialed her back. It rang and rang, but Harriet wouldn't pick it up.

Peter slammed the phone down and prowled around the room muttering now and then under his breath, until he remembered something—Harrie was his friend, and they had made a pact with each other not to see any questionable movies or videos. He came to the conclusion that if Harrie asked him to see an R–rated video, it must be very important.

He left his room, ran down the stairs and entered the family room where his parents were reading. They looked up as he entered.

"May I talk to you both?" he asked looking from one to the other.

His mother smiled. "Do you have to ask, Peter?"

Peter sat down across from them. "I'm going to ask you a very strange question. Try not to be too shocked, and please say yes. It's very important. I don't know why it's important, but apparently it is." He looked questioningly at each.

"Go on," his father said.

"Will you say yes, now?"

"That's a little hard to do not knowing what you're going to ask."

"I know, Dad, but I need your support."

Ed looked over at his wife and she nodded her head. "All right, son. Yes. Now ask the question."

"Will you both watch an R–rated video with me tomorrow night?"

From his parent's shocked expressions, it was clear that this was something they could never imagine him asking. His father looked over at his mother and again, but more slowly this time, she nodded.

"All right, son. I suppose we'll come to understand why?"

"I'm sure we will, Dad. Thank you! Both of you, thank you."

UNABLE TO CONCENTRATE, Peter's workday passed in a blur. The tasks and decisions he usually relished were dispatched by rote. Nervous and edgy, he left at 5:00, went to the video store and rented *the* video, feeling disheartened as he did so.

Dinner was a quiet affair, in contrast to their usual lively discussions.

Finally, they sat down to watch the movie. "This is the most unusual family home evening we've ever had, Peter," his father said, trying to add a little levity.

"Yeah," agreed Peter, unable to appreciate his father's efforts. His brows furrowing, he pressed the play button. The title of the movie appeared: *Flowers for Amy.* Peter fast forwarded to the beginning of the movie. A scene of a young woman walking quickly down a city sidewalk appeared. As the camera brought her in closely, Peter jumped out of his seat. "That's Jenny McDuffy!" He hit the pause button.

Totally shocked, his mother said, "It is!"

"It is?" his dad asked, his disbelieving eyes scrutinizing her.

"I'm afraid so, Dad. Now I know why Harrie asked us to watch it."

"Harriet asked you to?" his mother asked, surprised.

"Yes, I'll explain later. Right now, I'd like to make an introduction. Mom and Dad meet Jenny McDuffy alias Melba Beasley."

"Melba Beasley?!" they both exclaimed.

"Yes."

"I think, son," his dad said with some gravity, "that we should view the whole movie."

Peter nodded glumly. He released the pause button and rewound to the names of the stars. The name Jeni Logan appeared. "I've heard of her. It must be her stage name. Apparently she's very popular," he added, his heart feeling as heavy as a bowling ball.

They watched it all, the three of them uncomfortable a couple of times and a little embarrassed once. They found much of it amusing and would have laughed, but their disappointment was too great.

When it ended, his mother said, "That wasn't as bad as I

expected Peter." After a moment, she added, "She's a good actress, and a good comedian."

Ed turned to his son. "All right, Peter, tell us everything."

Peter filled his parents in, telling them how he discovered Jenny was Melba Beasley, omitting the part that led up to his getting punched in the stomach. He also explained Harriet's part in the whole saga.

"Well, what do you think?" he asked them, watching their expressions closely.

"I think," his mother began slowly, "that you need to hear *Jenny's* side of the story, that is, if you're interested in her at all."

"And," his father began, his sober expression contradicting the twinkle in his eyes, "I think you owe *Melba Beasley* a gift certificate and her fee for the photo shoot."

"And I," Peter stated bitterly, "don't know what to think."

Chapter Fourteen

All week long Peter tried to put Jenny out of his mind—muttering to himself every once in a while, "I knew she was too good to be true!" However, as the days went by, and as the initial shock wore off, Peter found questions forming in his mind. Why was Jenny living here and not in Hollywood? Where did she go when she left the apartment? Back to Hollywood to do another movie? Opening a drawer, he pulled out several pictures of Melba Beasley accepting the certificate. Why did she disguise herself? The only reason he could think of was to keep her fans from recognizing her. But why such an *ugly* disguise? And how can she justify starring in those kinds of movies and still be a good member of the Church?

Just then, Dan Markham, the advertising manager, walked in with some layouts in his hand. He was a short, stocky, energetic young man of thirty-five. His light brown hair was so straight and short that no matter how often he combed it, it stuck out in several places. And no matter how much he tried to look like an executive, his tie was always askew, and his suit always a little rumpled. As usual with each new project, his hazel eyes gleamed with excitement. "Have a minute, Peter?"

Peter nodded. Dan pulled up a chair and started to show Peter what he had come up with when he spied the pictures on the desk. "Hey. That's some female," he chuckled. "Why didn't you run those?"

"There were some complications," Peter stated with finality. "Let's see what you have, Dan."

Dan's eyes were still glued on the pictures. "I'll tell you, that would have captured and eye or two, Peter. What were the complications?"

"As I said, let's see what you have there," Peter repeated in a brisk, impatient tone.

Dan's brows rose in surprise. "Okay, okay." He plunked down the layouts.

BY FRIDAY AFTERNOON around 4:00, the unanswered questions about Jenny were bearing down on Peter unmercifully. He opened one of his desk drawers and pulled out Melba Beasley's gift certificate and the check Holmes Department Store owed her. Rewriting the check and filling out a new certificate putting the correct name on each, he left his office to take them to Jenny.

Driving toward her place, he tried to sift through his emotions. He decided they were like the ingredients of his mother's cake batter, all thrown in a bowl and mixed together, not knowing where one began and one left off. The main ingredient seemed to be a feeling of apprehension that things might really be what they seemed. Mixed in with that was uneasiness over his ability to influence her in any way. Peter knew Jenny McDuffy was no pushover—the punch in the stomach confirmed it! This was a new experience for him. He had always been able to sweet talk any girl he chose. His hands gripped the wheel, wondering whether he would even be able to get a foot inside Jenny's door. But through the melange of emotions, one thing was clear—he very much wanted to see Jenny again.

Pulling into the guest parking, he picked up the certificate and check, walked over to the short path and up to the door, his heart thumping against his chest. He pushed the doorbell and waited … and waited. He pushed it again.

The door opened, and Jenny stood in the doorway in white cut-offs and a blue shirt wiping her hands on a dish towel. She must have remembered to look through the peep hole, he surmised, because she didn't look surprised to see him. Neither smiling nor greeting him, she just waited for him to speak.

"I came to deliver the certificate and check Holmes Department Store owes you," he said handing them to her.

She stared at them a moment then took them. "Thank you," she said as she started to close the door.

Peter held it open. "Please, may I come in?"

"I'd rather you wouldn't."

"You owe me an explanation, Jenny," he stated emphatically.

The fire in her blue eyes emitted sparks. "I owe you nothing, Peter Holmes." Once more she attempted to shut the door.

Peter's hand held it open. "Please, Jenny."

Surprising Peter, Jenny opened the door wide, waving a fist in his direction. "How dare you! You … you big bully!"

Peter took a step backward, holding up his hands, palms outward. "Don't hit me, Jenny, please. You have a mean right hook," he said, grimacing and rubbing his stomach.

A flicker of amusement in her eyes came and went. "If you think you can intrigue me like you have every girl you've ever known, you're not mistaken."

"I haven't intrigued every..." he began. *"Not* mistaken?" he asked, certain he hadn't heard right.

"Not mistaken," she repeated. "You might as well come in for a few minutes, Peter."

"Thanks!" he said, stepping inside. Jenny didn't offer him a seat so he remained standing in her small entry. "You mean I've got you intrigued?" he asked in disbelief.

"Yes."

"Well, you could've fooled me. That sock in the stomach was ..."

"Deserved!"

"I know," he admitted, "but how have I intrigued you?" he persisted.

"How did you manage it with all the other girls?"

"What other girls?"

"All the girls you've ever known."

Peter was puzzled. "What in the heck are you talking about? They all hate me, or they act like it anyway."

"Of course they act like it because they're trying to resist you."

Peter laughed. "You've got to be kidding."

"You ... you really don't know, do you?"

He shook his head, the puzzled expression remaining.

How refreshing, she thought, *after dealing with all those self-centered male stars in Hollywood. Peter Holmes was a rarity!*

"Hey, wait a minute, Jenny. How come you know anything about the girls I've known?" he asked suspiciously.

"Harriet told me."

"Oh. She and I grew up in the same ward and the same stake. What a snitch," he said, hoping that was all she had told Jenny.

"She also told me that she suggested that you uh …" Jenny studied a fingernail a moment, "watch a certain video."

"Yeah. She's one busy girl."

Barely finding her voice, she asked, "Did you and your parents watch it?"

Peter's face turned grim, and Jenny felt like crying. "Please leave, Peter. I get the message."

"What message?"

"The message that you're totally disappointed and disillusioned in me."

"I just want some answers, Jenny. You owe me that much."

"I owe you? You keep saying that." Her eyes blazing again, she repeated, "I do not *owe* you *anything*, Peter Holmes."

"No, I guess you don't, it's just that …" Nervous about finishing his thought, he became silent, running his hand through his hair. He looked away, then walked to her front window and stared out, thinking. Turning abruptly, he blurted out, "Jenny, I'm miserable not knowing the answers about you."

"Why?" she insisted.

Peter took a step toward her, loosened his tie and gazed down at her blue eyes, her tantalizingly full rosy lips, her slightly upturned nose, her freckles. "Because … because you are the most beautiful girl I've ever seen in my life."

Acute disappointment cut deeply. She had hoped for more than superficiality. "Please leave, Peter."

Surprised and puzzled, he asked, "Why did *that* offend you, Jenny?"

"I don't want to discuss it."

Frustrated, Peter stated, "You are the most complicated and confusing girl I've ever known, Jenny. Any other girl would be pleased at that compliment."

"I'm sure they would."

Peter gave up trying to understand. "Uh, about the movie we watched, Jenny—please, will you tell me *your* side of the story?"

Something in Peter's eyes softened her resolve. She looked away, thinking. Finally raising her eyes to meet his, she said, "I have one request, Peter."

"What is it?" he asked, his hopes rising.

"If I tell you my side and answer your questions, could it be in the presence of your parents?"

Peter was incredulous. "Why?"

"Because they have been involved in my—deceit, as *you* put it."

"All right, when?"

"Whenever it's convenient for you and your parents."

"How about tonight if it's convenient for my parents?"

"All right."

"May I use your phone?"

"Yes," she said pointing to it.

He picked up the phone from the lamp table and dialed. "Mom, what are you and Dad doing tonight?... Jenny would like to talk to all of us ... All right, I'll ask her." He put his hand over the receiver. "She wants to know if you can come for dinner."

Touched by Mrs. Holmes' kindness, Jenny shook her head,

knowing she couldn't eat a bite under the circumstances. "Tell her thank you, but no, I'll be over later after dinner."

Peter relayed the message, thanked his mother and hung up. Looking at his watch, he noted that it was 5:20. "Could you come over at 7:30?" She nodded.

Peter stood up to leave, and grinned. "I smell something good."

"I'm baking cookies for a ward party."

Peter's eyes brightened. "Any cookie dough left?"

She couldn't help smiling. "Yes. Want a spoonful?"

Chapter Fifteen

As Jenny drove toward the Holmes residence, the tension in her shoulders increased. She had told the bishop everything, and also her new friend, Harriet Flower, but she felt more nervous about opening up to Peter and his parents. She hoped fervently that they would understand. Why did she care? And why did she consent to do this? She had asked herself several times, and the answer was always the same. Even though she didn't intend to have anything to do with Peter personally, it was still important, for some reason, that he think the best of her.

Pulling into the Holmes' driveway, she studied the attractive house before her. It was a two-story cream stucco with a burnt orange tile roof. The windows were arch-shaped, one on each side of the house and one on the second floor. Beneath each were black wrought iron planters housing flowers. They were attractive accents to the low wrought iron fence surrounding the yard, and the black wrought iron gateway. Citrus trees with white painted trunks adorned the front lawn. Flower beds, filled with a variety of colorful flowers flanked each side of the porch.

Parking on the wide driveway, she stepped out into the April night and shivered, not because it was cold, but from the uncertainty that lay ahead of her. The delicious fragrance of orange blossoms drenched the air, filling her heart with a feverish longing. She knew it had something to do with Peter Holmes, but her despair over his lack of remorse fought furiously with the ardent emotions evoked by the blossoms.

She stopped to button the last two buttons of her delicate blue damask-like floral, short-sleeved shirt jacket, cropped short over a blue tank dress. Filling her lungs with the sweet air to calm her racing heart, she resumed her walk along the path that led to the front porch. At the door, she paused a moment before pushing the bell.

It was Peter who opened the door. She sucked in her breath at the sight of him. The scent of his masculine cologne brought back some of the painful yearning the orange blossoms had evoked. He gazed at her a moment. His eyes, it seemed, reflected the same emotion, mixed with uncertainty. Time stopped for them as she returned his gaze. They remained this way for several seconds, then a wide contagious smile spread across his face, breaking the spell.

"Come in, Miss Jeni Logan."

The smile that had started across her own face, disappeared. "Peter Holmes! Don't ever, ever call me that again."

Peter's brows rose at her vehement reaction. "All right. I won't. Come on into the family room, Jenny. Mom and Dad are waiting for you."

They entered the room she had been in for a short time once before. It was homey and pleasant with a blue and cream floral sofa and two large blue and cream plaid overstuffed chairs. Accent pillows were thrown on the sofa for comfort. A large attractive off-white coffee table held a large bowl of rose silk flowers, a small green plant and a plethora of magazines. Off-white book cases, filled with books, framed the attractive entertainment center. The connecting kitchen was bright and cheery with accents of blue and rose.

Peter's parents greeted her. His father shook her hand. His mother held Jenny's hand in both hers and said, "Thank you for coming over, Jenny."

Their kindness helped her relax a little, and she seated herself where Peter indicated. Carefully, she took in and let out a tremulous breath, grateful that this first step was over.

It seemed to Jenny that Gladys Holmes was aware of her uneasiness and made pleasant small talk: asking her how she liked Phoenix; if she missed California, and so forth. After Jenny's own questions about the Holmes family, Gladys resumed telling her how all their children were born in Phoenix and grew up in that house. She explained that her three daughters and their husbands and families were living in other cities now. When it was apparent that she was no longer nervous, Gladys became silent.

Jenny took her cue. "Brother and Sister Holmes, I owe you both and Peter an explanation."

Peter raised his eyebrows."Oh? You owe *me,* too, do you?" His eyes held an expression of delight over catching her contradiction.

Color infused Jenny's cheeks, and her shoulders straightened in defiance. "It's out of pure courtesy to your parents, Peter, that I'm including *you.*"

Peter, surprised at her frankness in front of his parents, sat back in his chair and grinned. "Thank you for your courtesy, Miss McDuffy."

Ed and Gladys glanced at each other.

Jenny gave Peter a condescending look, then turned her gaze to his parents. "I need to start at the beginning if you don't mind."

"We would like that very much, Jenny," Gladys said, smiling warmly.

"Thank you," Jenny said, a small nervous smile on her lips. "I uh ... graduated from college in elementary education, but because it happened to be in the middle of the school year when I graduated, I couldn't get a teaching job until the next fall. I had to work for a while. With the help of a friend, I got a job in the makeup department of one of the major movie studios. I had been in plays in high school and college, but I found my greatest interest was in the area of makeup. Apparently I have a knack for it."

Peter and his parents chuckled. "That you do, Jenny," Ed stated.

The pink color came back into Jenny's cheeks, but she went on. "I quickly got promoted to doing the makeup on some of the major movie stars. One day, a new director came into the makeup area and talked to us. He kept staring at me as he talked. When he was through with his directions to us, he asked me to step outside with him. He said that I looked like a young Doris Day and asked if I had ever acted. I told him my limited experience, and assured him I was only interested in the makeup end of the industry."

She shifted in her seat. "To make a long story short, he insisted I have a screen test, promising that if it turned out well, I could make a lot more money than I was making doing makeup. I gave in because I needed the money, intending to make it only a short detour until I got a job teaching." She glanced at Peter and saw that he was leaning forward listening intently.

"After the screen test, I was shocked when they offered me a leading part in a major movie with a big star. I felt very nervous about the whole thing and told them why. The producer and director promised me that the movies would be like the early ones Doris Day played in. I knew the kind of movies Hollywood was putting out, so in case their ideas proved to be different than what they promised, I asked for a stage name. They liked my own name, but I refused to sign a contract for the movie unless they gave me a new name. As you know, they finally agreed.

"Also, I only agreed to sign a contract for one movie at a time. I didn't want to be hemmed in so I could do what I always wanted to do—teach grade school." She noted that Brother and Sister Holmes were listening with warm, sympathetic attention, and she continued with more confidence.

"The first movie was a comedy, and I was very surprised that I got rave notices from the movie critics, from the producers, and so forth. I made a big salary and royalties. The producers kept their promises for the most part in the first two movies, but they certainly weren't 'Shirley Temple' movies because of some profanity and suggestive lines given to a couple of other characters."

She sighed. "My parents are strict in their religious beliefs, and they raised me that way, so when the director wanted me to let the leading man slobber all over me in the name of kissing, I refused. In the fourth movie, they added more suggestive things. By the time I did the fifth movie, *Flowers for Amy,* all bars came down—in my mind, that is. As you know, I didn't do anything really wrong, but the plot was immoral, the language was worse, and the leading man forced me into the kind of kiss I had refused before and pushed me down on the bed. I fought it, but by the time I got free, they had already taken the shot. They promised they would take it out, but, as you are very aware, they kept it in so it could be rated R."

The kind, nonjudgmental expressions on Brother and Sister

Holmes' faces made her feel like crying, but a quick glance at the displeasure on Peter's face effectively stopped the threatening waterworks. *Is he displeased with me or the director?* she asked herself. Pushing this out of her mind, she continued.

"I, uh … could feel myself being drawn into the Hollywood environment and not minding it as much as I did in the beginning. And what was worse, my parents were getting caught up in my stardom and were encouraging me to continue—even when I voiced my concerns.

"The temptation of making even bigger money, and the pressures to continue from producers and my parents were wearing me down. I was about to succumb because I was tired of the war that was going on inside of me. At this critical point in my life, the sister missionaries knocked on my door."

"You're a convert?" Peter asked, astonished.

"Yes. I was far from happy when I answered the door that day, but I invited the missionaries in—simply because I needed a diversion from my thoughts and feelings. They started telling me about the gospel. It felt like they were throwing me a lifeline. I was totally amazed at how I felt. I took the lessons, and as I did so, I began to realize how far I had regressed. I was baptized one month later." Jenny was gratified as she watched the Holmes' reactions, but didn't allow herself to look at Peter.

"I gave up my movie career. This upset my parents terribly, but they were much more upset at me for joining the Church. They disowned me. The only one who stood by me was my brother, Kyle, who is a year younger and my only sibling."

"Oh, my dear girl," Gladys murmured.

Still not looking at Peter, she continued. "I decided it would be best for me to leave California, so I chose to move to Phoenix. My biggest problem was that everywhere I went, people recognized me and wanted my autograph. I thought if I could disguise myself for a few months, people would forget about Jeni Logan." Gladys Holmes nodded understandingly.

"Of course, I couldn't wear the disguise to church. I was disappointed to find out that so many people in the Church had seen my fifth movie and were excited about getting to know me.

"The only person who didn't recognize me was Peter." Involuntarily, she glanced at him, trying to hold back her feelings of admiration. She turned her smile of appreciation toward his parents. "I was shocked when I saw the man who had accosted me in the department store, standing by the refreshment table at the stake dance. I had no idea he was a member of the Church also. Well," she sighed, "I've told you about everything." She leaned back in her seat, grateful it was over.

Gladys was the first to speak. "That is one of the most inspirational conversion stories I believe I've ever heard, Jenny."

Ed added with a tone of wonder in his voice, "I've never heard of a movie star joining the Church and then giving up his or her career."

"Especially in the midst of their popularity," Gladys added.

Peter was thrilled at what Jenny had told them. Not only was there no deceit as he had suspected, but she was even more wonderful than he had first thought! "Jenny, I can't believe your courage and faith. You're a missionary's dream!" Jenny, averting her eyes, didn't respond.

"We're sorry about your parents disowning you, Jenny," Gladys said.

Her gaze lifting, she replied."Thank you."

"Can I ask a question, Jenny?" Peter ventured.

Slowly, she turned to Peter, observing his expression of happiness. Though his green eyes were thoughtful, they held that twinkle which always preceded a smile. "I'll answer it if I can."

"Why did you make such a grotesque disguise? Wouldn't just an ordinary one do?"

"Ordinary ones are what I usually did. It just so happened the day you first saw me, was a day I kind of got carried away with my creativity. Besides, I wasn't in the mood to talk to anyone on that particular day, and I found the more homely I could make myself, the more people avoided me. When you approached me in the store, Peter," she paused, and her eyes suddenly sparkled with amusement, "and I turned around and you saw my face, you hardly batted an eye." She laughed. "I was amazed you had the courage to go ahead and offer the dinner date. The problem was, after I accepted the date, I had to make sure my disguise was just the same, and it had to be just the same when I went up to the offices for a picture."

Peter chuckled. "I can't believe you had the guts to go to dinner with me looking like that. Why did you accept?"

"For the reason I said. I was new in town and didn't know the nice places to eat. I was lonely for my family, so I needed the diversion, and for some reason...," she hesitated a moment, "I wanted to see if you were the kind of man who would really go through with it. I'll have to admit you were a good sport and quite brave at that," she added, a soft smile on her face.

Surprised at the compliment, Peter responded warmly. "Thanks! I'll tell you now, it took all the courage I could muster to go through with it."

They all laughed.

Gladys, ecstatic at the turn of events, asked, "How about a dish of sherbet and a homemade cookie, Jenny?"

Jenny desperately wanted to accept, but didn't feel she could handle anymore personal interaction with Peter until he understood how seriously he had hurt her and why. She continued to hope, but so far, she hadn't seen any sign that a heartfelt apology was forthcoming. "Thank you, Sister Holmes, but I must be going." She noticed the disappointment on all their faces, mirroring her own.

"Why, Jenny? What's the hurry?" Peter asked.

"I have some things I need to do," she said, standing up. The other three did likewise. Feeling gratitude that they had listened with such kindness and acceptance, she added, "Thank you for letting me vindicate myself somewhat, Brother and Sister Holmes."

"You're welcome. We consider it a privilege that you chose to tell us the story," Ed Holmes said. His smile was as warm as the Arizona sun and just as comforting.

Gladys murmured her agreement.

Jenny couldn't help but admire Gladys and Ed Holmes. They were kind, gracious and warm, as well as a very attractive couple. Mr. Holmes was an older version of his son, but without the wide mischievous-looking smile that was unique to Peter.

"It was nice getting to know you a little better, Brother and Sister Holmes," Jenny said, giving them her genuine, sparkling smile. She took a step to go—only to trip over Peter's foot. He grabbed her as she lunged forward, setting her upright as he would an unbalanced Christmas tree.

Her freckles were suddenly hidden by the cherry pink color that rose in her cheeks. She grimaced. "Oh my! I'm such a klutz! My mother was too," she explained to the amusement of her audience. "I need to have a baby."

It came out of the blue, leaving the three speechless. Finally Peter asked tentatively, "Uh … why?"

"Because it will probably cure me of my 'klutziness.' My mother said she was a terrible klutz, but the minute I was born, something just righted itself inside her. Probably, she said, because she didn't want to stumble while carrying me in her arms. The natural protective instinct that a mother has apparently cured her."

"That makes sense. I think it's a splendid way to cure yourself," Peter said, his infectious grin looking more roguish than usual. "Have you picked out the baby's father yet?"

Jenny blushed furiously, but retorted quickly. "As a matter of fact, I'm taking applications as we speak."

Peter threw back his head and laughed. "Do you have a spare application on you?"

"Sorry, I just ran out. Good night to all of you," she said, flashing another sincere and beautiful smile at Peter's parents. Ignoring Peter, she turned and walked quickly toward the front door. Peter was close behind. She glanced at him, and with a quick twist of her wrist, turned the knob and let herself out. Peter followed.

When she had almost reached the driver's side of the car, he quickly stepped ahead and blocked her by leaning against the door. "I just wanted to walk you out," he said, grinning.

"Thank you, Peter. Now may I get into my car?"

"May I ask you a question first?"

"Do I have a choice?"

"No. May I take you to dinner tomorrow night?"

"Thank you, but no."

"Why, Jenny? Do you have plans?"

"Yes."

"How about the next night?"

"No."

"Are you putting me off, Jenny?"

"You figure it out."

"Why, Jenny?" he asked, surprised and alarmed at her continued refusal. "I'm impressed with what you told us tonight. Actually, I'm more than impressed, I'm inspired by your unusual conversion story and what you gave up—your family and career. I'm sorry for thinking you deceived me."

"Thank you for the apology, Peter. Now may I get into my car?"

Surprised that the apology made no difference, he tried once more."Will you go out with me, Jenny?"

"No."

"Why?" he asked, his frustration rising. "If you'll tell me you don't like me and that you don't want my company, I won't bother you anymore."

Jenny was silent.

"Is there someone else?"

In the dimming light, Jenny's eyes drifted from Peter's anguished eyes to his inviting lips. The desire to feel them upon her own astonished her. Never having felt such an emotion, she felt tongue-tied, foolish.

Summoning all the strength she had, she replied, her husky voice soft. "I'm not obligated to tell you anything, Peter. I'm not going out with you, so please don't ask me again. Just let me leave," she added with emphasis.

"All right! Have it your way." He stepped aside and opened the door for her.

"Thank you," she said. Tears dangerously close, she slipped in behind the wheel of her car. "Good night, Peter."

Peter was too angry to respond. He shut the door and waited until she started the car and drove off.

His heart had soared tonight as he learned what a truly unusual and wonderful girl Jenny was. *But*, he thought, *why would she come to my home and explain everything if she didn't intend to give me another chance?*

Abject misery descended upon him. "Why? Why won't she go out with me?" he asked aloud. So he had tried to kiss her a little forcefully, but hadn't he received his just punishment—a sock in the belly?

DRIVING HOME, JENNY'S hard-fought determination not to go out with Peter again began to wane. She felt utterly miserable. Never in her life had she met anyone like him. What was most amazing to her was that he was totally unaware of his charm, of his affect on the opposite sex. And more importantly—his values were just what Grandma McDuffy would totally approve of if she were alive today. And that was the very reason she had expected so much more of him—why he had so disillusioned her!

By the time she arrived home, she was fighting back hot tears. She got out of the car, stepped quickly into the house, and wept uncontrollably. Grabbing a box of tissues from the kitchen, she went into the living room, sat down on the couch, and cried until her eyes were red and puffy.

When her tears were spent, she blew her nose for the umpteenth time, gathered up the sopping tissues, went into the kitchen and threw them into the waste basket under the sink.

To renew her resolve she went to a closet where she kept a small box file, lifted the lid and withdrew the special article that Grandma McDuffy had given her on the day she turned sixteen. The article had turned yellow with age, and was torn in a couple of places. Carefully, she held it, gazing at it tenderly. She carried it into the front room and curled up on the couch.

Her mind went back to that day when she was visiting her grandmother:

Having just begun dating, Jenny had asked her grandmother advice about kissing boys, advice she had been too embarrassed to ask her mother. All her friends had been dating and were involved with boys in a way that made her feel uneasy.

Grandmother went to her old roll-top desk, unlocked a drawer, and pulled out a newspaper article. Her small, thin, heavily veined hand held the article carefully as she brought it over and sat down beside Jenny. She smiled lovingly at her. "My dear, I've been saving this for you for many years. A friend of mine, who was childless, subscribed to a paper called the Deseret News, published by her church. When she read this column, it impressed her so much, she cut it out and gave it to me. I read it to your father when he was old enough, and now I want you to have it, Jenny. It's advice I would have appreciated when I was your age. I've been waiting for just the right moment to give it to you. Read it out loud, and we'll discuss it." Jenny read the title:

Confidentially Yours

WHAT IS THE HARM IN KISSING?

By Mary Marker

Dear Mary Marker:

I have just started dating and I want to know what harm there is in kissing the boys I go out with? L.M.

Dear L. M:

To prepare for marriage, you will have gone with a great many nice boys. For that is the way you will develop understanding, judgement, and the right standards on which to base a marriage. You are just beginning your dating now, and if you see this boy every evening you are in a sense "going steady" with him—or at least other boys will think so and won't invite you to go out. So I would definitely restrict dates to not more than two a week. Spend some of your other evenings with your girl friends, and when possible go with other boys. At your age it is lots more fun to have variety in friendships—both boys and girls— than it would be to have one boy friend or just one girl friend.

There isn't any harm in kissing, L. M., when it is the right person, the right time, and the right age. In fact it is so special, if it means anything at all, it is well worth saving for that very special "person and time."

You wouldn't expect to wear your best party dress to scrub the floor, and still have it nice enough to make a big impression on your beau at a party. And neither can you expect to indulge in indiscriminate kissing with the boys you will be going out with in the next few years—and still have it mean anything when you finally do meet the boy you really care for. Incidentally, the boys will be far more intrigued with you if you stick to your own ideas in such matters. There is no need to be prissy about it, just be indifferent or laugh it off. But remember to save your party dresses for parties, and your kisses for the time when they will mean something sacred and wonderful to you!

The sixteen-year-old Jenny held the article in her hands thinking, then looked up at her grandmother. "Thank you, Grandma. This is the neatest answer you could have given me. Now I can plan ahead! I'll know how to act when a guy tries to kiss me."

The twenty-eight-year-old Jenny gently placed the article on the basket table, recalling how much the article had affected her. Knowing that this was her grandmother's view, she took Miss Marker's advice, putting it into practice from that day on. She remembered how much fun it was finding clever and funny ways to turn down her dates' efforts to kiss her.

She had carried these values on into college with her, finding it even more fun turning the boys down in kind, unique or humorous ways that wouldn't offend them. Not only were most of them amused, but they became more interested and her popularity increased, as Mary Marker and Grandmother had predicted. She had only kissed a couple of boys during her college days who, for a brief period, seemed special.

When her Hollywood career began, she felt she was compromising her ideals, but her mother had assured her she wasn't. By the time the fifth movie was finished, she *knew* she was on the way to abandoning those values. What she didn't tell the Holmes family was when the missionaries began teaching her, she felt her grandmother's presence helping her to hold fast to the goals she had made years ago. When she was baptized, all the guilt and remorse left. Her slate was wiped clean. She could once more put into practice what she had learned from Grandma McDuffy and Mary Marker.

When she had met Peter in the department store, she automatically, because of his looks, put him in the category of the self-absorbed men in the acting field. After going to dinner with him as Melba Beasley, however, she was terribly impressed.

She couldn't tell the Holmes just *how* thrilled she was to see Peter at the refreshment table—to realize that he, too, was a member of the Church! She could have cried in relief when he didn't recognize her. This meant that he didn't attend most of today's movies.

The picnic with Peter was wonderful, until he discovered her deception. She knew he was upset—but that was no excuse for him to try to kiss her the way he did! Angry, disappointed tears sprang to her eyes. The young men she had dated in college, as low-brow as some of them turned out to be, had all *respected* her more than Peter had that evening. Though none of them were members of the Church, not one of them had tried to forcibly kiss her as Peter had! She had expected so much more from *him*! "Oh!" she pounded a pillow. "He's ruined what possibly could have been between us!"

After some moments, her fists still clenched, she sat up and straightened her shoulders. Her head held high, she tried to make herself believe that eventually, a young man in the Church would come along who would respect her as Grandma McDuffy had convinced her she deserved.

Chapter Sixteen

April moved on. With a vengeance, Peter threw himself into work, his church obligations, and soccer. Ed and Gladys watched their cheerful son turn into a solemn, unhappy one. Each had tried to ask him about Jenny McDuffy only to be answered with a shrug of his shoulders. Special as their only son was, Peter was also the most stubborn of their children. They knew it had to be Jenny who was causing his unhappiness; they saw his feelings for her the night she had come over. They also saw and felt the undercurrents in Jenny toward Peter. Ed and Gladys were burning up with curiosity over what was behind it all. They were also very concerned.

One Friday evening late in April, Peter could take it no longer. After showering, he got into his car and drove to Jenny's place. His heart thumping hard in his chest, he got out of the car and was about to cross the street to the walk leading to Jenny's front door when he saw a nice-looking young man ringing her doorbell. He eased back near his car so as not to be seen, and watched. Jenny opened the door. She stood there a moment looking as though she couldn't believe her eyes. Squealing, she threw her arms around him, then pulled him inside.

Peter stood there, stunned and broken-hearted. How could this happen to him? He had found the most wonderful girl in the world, and she had just acted gloriously happy to see what appeared to be an old boyfriend!

Defiance soon replaced the anguish. That man didn't have a date with her anymore than he did. He had a right to knock on her door! He stomped up onto her small porch and rang the bell.

Apparently, she hadn't taken time to look through the peep hole because he saw the surprise on her face. Had he also seen a glimpse of happiness in her eyes when she first saw him? If he had, it disappeared quickly when she spoke.

"Hello, Peter." Her face held no welcoming smile.

"Hello, Jenny. May I talk to you a moment?"

"I'm sorry, Peter, but I have company."

"Well, uh, could you step out onto the porch a minute? I just need to ..."

"No, Peter. That would be rude," Jenny said, distracted by an unruly lock of blond hair on his forehead.

Peter noticing her glance at his hair, roughly ran his hand through it. The curly lock promptly fell back to its comfortable place. Jenny giggled. Peter, confused at her sudden change of mood, raised his brows questioningly.

"It didn't want to stay," she stated, her eyes twinkling.

"Wh ... what?"

"Your curl," she motioned with her finger to his head, "didn't want to stay back."

Bewildered, he shoved it back. "What does that have to do with anything?"

She smiled. "Nothing. I've got to go, Peter."

"But …"

"I have company, remember? Good-bye."

Peter found himself facing only the door. "What the heck!" he muttered under his breath. He turned abruptly and strode angrily back to his car.

ED HAD GONE upstairs to shower, and Gladys was reading when Peter entered. He snorted around the family room like an angry bull. His mother watched and waited. Next, Peter went into the kitchen, opened up the refrigerator, stared in for a moment, slammed it shut, opened up a cupboard, and slammed it shut.

"There's nothing to eat around here!"

"What's the matter, Peter?"

"Not a darn thing!" he stated emphatically.

"I believe that like I believe there's an Easter bunny," his mother said softly, trying not to smile.

"It's not funny, Mom!"

"I don't know who *it* is, so how could I think it's funny?" Gladys smiled in spite of herself.

Peter's sand-colored brows lowered menacingly as he plunked himself down in a chair across from her and muttered, "Clever, Mom, clever. And how do you know it's a *who*?"

Gladys laughed. "Because *its* don't make you angry, Peter."

"She has a boyfriend, Mom!"

"Who?" Gladys asked innocently.

"Jenny McDuffy, that's who."

"Well, of course she has. She's such a darling girl."

"You sound like you're on her side," Peter answered in a hurt voice.

Gladys smiled. "I didn't know there were sides, Peter. Do you want to explain?"

"She's refused to go out with me. I finally went over there tonight to see once more if I could change her mind, and just as I got out of the car, I saw a guy ringing her bell. She was so happy to see him, she threw her arms around him!"

"What did you do?"

"I waited for a few minutes, then I went over and rang the doorbell. She said she had company and wouldn't talk to me."

"Why do you think she has refused to go out with you, Peter?"

He shrugged his shoulders. "She won't tell me why."

"Well, this is a *first*, Peter, isn't it?"

"What do you mean, Mom?"

"The first time a girl has turned you down."

Peter frowned, thinking. "Yeah … I guess it is."

"You're spoiled, Peter."

"That's a fine thing for a mother to say to her favorite son. If I'm spoiled—you're the mother."

Gladys laughed. "Don't blame it on me, Peter. Every girl you've even had a minor association with has spoiled you."

"Just because I haven't had a girl turn me down, I'm spoiled?"

"Have you ever had to work hard to get a girl to go out with you?"

"Well … I suppose not."

"I rest my case."

"I can't do anything about Jenny McDuffy. She won't even let me get my big toe in the door. What do you expect me to do?"

"I'm not expecting you to do anything, Peter. You're spoiled."

"Hey, what's going on?" Ed's cheerful voice interrupted.

Peter stood up and walked past him to the stairs. "Nothing much, Dad, Mom is just slamming her favorite son." With that, he took three steps at a time and disappeared.

Peter went straight to the phone and dialed Harriet. Her grandmother answered.

"Is Harriet there, Sister Flower?"

"Oh, hello, Peter. How are you?"

"I'm fine, thank you."

"Harriet is out on a date, Peter."

"A date?" Harriet didn't go out on dates—she was always there when he needed her!

"Shall I tell her to call you?"

"Yes. Tell her it's very important." He hung up, feeling abandoned. Harriet on a date? Then he remembered how she had changed herself, lost some weight, how she fixed her hair and face, and dressed nicer. Of course she would be on a date. He was happy for her … in spite of the fact he needed to talk to her.

"Spoiled am I, huh?" he grumbled, pacing around the bedroom. "That's a fine way for a mother to talk to her son! I was hinting for suggestions, but did she give me any? She always has more advice than a cactus has thorns, but tonight when I needed some, did she give me any? No!"

With nothing else to do, he got ready for bed, flipped on the television and watched an inane show until he was so bored he went to bed. He lay in the dark thinking. *I can't let Jenny get away! I have to do something. But—if she likes this other guy and doesn't like me, maybe I ought let it go.* "But I don't know that," he whispered. He remembered that flitting expression of happiness in her eyes tonight when she opened the door and saw him. Maybe he was imagining it, but maybe not.

He slipped out of bed and offered a long and fervent prayer.

Chapter Seventeen

Saturday morning, Peter was outside cleaning the pool when his mother called.

"Peter, you're wanted on the phone."

Peter ran over to her and took the phone. "Thanks, Mom." Settling himself on a patio chair he said, "Hello?"

"What's so important, Peter?"

"Harriet, sweetheart!"

"I only want a buddy, not a sweetheart ..."

"Then why in the heck are you going out on dates making yourself completely unavailable to me?"

Harriet laughed. "I guess, secretly, I do want a sweetheart after all."

"Fine thing, Harrie! How can you be there for me while you're out trying to find a sweetheart?"

"What's the matter, Peter?"

Peter told her of the man who apparently had become his competition.

Harriet felt disappointed. If there was ever a girl who was right for Peter, Jenny McDuffy was! "I'm going over there right now to talk to Jenny."

Peter smiled in relief. "Thanks, Harrie, I knew I could count on you. By the way, did you find him?"

"Who?"

"Your sweetheart?"

"Of course not. As I've said before, you're a hard act to follow, Peter. I wish I could find a guy with your qualities, but I think they're all married by now."

"No, Harrie. There's a special man out there for you. I've always told you that."

"I know you have. I hope you're right. I'll call as soon as I have something to report."

"Thanks, Harrie."

Harriet hung up the phone, frowning. What could she do about it if Jenny *did* have a boyfriend? At the moment, she couldn't think of a thing, but maybe she could later.

Changing to tan knee-length shorts and a wine T-shirt, she looked at herself in the mirror, still pleased at her new figure as she tucked in the shirt. Mascara, eyeshadow, and wine lip-gloss were added. With a quick brush through her shiny dark hair, she grabbed her purse and went into the kitchen to tell her grandmother where she was going.

While driving, Harriet thought of several things she could say to Jenny, only to decide against each of them. Two weeks ago, Peter had told her of the forthright explanation Jenny had given to him and his parents. He had then begged her to find out why Jenny refused to go out with him. She had tried, but Jenny wouldn't say.

Upon arriving at Jenny's condominium complex, she parked in the guest parking, ran to the condo, and rang the bell.

Presently the door opened, and she found herself gazing up into the sky blue eyes of Peter's competition. Her heart did a flip-flop. All she could do was stare at the angular features of this clean-cut, nice-looking man with strawberry blond hair. Medium height, he was dressed in chinos and a blue knit shirt.

The man, momentarily surprised, quickly gave her the once over. A slow grin spread across his face. "Well, if you aren't the prettiest cactus flower I've seen since I arrived in Arizona. What can I do for you?"

Harriet, totally unprepared for this kind of greeting, just stared at him. Then her loyalty and sense of fair play emerged. "Well! If you're a boyfriend of Jenny's, you're certainly not acting like one! Besides—she's taken!" she blurted out.

Surprised by her indignant outburst, the young man angled his head to one side, a bemused expression on his face. "Please come in, miss. May I have your name?"

"Miss Flower."

"I was right!" he grinned. "You *are* a cactus flower."

Harriet stepped inside, flustered at his manner. "I came to see Jenny," she stated with abruptness.

"Please have a seat, Miss Flower."

She seated herself and he sat across from her.

"Where's Jenny?"

"Oh," he replied as if he'd forgotten all about Jenny. "She went to the grocery store to pick up something special for breakfast."

"She invited you to breakfast?" Harriet asked, surprised.

"Well, yeah. I guess she had to since I stayed here last night."

Shocked, Harriet couldn't speak for a moment. Her heart plummeted. Still not wanting to believe it, she stood up and glared down at him, her hands on her hips.

"You … you stayed *here*?"

"Of course. Jenny and I are, you might say, good friends." He grinned.

"But it doesn't look right. It …"

"There are two bedrooms," he interrupted. "I assure you it was perfectly innocent. I stayed in one and she in the other."

"It still doesn't look right!"

Ignoring her outburst, he said, "You mentioned something about Jenny being taken, I believe."

"Yes. She is," Harriet said sitting down again. "You're wasting your time. She has a boyfriend."

"I can hardly believe that. What's his name?"

"Peter Holmes."

"She didn't tell me anything about being a girl friend of a Peter Holmes."

"How long are you here for, Mr …"

"My name's Andrew."

"Uh, Mr. Andrew, how long are you going to be visiting Jenny?"

"I don't know yet. But I'm taking Jenny out to eat at the Terrace Dining Room tonight at 6:00. Want to come along?"

This propelled Harriet to her feet and to the door. She couldn't believe the man's crass insensitivity. "No thank you! How can you invite another girl to go on your date with Jenny without asking *her*?

Good-bye, Mr. Andrew." She opened the door, stepped out quickly, slammed it shut, and ran to her car.

She fumed all the way home. "What can I tell Peter?" she asked aloud. One thing for certain, she wasn't going to destroy him by revealing that Mr. Andrew stayed the night at Jenny's.

By the time she arrived home, an idea had come to her. Greeting her grandmother, she went directly to the phone and dialed Peter. Peter's hello came before it could ring twice.

"I met him, Peter."

"You met him?" he asked in amazement. "He was there at Jenny's this early?"

"Yes."

"What happened? What did Jenny say?"

"Jenny wasn't there. She had to run an errand, but I did tell Mr. Andrew that Jenny was taken and that he was wasting his time."

Peter's silence lasted only a moment, then he burst into laughter. "You didn't."

"I did."

"What did he say?"

He didn't believe me. But I found out that he's taking her to dinner at the Terrace Dining Room tonight at 6:00.

"So what can I do, Harrie?" Peter asked, feeling miserable and helpless.

"I think you and I ought to go out to dinner there also and get a table right next to theirs."

"Why?" The thought of watching Jenny with someone else was so unsettling, his hand clenched.

"I want you to flirt with Jenny right in front of him—because you know what he did?"

"What?"

"He flirted with *me!* And to top it off, he asked if I wanted to come along on their date."

Peter was incredulous. Even though Harrie was attractive, he wondered how a guy could be disloyal to a girl like Jenny. Outraged, he almost broke Harriet's eardrum. "What a two-timer! I'll try to put a stop to that relationship," he stated grimly. "Let's go. I'll pick you up at 5:00. I would like to get there early so we can get a table near them. Oh, and dress up. It's a pretty nice place."

"I forgot, Peter, you have soccer tonight."

"What soccer?"

Chapter Eighteen

Peter and Harriet arrived at the restaurant at 5:30 informing the maitre d' they had a reservation at 6:00. "We came early because we'd like you to arrange a table near our friends. I believe the reservation will be under the name of Andrew."

The maitre d' looked at the reservation list. "I'm sorry, sir, but we don't have a reservation under that name."

"Do you have one for McDuffy?"

He looked. "Yes, we do at 6:00. But I'm sorry I don't believe I can arrange a table near them."

Peter slipped him a $20 bill. "We'd like to be seated right next to the McDuffy party."

"I believe I can arrange that right now, sir. Follow me."

They followed him to a table for two and the maitre d' pulled out the chair for Harriet, then nodded formally at Peter. "The waiter will be with you soon."

Harriet grinned at Peter. "Well, if you aren't a smooth operator, Peter Holmes."

"Thanks, Harrie. All it takes is a little money under the table to make one smooth."

Harriet looked around at the ambience of the restaurant. "This is some fancy place, Peter. Mr. Andrew must be well-off. I remember now, you've been here before."

"Once," he smiled, remembering his date with Melba Beasley. "That's why I said we'd better dress up."

Harriet's heart was aflutter. She was anxious over Peter and Jenny, but her pulse quickened whenever she thought about Jenny's escort. She had gone over her new wardrobe carefully, and had chosen an apricot rayon-linen dress with princess seams that showed off her new figure, flaring softly from the waist to below the knee.

Peter's heart was a little erratic also. He was concerned at how Jenny would react when she discovered their presence. Pulling himself together, he smiled at Harriet and for the first time noticed the rosy flush of her cheeks. "You look nice tonight, Harrie."

"Thank you, Peter," she said, pleased at the sincere admiration she saw in her friend's eyes.

It wasn't long before they became aware that the maitre d' was seating Jenny and her date. Peter's eyes gazed admiringly at Jenny. She was wearing a dress the color of her hair. Then she flashed one of those glowing smiles at her escort, and Peter's insides twisted in knots.

Harriet stared at Jenny's date. He was even better-looking tonight in his taupe pinstripe suit accented by a colorful tie with some of the same hues as his reddish blond hair. Her heart did that annoying flip-flop again. She would have felt very disloyal to her friend if she hadn't felt so sure that Jenny was right for Peter. The subject of her scrutiny turned and caught her gaze.

"Well, if it isn't the little cactus flower who appeared on your doorstep this morning, Jenny," he said loudly while gazing at Harriet.

Jenny looked over at Harriet, whose cheeks were now infused with color from embarrassment over the flirtatious remark.

"Harriet!" Jenny exclaimed. "How fun to see you here." Her eyes moved across the table to Harriet's escort, and her heart sank. *Was Peter dating Harriet?* she wondered. "Hello, Peter," she greeted hesitantly.

"Hello, Jenny," Peter said, trying to sound casual. Then to Jenny's date, he said through clenched teeth, "I really don't appreciate you calling my date a 'cactus flower.'"

Jenny's brows rose at Peter's ominous tone, but her escort only looked amused, increasing Peter's annoyance.

The man stood up and stepped over to Peter. "I don't believe I've had the pleasure. My name is Andrew and yours?" he asked holding out his hand.

Peter scooted his chair back, stood up, and looked down at Andrew, who was a couple of inches shorter, trying to squelch his jealousy enough to be cordial. "Mr. Andrew, my name is Peter Holmes."

"Andrew is my first name," he corrected, then his brows rose. "Ah … so you are Peter Holmes. This lovely cactus flower here told me you were Jenny's boyfriend." He turned to Harriet. "Isn't that right?"

Peter was speechless. He couldn't believe the man's lack of tact! He glanced at Harriet, who looked as though she couldn't utter a word if she had to. It was Peter who rallied first. "Out of consideration to your date, Andrew, I once again suggest very strongly that you refrain from calling my date a 'lovely cactus flower.'"

Andrew turned to Jenny. "Do you mind me calling this lovely girl here," he indicated with a flourish of his hand, "a cactus flower?"

Her eyes alight with amusement, Jenny said, "Of course not, Andrew, dear."

Peter and Harriet stared at Jenny in stunned silence.

Andrew broke the silence. "Why don't the both of you join Jenny and me at our table?"

Peter and Harriet looked at each other totally puzzled. Peter turned to Jenny. "Is it all right with you, Jenny?"

"Anything my wonderful Andrew wants is what I want," she answered in sickening sweet tones while gazing at Andrew with puppy-dog eyes.

His brows hovering over his eyes, Peter wondered if he really knew Jenny after all. "We'll join you," he mumbled as began to pull his chair over to their table.

The maitre d' appeared suddenly. "May I help you, sir?" he asked Peter.

"Yes. We would like to join our friends here."

"Your waiter will be here momentarily to assist you."

"Thank you." Peter moved Harriet's chair over and seated her. He sat across from her, seriously wondering if coming here tonight was a good idea. He could tell Harriet was feeling the same way.

The waiter appeared and set glasses of water, silverware, and napkins at their respective places. When all four had declined an alcoholic drink, he handed them each a menu. Jenny and Andrew discussed the choices, making remarks and laughing at inside jokes. Harriet and Peter studied their menus in silence, wishing they were elsewhere.

After the decisions were made and the orders taken, Harriet made a stab at conversation, awkward as it was. "Where are you from, Andrew?" she asked.

"California."

"How long will you be visiting our sunny Arizona?" She wanted to add, *and when will you be staying somewhere besides Jenny's?*

"That depends." He gave Jenny his own sickening puppy-dog look. "My sweet Jenny doesn't know yet, but I may be moving to Phoenix."

"Really?" Jenny asked, sincere excitement in her voice.

"Would you like that, sweet Jenny?"

Harriet felt like throwing up, and Peter looked like he couldn't eat a bite.

"Oh yes, dear Andrew," she gushed.

Harriet rolled her eyes. "Oh come on, you two! Are you for real?"

They both laughed—a little too long, Harriet thought.

Jenny reached for Andrew's hand and held it across the table. "We are for real, Harriet. Aren't we, dear Andrew?"

A sappy smile on his face, he answered, "We are … oh yes, we are."

When Jenny withdrew her hand from Andrew's, she hit Peter's glass of water, knocking it over. He scooted back quickly and stood up, but not quickly enough. The water had run over the table onto his suit pants, leaving a large wet mark in a conspicuous and embarrassing spot.

"Oh my! I'm sorry, Peter. And that's such a nice suit."

"It was a nice suit," he muttered as he tried to wipe his pants.

Andrew was grinning from ear to ear. "Jenny, you are such a klutz!"

The waiter came with the salads. Seeing the problem, he placed them on Peter and Harriet's recently vacated table instead, suggesting they all move there.

As the other three stood and the four started over to the next table, Jenny tripped over a chair leg. Peter caught her just as she tried to grab hold of the table to catch herself, grabbing only the drenched table cloth instead, pulling it with her, glasses of water, silverware and all.

Peter held her upright while they watched the table cloth and everything on it go crashing to the floor. Grinning, Peter said, "Have you any spare applications on you?"

Flustered and embarrassed, she began to giggle. Then realizing Peter still had hold of her, she tried to pull her arm away. "You may let go now."

Instead, Peter picked her up in his arms and carried her to the next table and sat her in one of the chairs, seemingly unaware of the stares from surrounding tables.

Andrew watched quizzically. "Looks like you're the hero of the day, Peter. Don't you think so, Harriet, my cactus flower?"

Harriet, who had been fighting laughter over Peter's conspicuous wet spot, suddenly sobered. "I am not *your* cactus flower. Remember your *sweet* Jenny?"

"Oh yes, but when I look at you, I almost forget."

Reseating herself at the other table, Harriet almost shrieked. "Did you hear that, Jenny?"

"I did," she sighed dramatically. "Andrew is just a little fickle sometimes."

"A little fickle! Jenny, you are the last person I would think would put up with a fickle guy."

The waiter arranged the salads in front of each of them along with a fresh glass of water. After he left, Peter glared at Jenny. "I agree with Harriet, Jenny. You haven't let *me* get away with a thing. How come you're letting this guy get away with flirting with Harriet?" Before she could respond, he turned to the man himself. "I don't know what's going on with you and Jenny, but you don't deserve her. I want you to treat her right. Jenny's *my* girl."

"Your girl? I am not your girl!" Jenny exclaimed as she pulled the napkin to her lap, sending two forks flying to the floor. "Oh my!" She and Peter bent over to pick them up at the same time and bumped heads. Jenny, in her unbalanced state fell sideways and grabbed at the table for support, but once more only managed to pull the tablecloth, upsetting water glasses and spilling a bowl of salad on top of Peter's legs while he was trying to stop her from falling. Not succeeding in catching her this time, Peter slipped off his chair to his knees and Jenny fell to the floor.

Jenny looked at Peter in dismay, her face crimson. The other two at the table, having caught the table cloth before everything went off, were frantically trying to mop up water. The maitre d' and the waiter came running over. They stood staring at the table and then at the two on the floor. The maitre d' trying to keep his voice under control, addressed Peter. "May I ask you, sir, how in the world this happened?"

Peter looked up at him, shaking his head. "I have no idea." He started laughing, unable to stop. Harriet and Andrew, who had both been fighting back laughter, let loose. Jenny, her face still crimson and the only one not laughing, looked up at the maitre d' and pointed a finger at herself as the one who had caused the catastrophe. Getting to her feet as ladylike as possible, she waited for Peter, who was still on his knees laughing. Finally, getting control of himself enough to stand up, Peter brushed the salad off his pants.

The maitre d' looked around uncomfortably at the other patrons who were clearly upset at the disturbance. He cleared his throat several times, glaring at the three who were still trying to stop laughing. In frustration, he pointed to the other table. Peter stepped over to their recently vacated table which had just been freshened up, pulled out a chair for Jenny, and waited for Andrew who was, by now, seating Harriet. Both men seated themselves. Harriet pulled a tissue from her purse and blew her nose.

The waiter began cleaning up the other table and the maitre d' hovered over the four. Finally, he said with great irritation, "I know we didn't serve you drinks here, but did you four consume liquor before arriving?"

The four looked at each other and burst out laughing. The maitre d' threw up his hands and walked away. Patrons at the tables nearby, already shocked at the unseemly accidents happening one after the other, were now more irritated at the laughter they felt had gone on far too long.

When, at last, their amusement subsided, the four of them felt relaxed and more comfortable with each other. However, Peter was still puzzled at Jenny and Andrew's strange relationship and more than a little worried.

Another round of salad bowls were placed on the newly changed tablecloth along with fresh glasses of water. They got through the salad without mishap. The conversation consisted mostly of Andrew asking Peter questions about his work and his family. Peter, trying his best to be cordial, answered in as few words as possible. He couldn't think of a single personal question he wanted to ask Andrew. All he could think of was that he wanted him out of his life!

The orchestra began playing, and the lights dimmed on the dance floor.

"How about us dancing until the main course comes?" Andrew suggested.

Peter nodded, but groaned inwardly at the thought of Andrew taking Jenny into his arms. Out of courtesy, he asked, "How about it, Harrie sweetheart?"

From habit, she sang softly, *"I only want a buddy, not a sweetheart …"*

Andrew stared at her in astonishment.

She blushed. "Oh, sorry, this is always how Peter and I greet each other."

Andrew laughed. "Neat! And you have a great voice."

"Thank you," she responded, more pleased than she wanted to be. After all, Jenny was her friend. She hated the fact that she was attracted to her boyfriend.

Andrew turned to Peter, a puzzled frown on his face. "I believe I heard you call this beautiful little cactus flower, Harry."

Peter seethed at Andrew's total disregard of his date. "So?"

"That seems a little masculine for one so feminine."

Peter jumped up from the table, stepped over to Andrew, grabbed him by the scruff of the neck, and pulled him up, knocking his chair over. "I'm tired of your rudeness and disregard of the girl you brought here tonight!"

The other diners, who had watched with both abhorrence and fascination the machinations of this foursome, were now disturbed at what looked like forthcoming violence. The maitre d,' who had been keeping an eye on the group, rushed over and spoke low and menacingly to Peter. "I'm afraid I'm going to have to ask you and your group to leave the restaurant."

The giggles that Jenny had been stifling broke out into full blown laughter. And, to Peter and Harriet's surprise, Jenny's date was also laughing. Confused, Peter abruptly let go of Andrew, who had to step back quickly to keep his balance. Picking up his chair, he sat down, red in the face from laughter.

Suddenly, voices of diners around them buzzed loudly, and two women from adjacent tables came over to Jenny. One of them ventured, "Aren't you Jeni Logan, the movie star?"

Jenny immediately sobered. "No, my name is Jenny McDuffy."

"But I know you're Jeni Logan," the other woman stated with conviction.

A man stepped over to the group. "You *are* Jeni Logan. I want to tell you how much I enjoy your movies."

Jenny finally succumbed. "All right, I *was* Jeni Logan, but that's only my stage name. I've retired from the acting field."

"Oh no!" one of the women exclaimed. "I love your acting and your sense of comedy."

"Have you seen my fifth movie, *Flowers for Amy?*"

"Oh yes!" the women said almost simultaneously, and the man nodded, smiling.

"Well—you should all be ashamed of yourselves."

The three strangers stared at Jenny, not quite believing their ears. Andrew was grinning with amusement, and both Peter and Harriet's mouths were agape with surprise.

Jenny continued, "I would suggest that all of you be more

discerning about the movies you see."

"But ... but, Miss Logan...," spluttered one of the women.

"You may return to your tables." She flashed a wide smile. "And have a good evening."

Peter smiled and clapped. Harriet joined him. The confused threesome returned to their table. Only the confused maitre d' remained. "Are you r–really Jeni Logan?" he stammered.

"I *was* Jeni Logan."

"Uh, I'm sorry I asked you to leave, I ..."

"You should have asked us to leave. We've disturbed the pleasant atmosphere of your restaurant. We'll try to be better behaved for the rest of the evening."

"Thank you, Miss Logan."

"Miss McDuffy," she corrected.

"Oh yes, Miss McDuffy." He backed away, smiling.

The waiter arrived, placing the main course before each and pouring fresh water in the glasses, leaving Jenny's half full. Jenny looked up at him, amused and said, "Thank you." The waiter coloring slightly at being caught, nodded.

Peter was supremely proud of Jenny, but was still ticked off at Andrew. "Now, back to your behavior, Andrew," Peter began grimly. "I ..."

"Peter," interrupted Jenny, "I would like you and Harriet to meet my *brother*, Kyle Andrew McDuffey. He goes by Kyle rather than Andrew."

"Your brother?" Peter asked, astonished. Instantly, a broad grin of relief spread across his face.

"Your brother?" Harriet repeated, feeling almost as much relief as Peter. She wasn't being disloyal to Jenny after all!

After the disclosure had totally registered itself upon them, Peter and Harriet began to understand the sickening interaction between Jenny and 'Andrew.' They looked at each other, and Harriet asked, "Why didn't we guess before, Peter? Their conversation was so nauseating and overdone." Turning to Jenny and Kyle, she added, "I didn't think you were for real, but still, I wasn't sure."

"I think it was kind of a dirty trick to pull on us," Peter stated.

"I agree!" Harriet exclaimed. "You made us look like a couple of dunces."

"Wait a minute here," asserted Kyle, gazing directly at Harriet, "we didn't ask you to come over to Jenny's place and indignantly tell me that Jenny was taken."

"But … you …" Harriet spluttered.

"And," he continued, "we didn't ask you to follow us here to The Terrace Dining Room and arrange for a table next to us."

Peter, also feeling cut down to size, chuckled. "I guess we did have it coming, Kyle."

"But I do have to thank you, Peter, for looking out for my sister."

"You're welcome. Now can you put in a good word for me? She won't go out with me."

"That's what she told me." He turned to his sister. "I think you ought to go out with Peter, Jenny. He's a passable enough guy." He grinned.

Peter grunted. "That was a halfhearted endorsement."

"Maybe I can do better after I get to know you. Now, how about us focusing on this delicious-looking food. I'm starved."

In spite of their still curious audience, Jenny's revelation that

Kyle was her brother made it possible for all four to converse more easily. Later, after dessert and after the girls had returned from the powder room, Kyle smiled at Harriet.

"May I have this dance, Miss Cactus Flower?"

"I wouldn't dare refuse now," she responded. Smiling at Jenny and Peter, she said, "See you later, you two."

Stepping onto the dance floor, Kyle looked down at Harriet, his eyes intent. "I didn't know I was going to be lucky enough to see you so soon." He slid his arm around her and held her close, his face pressed against her upturned one. The orchestra was playing a slow number.

The music may have been slow, but Harriet's heart was beating a fast tango. *This is just my luck!* she thought, unhappily. *The first man who really attracts me since Peter, has to be a non-Mormon!*

"You know what?" Kyle whispered in her ear, "The fire in those brown eyes of yours this morning set my heart ablaze."

"If you weren't Jenny's brother, Kyle McDuffy, I would say you were full of baloney."

Kyle pulled back and looked at her in amusement. "Not only are you a beautiful cactus flower, but you're a *prickly* one." Pulling her close again, he asked, "And since I am her brother, what would you say?"

Harriet thought about it a moment. "Using an expression my grandmother uses, I think you're a charming snake oil salesman."

Kyle threw back his head and laughed.

Harriet studied him. "I should have guessed you were Jenny's brother. You have the same charisma she has."

Kyle grinned. "Thanks."

"How old are you, Kyle?"

"Twenty-seven. How old are you?"

"The same. Twenty-seven."

"Just a kid."

"And you, I'm sure, are a man of the world."

Tightening his embrace, he admitted, "That I am, I'm afraid."

Their table was close enough to the dance floor for Jenny and Peter to watch Harriet and Kyle.

"This has been a strange, but enlightening evening," Peter remarked.

Jenny pulled a face. "And almost a disastrous one."

Their heads turned to the dance floor as they heard the fast beat of the new song. Harriet and Kyle were now doing the swing. They watched, fascinated at how well they danced together.

Peter reached for Jenny's hand. "How about it? May I have the next slow dance? I'm a little nervous about starting out with a fast one."

"Are you afraid of my klutziness?"

"No, I'm afraid of mine. You've got me feeling totally off balance, Jenny."

She pulled her hand away, her smile crinkling the corners of her eyes. "You wouldn't dance with me when you brought me here before, why should I dance with you now? Are you prejudiced toward homely women?"

"No," he grinned. "I'm prejudiced against getting plastered with thick makeup. As it turned out, you left an unsightly blob of it on my suit one time, remember?"

"How could I forget. I shudder when I think of it. And now your suit is all wet and smudged from the salad and water I spilled on you. Are you sure you want to get up and dance looking like that?"

"I sure do." He grinned. "Who will be looking at me when I have you in tow?"

The next dance was a slow one. Peter stood up and held out his hand to Jenny who took it. When they reached the dance floor, Peter paused a moment, his eyes taking in every inch of Jenny's face. Unable to hold out another moment, he pulled her close, bent his head to touch his face to hers. The thrill of finally holding her in his arms almost stopped his feet, moving only enough to make a pretense of dancing. Without even thinking his lips pressed against Jenny's temple. He felt her stiffen. She tried to pull away, but he held her tighter and began dancing seriously.

When the song ended, Peter led Jenny over to the orchestra and requested another slow one. Several members of the orchestra recognized her as Jeni Logan. They grinned and nodded vigorously.

"Peter," began Jenny, as he led her back to the center of the floor. "I didn't accept another dance."

"You didn't? I swear I saw it in your eyes." Ignoring any further refusal, he held her close again. "This is a little bit of heaven, Jenny," he whispered in her ear.

If Peter could have seen Jenny's face, he would have been happy to see the distressed frown melt away after only a few bars, replaced by a dreamy expression.

As the music ended, Peter reluctantly led Jenny to the table. "We have to talk," he said, pulling out the chair for her. "It's time now that you to tell me why you won't go out with me."

"It's personal, Peter. Besides—you should *know*."

"But I don't!"

"That's what hur... I mean that's what's so frustrating, Peter, that you *don't* know." She almost slipped and told him how hurt she was. If he didn't know that, there was no chance for them to get together!

"You're frustrated? Well, join the club, I've never felt so perplexed in my life. What do *you* have to be frustrated about, Jenny? I'm the one who's getting the cold shoulder, and for reasons you won't tell me."

She looked down—silent—her full lips trembled momentarily, then compressed tightly.

Peter let out a baffled sigh. "I'm sorry for whatever I've done, Jenny."

Hastily, she scooted back her chair, stood up, and folded her arms tightly across her mid-section, her blue eyes spitting fire. "You most certainly are *not* sorry, Peter Holmes! How can you be sorry for 'whatever?' You are an insensitive, obtuse, bull-headed man!"

Peter stared up at her, taken back by the unexpected outburst. Nevertheless, he was instantly intrigued and amused by it. "I'll try not to be bull-headed, my little powder-puff pigeon, if you'll just ..."

"I'm not your powder-puff pigeon! I'm not your *anything*!"

Harriet and Kyle had walked up just in time to hear the exchange between the two. The people at the tables close by were all watching and shaking their heads, intrigued by the latest crises involving Jeni Logan.

"Ah, give the guy a break, sis," Kyle said, grinning.

"Well of all things!" Harriet exclaimed. "You men do stick together, don't you? Well, just go ahead and stick together. Jenny and I are going home. You two can be bosom pals all the rest of the evening. Come on, Jenny," she said, grabbing her purse.

"Thanks, Harriet," Jenny said, smiling, gratefully. "Throw me your keys, Kyle."

Dumbfounded, Kyle did as he was told and threw the car keys to her. The two bewildered men watched their partners walk briskly off toward the front door.

Chapter Nineteen

It wasn't long before Peter and Kyle left the restaurant. They felt altogether deflated and confused. Peter drove Kyle to Jenny's apartment only to find she wasn't home yet.

"They're probably over at Harriet's, Kyle. Do you have a key?"

"No. I'll just wait here on the doorstep until she comes."

"That may be a long time. How about coming over to my house?"

"No thanks, Peter. I'm waiting right here. I intend to give my sister a few succinct words when she arrives."

Peter sat down on the doorstep beside Kyle. Both men, still puzzled over what had happened, sat in silence. Finally, Peter spoke. "Would you do me a favor, Kyle, and try to find out why Jenny won't go out with me?"

"I've already tried. She won't tell me a thing. I asked her after Harriet came over and told me you were Jenny's boyfriend. We've always been close, and only a couple of times has she ever held anything back from me. It must be a very sensitive issue with her, or she would have confided in me."

"That bit of info concerns me even more, Kyle."

Just then, Jenny drove up and into her garage. Peter and Kyle stood.

"I guess I better get outa here so you can have a talk with your sister."

"Okay. Hope to see you again, Peter. And I hope to see Harriet Flower again, too."

"Wel–l–l, good luck on that one."

Before Kyle could ask him what he meant, Peter was off, sprinting toward his car. Kyle pushed the bell. Jenny opened it, greeting him with that acrimonious look he knew so well.

He stepped in. "Thanks. I thought I might have to sit on the porch for hours."

"I thought you and your buddy, Peter Holmes, would be having a great time for hours."

"Don't take it out on me, Jen. It seems to me that you overreacted tonight."

"You know nothing about it, Kyle McDuffy!"

Kyle's brows rose knowingly. "Something's really bothering you for you to become that angry. Tell me about it, sis."

"You wouldn't understand."

"Hey, that's not fair, sis."

"I know you, Kyle. You'd sympathize with Peter."

"I've changed, Jenny."

Jenny threw him a skeptical glance as she walked away. "I'm getting ready for bed. And by the way, I'm going to church in the morning at 9:00. If you want to come with me, be ready."

"No thanks, sis. I'm going to *my* church."

Eight-thirty Sunday morning, Jenny and Kyle left for their respective churches. Kyle waited until Jenny's car was half a block away before he followed her. He had a wonderful surprise for her, and he was going to let her in on it when he walked into church and sat down beside her in the chapel.

When his sister gave up being a successful actress because of the church she had joined, Kyle became suspicious of that church. When Jenny moved to Arizona, he investigated it for one reason only, to prove that it was a cult of some kind. *What else could have drawn her away like that?* he had asked himself.

Checking into it, he had agreed to let two young missionaries come to his apartment and teach him, and to his surprise, everything they said gave him a feeling he had never felt before. He read the Book of Mormon for one reason only—to discredit it. As a young boy he had been taught to pray. So, when the missionaries suggested he pray about the book, he did. He prayed that he would be able to see it for what it was, expecting to find out its falseness. Instead, the book and the Spirit converted him. Six weeks later, he was baptized. His desire to have Jenny come to his baptism was overridden by his desire to surprise her.

Excitement pumped adrenalin into him as he followed her. Allowing a car to get between them so she wouldn't see him, a red light stopped them, but Jenny went sailing on. When the light changed, the car in front of him stalled. The traffic in the left lane was busy, and by the time he could pull out from behind the stalled car, he could no longer see Jenny's car. Where had she turned?

"Doggone it!" he muttered. "Now what am I going to do?"

Turning at several corners, he couldn't find an LDS Church anywhere. *Well, so much for trying to surprise Jenny,* he thought miserably. Finding a service station, he stopped and looked in a phone book for a ward building close by.

Eventually, finding one, he cruised around the parking lot looking for Jenny's car, but as he had expected, it wasn't there. This wasn't her ward building. Nevertheless, he parked, got out and went in to attend church anyway.

PETER'S SPIRITS WERE up in spite of Jenny's actions the night before. Finding out that Kyle was Jenny's brother instead of a boyfriend gave him hope that he could still win her over. Since she wouldn't date him, he was determined to find a way to be around her, a way that would let them become better acquainted.

After church, he and Harriet walked to the parking lot together. "Okay, Harrie, why did you turn on me last night and leave Kyle and me in the lurch?"

"For the reasons I said, Peter. You guys stick together, no matter what."

"That's not true, Harrie. The only reason we did last night is because neither of us understand what in the heck Jenny is so upset about. She won't tell you, she won't even tell her own brother. What were we to do?"

"Find out what's bothering her," Harriet said flatly.

"How the heck can I do that, Harrie?"

"I don't know, Peter, but I would suggest that you look inside yourself and do a little self-analysis—something guys don't do very often."

"I have."

"Dig deeper then." She opened her car door and got in. "Got to get home, Peter. It's my turn to get dinner."

Peter watched the friend who usually helped him out in every situation drive off, leaving him alone in the most puzzling dilemma he had ever been in.

LEANING ON THE wall next to the garage door, Kyle waited for Jenny to return from church. When she arrived, he entered the garage and followed her inside.

"Did you have a nice meeting, Kyle?"

"Yes, but I need a key to your condo, Jenny. I can't get caught outside each time. I'll need to stay here for a while until I can find a place of my own."

Jenny squealed. "You really are moving here?"

"Yes. I thought maybe you needed some family. Mom and Dad have each other, so I'm moving my office to Phoenix. I can arrange to find a good assistant as an on sight manager for our properties in California, and I'll look for new investments here for us."

Throwing her arms around him, she shed a few tears. "I'm so happy, Kyle. I've been lonesome."

"Me too, sis," he said, hugging her, wanting to tell her that their parents had also disowned *him* for joining the church.

"Let's change and get dinner while you tell me everything. But first, tell me how long you're going to be here now?"

"About a week. Then I'm going back to California to arrange for a moving truck to move my business and personal things. I need a week to find an office and—to date Harriet Flower."

Jenny laughed. "I knew you were taken with her the moment you called her your little cactus flower. She's a wonderful girl, Kyle." A troubled expression slowly erased the happy one. "But Kyle, I don't know how far you'll get with her. I'm sure she doesn't want to get too involved with a non-member of the Church—my church."

"Hey, I'm the charmer remember?"

"Hey yourself, Kyle. You have no idea what deep water you'll be getting into."

"I've never been turned down yet, have I?"

Jenny studied her brother, remembering sadly how she had tried to tell him about the gospel, and how he had refused to listen.

KYLE MCDUFFY STOOD on Harriet Flower's porch. Confidently, he pushed the bell.

A nice-looking woman opened the door. Her short dark hair displayed only a few strands of gray and her brown eyes were warm and friendly. She smiled. "Hello."

"Hello. I'm Jenny McDuffy's brother, Kyle."

The woman's eyes lit up in acknowledgment. "Oh yes. Come in." She stepped aside. Closing the door, she said, "I haven't met Jenny yet, but Harriet has talked about her. I'm Harriet's grandmother, Camille Flower."

"Glad to meet you, Mrs. Flower. Is Harriet home?"

"Yes, she is. Have a seat, and I'll go get her."

"Thank you," he replied. Remaining on his feet, he looked around the nice living room with its comfortable-looking chairs and sofa. The predominant colors of blue and lavender set off the lovely antique pieces that filled the room. "A lot of money is represented in this room," he muttered.

"What did you say, Kyle?" Harriet asked, delighted to catch him talking to himself.

"You caught me," he grinned. "I like antiques and have priced them. Your grandmother has a lot of valuable ones in here."

"I know. I have my eye on a couple. Have a seat, Kyle."

They both sat down, Harriet in a chair and Kyle on the sofa next to it.

"Hey, you look just as lovely casual as you do dressed up," Kyle said, perusing her.

A smile hovered around her lips and her eyes narrowed. "And I still think you're a snake oil salesman, Kyle McDuffy."

"How can you say that about Jenny's brother?" he asked, putting on a face of wide-eyed innocence.

"Hmm, are you an actor, too?"

He smiled. "Naw, I'm just a boring investment broker. I don't sell snake oil, just investment packages."

"That doesn't sound boring at all. Tell me about how you came to be an investment broker."

"I graduated in business and tried working for a couple of big companies. I got frustrated, so I saved and started investing. I was lucky, so I quit my job and began doing that full time. When Jenny went into the movies, she asked me if I would help invest her money. We've been fortunate in that also. Since I'm moving here, I'll be looking to invest our profits in something here in Arizona."

"Sounds impressive. I'm sure it helps to have a smooth tongue."

"A smooth tongue? You don't believe me when I say you're the prettiest little cactus flower I've seen since arriving in Arizona."

"How many cactus flowers have you seen in Arizona?"

One brow rose at her astuteness. A half-smile on his face, he replied, "You've got me there. How about we go out into the desert together and compare? I'm positive all the flowers will come in second to you."

Harriet smiled. "Thanks, but no thanks."

Undaunted, he went on, "I'm going to be around for about a week before I go back to California and arrange for my move. How about dinner tomorrow night?"

Harriet, finding that she was still terribly attracted to this charismatic man, had to force herself to turn him down. "I love Jenny, and I'm glad for her sake you're moving here, but I, uh … don't think we'd better go out."

Surely she can't be serious, he thought, then aloud, "Why not?"

"I'm sure that I'm just one of the many girls who are attracted to you, Kyle, but I can't go out with you."

"You're attracted to me?" She nodded. "Great!" he grinned. "So let's go out."

"No."

Disconcerted over this new experience, he frowned. "Hey, come on. Tell me why."

"Because I'm *too* attracted to you, and you aren't a member of my church."

Darn! he thought. *If I had made it to church with Jenny I could tell her that I am a member*. He was tempted to set her straight, but thought better of it. *Jenny should be the first one to know.*

"I admire you for that, Harriet," he said sincerely. He reached over and took one of her hands and kissed it.

Harriet's heartbeat accelerated. She tried to retrieve her hand, but Kyle held it firmly.

"So what are we going to do about this situation?"

"You can look into the Church."

"Jenny wanted me to, but I felt it must be a cult to be able to pull her away from the movies. Mom and Dad agreed with me."

"Well," bristled Harriet, pulling her hand away forcefully, "you can find out for yourself, Kyle."

Quickly changing the subject, he said, "Well, Harriet, my lovely, but *prickly* cactus flower, I might as well go back to California as soon as I locate an office here in Phoenix if you won't go out with me." He found himself more disappointed than he thought he would be. "Why should I stick around?"

"I wouldn't know, Kyle. Why did you come in the first place?"

"Wow. I don't believe I've come across a woman like you, Miss Harriet Flower. I guess I'd better leave." He stood up to go.

"You didn't answer my question. Why did you come here?"

"To visit Jenny, of course, to locate an office for my business—and to find *you*."

Chapter Twenty

Three days later, on a Wednesday evening, Maribell Gunther and Muriel Martin were having a good laugh.

"I wonder what Peter Holmes would say about what we've just seen, Muriel?"

"I wonder too. Just like all the other guys in the ward, he's after Miss Jenny McDuffy because she's *new*, and because she's Jeni Logan!"

"Maybe Peter ought to learn that not everybody loves her latest movie. Maybe he'll think twice before trying to date her."

"How about calling him and telling him what we've just seen, Muriel?"

"That's a great idea, Maribell. But you do the calling. You know him better than I do."

"Okay." She picked up the phone and dialed.

Peter answered. Surprised to hear the familiar whiny voice, he chuckled to himself. "Hi, Maribell. You calling to apologize for treating me so badly?"

"Far from it, Peter," she gloated. "I called to ask you if you ever found out who Jenny McDuffy is?"

"Yes. No thanks to you."

"Well, I thought you might like to know that not *everybody* likes her last movie, *Flowers for Amy.*"

Peter's brows rose in greater surprise. "Oh? Who doesn't?"

"The movie is now showing at a discount theater, the Palm, and it's being picketed."

"Picketed?"

"Yes. There's a red-headed woman picketing. She's walking back and forth in front of the theater carrying a large sign that says: 'This movie is inappropriate for anyone to see.' Boy, is she getting flack from the movie goers. They're calling her names. Only two mothers who have come out of the theater with their children agreed with her."

Peter was speechless for a moment. "Have you seen it, Maribell?"

"Yes. And I agree with the picketer!"

"You do?" he asked, surprised.

"Yes! What I want to know, Peter, is why you, of all people, want to date her knowing she was *in* an offensive movie?"

Peter was annoyed with Maribell, but he felt a little uneasy over what she had told him. Something didn't quite add up. *Odd,* he thought, *that only one woman would picket.* Then it struck him. "What did the woman look like, Maribell?"

"I told you she's a red-head."

"Did she have a lot of makeup on?"

Maribell thought about it for a moment. "I think so. Yes! She did."

"Thanks, Maribell. I appreciate you calling me. Talk to you another time, good-bye."

Maribell hung up, a self-satisfied smile on her face. "I think Peter may know the woman who's picketing, Muriel. In any advent, this may show Peter what kind of movies Jenny McDuffy is in, and cool his interest in her."

"Good! How about we call some of the other guys in the ward about the picketer."

"Good idea, Muriel."

Upon replacing the phone, Peter informed his parents he had an important errand to run. He hurried out of the house, got into his car and headed for the Palm Theater. "Dang! That imprudent girl is going to get herself in hot water doing this."

Arriving at the theater, he drove directly in front to get a good look at the woman who was picketing. He could tell by her figure that it *was* Jenny! Alarmed, he saw that she was now standing toe to toe with one of the hecklers, her eyes blazing. It was clear that the young man was becoming so agitated, it looked as though he might grab the sign away from Jenny and hit her over the head with it. People were standing around watching the episode. Parking quickly, he ran over.

Jenny saw him immediately and glared at him.

"Miss," he said, getting between her and the heckler, "do you have another picket sign I could use?" Since Peter was twice his size, the angry young man backed off.

She stopped and stared at him in disbelief. "You want to join me?" she asked.

"You bet!"

She dug through her small purse and handed him her car keys. "There's one in the trunk. My car is parked right there next to the street," she said, pointing.

Before long, Peter was back with the sign and one extra he had found. "Anybody want to join us?" he yelled at the spectators.

One woman slipped out from the crowd and nodded. Peter gave her the sign and they began walking back and forth in a line.

The jeering started up again. Arguments broke out, and soon the manager of the theater came out and ordered them to leave. "This is private property. Get off or I'll call the police." A bunch of teenagers clapped and cheered.

Jenny went up to him. "You ought to be ashamed of yourself for showing this movie!"

The man looked at her as if she were crazy. "Are you going to leave, ma'am, or am I going to have to call the police?"

"Call the police," she stated defiantly.

Concerned, Peter said, "Miss, let's leave."

"No! I'm staying."

She turned to walk on and stumbled over someone's foot. Peter dropped the sign and caught her, but in doing so, knocked her wig a little askew. Laughter swelled around them. Without pausing, Peter scooped her up and carried her struggling, kicking, and shouting imprecations. "You bully! You unmitigated brute! Put me down! Right now!"

When Peter failed to respond, she continued, "You … you department store Lothario!"

In spite of himself, Peter had to smile at Jenny's colorful choice of words.

Still holding her in a vice-like grip, he freed one hand. Reaching down, he opened her car door and dumped her unceremoniously onto the front seat. The crowd cheered and clapped. The lone supporter, mouth open, slowly put down her sign.

"How dare you!" Jenny said, a tear teetering on the edge of her lower lid.

"You don't want to get arrested do you?"

Her chin trembled. The tear finally making its way down her cheek, she asked in a subdued, but incredulous voice, "How did you know I was here?"

"I have my sources."

Once more, she mustered her indignation. "How dare you carry me off like that?!"

Peter turned serious. "Jenny, you aren't helping by picketing. You're only encouraging people to go see it just to see why someone would demonstrate against it."

"That kind will go see it anyway," she argued. "Several families came up and thanked me for letting them know, then bought a ticket to another movie."

"Another movie?"

"Yes."

"But the other movies at that theater are even more unsuitable, Jenny. Your movie is the least objectionable one there."

"Oh."

She looked so deflated, Peter spoke softly, "Let's go home, Jenny."

"All right," she said in a small voice. "You still have the keys." She held out her hand, and he gave them to her. "Would you mind going and picking up the signs we dropped?"

He nodded and sprinted back. Quickly gathering the signs, he headed back to Jenny's car just in time to see her drive off. He watched, his anger rising. "Dang that girl!" he muttered. He ran to his car, placed the signs on the back seat, and sped off in pursuit.

Reaching Jenny's condominium complex, Peter arrived in time to see her drive into the garage. He got out, slammed the door, and walked rapidly to the porch. Pushing the bell, he waited, and waited. He rang it again with no luck. Frustrated and angry, he strode back to his car, wishing he could give her a good shaking, or better still, a good spanking!

By the time he got home, Peter's anger had expended itself, leaving only a feeling of hurt—for Jenny. She was trying to make amends for acting in the kind of movies she felt were not right. How could he help her?

An idea came as he was walking into the house, but he would need his dad's help. Relieved to see both his parents in the family room, he sat down.

"I need your help, Dad, and your input, Mom."

"Sure. What is it?" his dad asked.

He related Maribell's call, his dash to theater, and everything that had happened thereafter. His parents laughed, helping him to see the humor in the whole episode, then sobered as he recounted how hurt he felt for Jenny and his desire to help her in what she was trying to do.

His mother was touched by his concern. "Jenny is such a dear girl, such an *idealistic* girl. We need more of her kind today."

Ed nodded thoughtfully. "So what is it we can do for you, Peter?"

"I've thought of something Jenny can do to make amends and

help every single adult in the stake. Since you're on the high council, Dad, maybe you can talk to the stake president about what I have in mind. First of all, Jenny's conversion is a very unusual and inspiring story. Since most singles in the stake know who Jeni Logan is, they would come out in flocks to hear her speak. She could tell her conversion story and how she feels about her last movie. Rather than making it into a fireside, perhaps it could be held in the cultural hall and be called an evening of entertainment because she has a beautiful singing voice. Maybe to start with she could sing a duet with Harriet and then a solo. The evening could begin with several fun songs, then a spiritual song could lead into her talk." He looked from one to the other. "Well, what do you think?"

"I think that's an outstanding idea, Peter," Ed said. "The bishops and the stake presidency are very concerned over the moral issues facing our teens and single adults. This could be a great help."

"I agree with your dad, Peter," his mother said, smiling. "And, I suppose you will accompany Harriet and Jenny since you have always accompanied Harriet when she sang."

Peter gazed at her a moment, then almost let out a war whoop. "Yes! That's the way! I hadn't even thought of that."

"What are you talking about, Peter?" Gladys asked, puzzled.

"Since Jenny won't go out with me, I was trying to think of a way for us to be around each other, a way we could get better acquainted. This is the answer!"

"Well then, perhaps we can arrange for several other stakes to use her also," Ed said, smiling, half serious.

"Then there are rehearsals, Peter," his mother added helpfully.

"Yes!"

"But why won't she go out with you, son?" his dad asked.

"I don't know. She won't tell me."

"This is certainly a new experience for you, Peter," his father said. "I like Jenny. I hope you can figure out a way to break the wall down."

"Me too, Dad."

Chapter Twenty-One

Before returning to California, Kyle had secretly met with Jenny's bishop and told him how he wanted to surprise his sister. The bishop had greeted him heartily, welcoming him into the Church and the ward. He explained that Kyle's first task upon arriving in Los Angeles was to make sure his ward clerk immediately transferred his records. Since the transfers came quickly because of the computer, the bishop promised Kyle that he would hold them and read in his membership the Sunday he arrived.

Now, twelve days later, the tenth of May, he had found an office for his business, moved from California to Phoenix, and settled in with his sister. He had left the day-to-day management of his and Jenny's properties with an assistant in California. The profits from Jenny's movies were still coming in big and he had a lot to do to find investments here in Arizona for her.

It was Friday, and he had planned an even better way of surprising Jenny on Sunday. He was going to attend church with her and, hopefully, his records would be read in. His desire for his sister to know that he had a testimony of the gospel, and that he had joined the Church was about to eat him up. He could hardly wait until Sunday.

Kyle was also excited about telling Harriet Flower about his conversion. She had been on his mind non-stop since he left. He realized he had been attracted to her the minute they met, but thought it would pass as it had with all the other women he had momentarily been attracted to. This *wasn't* going to pass. He knew it. And he hoped, with a fervor that was unfamiliar to him, that he could make some inroads with her.

KYLE WATCHED JENNY hang up the phone almost in a daze, she was so happy.

"What is it, sis?" he asked. "Who called?"

"You wouldn't know if I told you, Kyle."

"Try me and see."

"The president of our stake called me."

Feigning ignorance, he said, "I think you explained that office to me once."

"Oh. Well, he asked if I would speak to a meeting of teenagers, singles and single adults and tell my conversion story. He also wants me to sing several solos and work up some musical numbers with Harriet."

Kyle's face lit up. "Harriet? Can I come to the practices?"

"It won't do you any good, Kyle. Harriet told me you asked her out, and she said me she was too attracted to you to accept because you aren't a member of the Church."

"That's a little narrow-minded."

"You don't know a thing about it, Kyle," she said placing her fists on her hips, her eyes emitting sparks. "So quit judging."

"Okay, okay. You invited me to go to church when we were in California. Aren't you inviting me here?"

"Only if you really want to."

"I'll think about it."

"Don't do me any favors, Kyle."

SATURDAY EVENING, JENNY, with Kyle tagging along, drove into the Flower driveway and parked. Harriet had been asked by the stake presidency to organize Jenny's program, which would be held the following Saturday evening in the ward cultural hall. It was to be announced in sacrament meeting the next day in both Jenny's and Harriet's wards.

Harriet was surprised when she opened the door. "Kyle! When did you get back?"

"A few days ago. Do you mind if I'm a tag along at your practices?"

"If your sister doesn't mind, it's all right me." She turned to Jenny. "Come on into the parlor where the piano is, and we'll decide what songs you'd like to sing solo, which ones we'll do in a duet and in what order."

"I'm glad you're the one organizing this, Harriet. I would rather work with someone I know. And I'm happy that we're going to sing some duets."

"It will be fun," Harriet agreed, as they moved into the front room.

Peter stood up as they entered. "Peter!" Jenny exclaimed. "What are *you* doing here?"

Before he could answer, Harriet said, "Peter has always accompanied me. He's the best around. I asked him to accompany us."

"Oh," she said, surprised to hear that Peter could play the piano. Still miffed over the incident at the theater, she turned away from him.

"And it's good to see you, too, Jenny," Peter said, grinning. His gaze traveled to her brother. "How are things going, Kyle? Are you all moved?"

"I am. I've rented an office, and I'm open for business. I'll be staying with Jenny for a while until I can find a place."

"Great! Why don't you come on out to church with us tomorrow?"

"Thanks. Jenny has already halfheartedly invited me to go."

"Sit down everyone," Harriet said, "and I'll go over the songs I've picked out. We'll choose which ones we think are best. Hopefully, we can go over them tonight."

They chose two duets. Jenny insisted that Harriet sing a solo, and Harriet insisted that Jenny sing three. They chose a couple of old familiar hymns and one new one. The other two were popular songs of the day. Just before Jenny's talk, they decided that she should sing a hymn to prepare everyone, and the other hymn afterward to end the evening. They went through them once and set up practices for Sunday, Tuesday and Thursday nights.

Camille Flower came in during the last part and clapped. "Sounds wonderful already. Jenny, you have a lovely voice."

"Thank you, Sister Flower."

"How about some homemade cookies and a bowl of ice cream?" Camille asked.

"Sounds great, and maybe we can play a game afterward," Peter said, anxious to keep Jenny around awhile. He had thoroughly enjoyed hearing Jenny sing. The husky tonal quality of her voice had a sweet, tender mellowness to it. While accompanying her during the hymns, he had to blink away tears a couple of times. The sincere emotion that came through while she sang touched his heart. He felt she was going to touch a lot of hearts with her voice and her testimony.

Kyle was also impressed by his sister's sincerity and testimony that came through her songs, but his attention had been focused mainly on Harriet and her rich dulcet voice. He was amazed at how well it blended with Jenny's. Harriet was still a little formal with him, even through the dessert and games, but he knew that would change Sunday when he told her he was a member of the Church.

Jenny, herself, felt touched by the hymns as she sang them in this intimate atmosphere with friends. But like her brother Kyle, her focus kept straying. Peter's ability to accompany was exceptional. A man who could play the piano was always attractive to her, but since she already found Peter too wonderful, too attractive, it was just one more thing to resist! The theater incident was minor compared to the other problem with Peter. She felt badly for how she had treated him. Many times she about broke down and told him how he had hurt her, but she couldn't quite bring herself to do it. Unless he realized it himself, his apology wouldn't come from his heart.

If only she could make Peter understand how her ideals had soared that day Grandma McDuffy handed her the article. She had applied it to her life from then on, that is, until she unwillingly entered the movie industry. It was painful to remember how her ideals had begun to slip. *But*, she reminded herself, *the sister missionaries came to my aid, and the gospel rescued me!*

She asked herself an uncomfortable question. *Am I being too idealistic? Maybe I shouldn't allow myself to be so disappointed over Peter's actions and his lack of remorse.* But no matter how she argued with herself, the hurt wouldn't go away.

Chapter Twenty-Two

Jenny was both nervous and excited about Kyle attending church with her this morning. As they walked into the building, she glanced at him and noticed that *he* wasn't nervous at all. In fact, he seemed to have an air of excitement about him. *That's odd,* she thought. *Maybe he's interested in the Church.* She squelched the idea, afraid to get her hopes up.

In the foyer, she was greeted by several people, and she promptly introduced Kyle. They greeted him with enthusiasm and warmth. Leading him to her usual spot in the center about five rows from the front, they sat down.

Kyle looked around. "Hmm, nice building."

"It's a new building. The Latter-day Saint population is growing in Phoenix."

The bishop was conducting, and when it came time for announcements, he welcomed a new member of the ward and asked that he please stand as he read his name. "Kyle Andrew McDuffy …"

That was all Jenny heard, her shock was so great. Her mouth slightly open, she watched her brother stand and the ward members raise their hands in welcome. She was too dumbfounded to raise her own. When he sat down, he turned to her and smiled, then took her hand and gave it a squeeze. She tried to mouth some words. They wouldn't come, but the tears did. When she saw the moisture in Kyle's eyes, she almost burst. Swallowing hard and wiping her eyes, she managed to whisper, "Really?"

He nodded, his eyes soft with emotion. By the time the sacrament has been passed, she had used up every tissue in her purse. For the rest of the meeting, she held onto his arm, her heart full and her mind reeling with questions.

The moment the meeting was over, Jenny led Kyle out quickly. When they reached the foyer, she hugged him and cried. Friends gathered around them, shaking Kyle's hand and welcoming him into the ward.

When everyone had dispersed and gone their different directions, Jenny said, "I can't wait to hear about your conversion. Let's go home, Kyle."

"Okay! I can't wait to tell you."

Jenny had to have Kyle drive, because tears kept blurring her vision. When they were finally seated on the couch together at home, Jenny, with a box of tissues by her side, said, "Okay, Kyle McDuffy, tell me everything from start to finish."

He smiled and told her everything, beginning with his desire to prove the Church a cult, and ending with his decision to get baptized. They laughed, they cried and, in the end, knelt together in a prayer of gratitude.

"Now," Kyle began, grinning as he spoke in exaggerated tones, "my *sweet* Jenny, I guess you know who I'd like to tell next."

"Harriet."

"Right on, sis. You have a practice over at Harriet's tonight. I'd like to tag along for obvious reasons. And, of course, Peter will be there. He's the next person I'd like to tell my good news."

WHEN JENNY AND Kyle stepped into Harriet's house that night for practice, Harriet immediately noticed the glow of happiness on Jenny's face. Peter also noticed and was hoping it meant that her heart had softened toward *him*.

"What's going on with you, Jenny?" Harriet asked.

"Kyle and I have something to tell you and Peter. Maybe your grandmother would like to hear it also."

Harriet looked puzzled. "Oh, okay. I'll go get her."

When Kyle and Jenny greeted Camille, and everyone was seated, Harriet looked at Jenny expectantly. "Okay, what is it you have to tell us?"

"Well, the bishop of our ward today in sacrament meeting welcomed a new member into our ward. His name is Kyle Andrew McDuffy." There was silence. For a moment no one grasped the significance of Jenny's announcement.

Peter reacted first. "You're a member of the Church, Kyle?" he asked, surprised. "I thought Jenny said she was the only member in her family."

"Jenny didn't know anything about it until this morning. I joined the Church three months ago."

Relief raced through Harriet, and when she could speak, her words rushed out breathlessly. "How wonderful, Kyle. Congratulations."

He smiled at her, his eyes saying more. "Thank you."

"Yes. Congratulations, young man," Camille added. "Will you tell us your conversion story? You see, I've been a member all my life, so conversion stories always add significant light to *my* testimony."

"Is there time with the practice and all?"

"You bet!" Peter confirmed with enthusiasm.

Kyle's small audience listened with rapt attention as he began, especially Harriet.

As he retold his conversion story, he felt the Spirit again so strongly that when he finished and felt the warmth from Harriet's brown eyes, he bore his testimony.

After a charged silence, Peter got up, went over and enthusiastically shook Kyle's hand. "Thanks, Kyle. That was an inspiring story."

Camille was next. "That's a story that should be written up, young man. Be sure to record every detail in your journal."

"Journal?"

"Yes. I'll let Harriet tell you about that."

Harriet was next, she went over to him and shook his hand. "Thank you for telling us about it, Kyle. I'm so happy for you."

Kyle held her hand fast, smiling, his eyes eager, "You're welcome. Will you go out with me now?"

Harriet caught her breath, but still, she hesitated. "I think we had better get on with the practice."

PETER WENT HOME that night still discouraged. He thought that maybe Kyle's wonderful news would have softened Jenny's heart toward him. It hadn't. She was friendly, but still not warm. Never in his life had he been so baffled and disheartened.

Once again, he went over in his mind a conversation he had had with Jenny. He told her that if she didn't like him he wouldn't bother her again. But she had refused to say that! She was definitely giving him mixed signals and, as long as she was, he wouldn't give up.

His hopes soared at the thought of their continuing association during the practices and programs. Something would have to give. Jenny couldn't hold out indefinitely—and he was prepared to keep trying for as long as it took.

JENNY STILL HAD to pinch herself as they arrived home after the practice. It felt too good to be true that her one and only sibling was actually a member of the Church!

"What's the matter, Kyle?" Jenny asked, surprised to see his pensive face.

"I asked Harriet if she'd go out with me, and she still put me off."

"I noticed." Jenny was thoughtful a moment, then smiled. "Has it ever crossed your mind, Kyle, that a girl might not want to go out with you?" The surprised expression on his face made her laugh. "I thought so."

"You really think she doesn't want to go out with me?" he asked, suddenly more concerned.

"I can't imagine a girl not dying to go out with you, Kyle, and that includes Harriet."

"Thanks, sis, but since that doesn't seem to be the case, what should I do?"

"Don't give up. Keep trying. Come with me to all the practices and the programs so you can get to know each other better."

"All right, but patience isn't my long-suit."

"What choice do you have?"

"I can ask her over and over."

"Okay, but if I were you, I'd keep her guessing whether or not you're going to ask her out again."

"That's game playing."

"No. That's being smart."

"Maybe I should give Peter this same advice."

"Kyle, our situation is totally different from yours and Harriet's."

"Oh? Tell me how it's different?"

"No. As I said, you wouldn't understand."

"Okay, if that's the way you want it, Jenny. But don't push it too far. Peter might lose interest."

"What makes you think I would care?"

Chapter Twenty-Three

The program Saturday night was a huge success. The cultural hall was filled with members of the singles ward and Jenny's ward. All three members of the stake presidency were there and were more than pleased at the messages that came over in such a delightful and inspiring manner. They immediately planned on this as a ongoing program until all the wards had seen it. Peter's father, one of the high councilmen in attendance, was there accompanied by his wife.

Afterward, Gladys invited the four over for ice cream and cake. The evening was enjoyable. Peter and Kyle seemed to feed off each other with their wry humor and clever quips about anything that came up in the conversation. The girls' and Gladys' laughter only egged them on. Ed soon joined in with his wit which kept it going until the conversation shifted to the gospel and Kyle's conversion, ending with a gospel discussion.

As Harriet prepared to leave, Kyle asked if he might drive her home since Peter had picked her up.

Harriet hesitated, then asked, “You'll be coming along won't you, Jenny?”

The glance Kyle threw Jenny put her in a spot she didn't relish. *Without a ride* ... Before she could even complete her thought, the inevitable happened.

“I'll drive you home, Jenny,” Peter quickly offered.

Casting a withering glance at Kyle, she replied, “Thank you, Peter.”

After thanking the Holmes for the refreshments, the four left in their respective automobiles.

“HEY, YOU DID a great job singing tonight, Harriet,” Kyle said as they drove toward her grandmother's house.

“Thank you, Kyle.”

“You have a voice good enough to go into the recording business.”

“I've been out in California trying to find an opportunity for that very thing, but I don't know anyone who knows anyone, so I wasn't successful.”

“It's a ruthless business and very competitive. I don't think you'd be happy doing that.”

“Why?”

“For the same reason Jenny wasn't happy doing movies.”

“Surely, Kyle, the recording business isn't as ...”

”Yes, it is. I have friends in the business.”

“Oh.”

“Besides,” he said, turning into her driveway, “you have

something more important to do here."

"And what is that?" she asked, surprised.

"You have to go out with me." He turned off the ignition and grinned.

Harriet laughed. "That will take the place of me trying to support myself?"

"Of course. When we're married, I'll support you."

"Kyle McDuffy! You're the most presumptuous man I've ever met."

"I mean it, Harriet," he said, caressing her hair, his face suddenly serious. "I know it's a little soon to be telling you this, but I'm no good at games. I think I fell in love with you the first time I saw you. I didn't quite realize it then, but when I left for California, I couldn't think of anything else but getting back here to see you. I could hardly wait to tell you I was a member so you'd go out with me. I love you, my beautiful cactus flower."

Harriet was speechless for a moment. Her heart pounded, thrilled over his expression of love, yet she felt a little distrustful of it. "I'm touched, Kyle. But you hardly know me." Not trusting her emotions, she said, "I think I had better go in."

Deflated for a moment, he rallied. "Will you invite me in so we can talk?"

"All right."

After Harriet went in to tell her grandmother she was home, they settled themselves in the front room.

Kyle felt a little concerned. "What's on your mind, Harriet?"

"Kyle, I'm very flattered over how you say you feel about me, but … well, I'm wondering how many other women you've said this very thing to."

He blinked and turned away, stunned at her perception. He got up, went to the window and stared out. What could he say? Of course he had told a few women that he loved them. It was what they wanted to hear, wasn't it?

Harriet knew she had touched a sore spot, and her heart sank with disappointment.

Kyle turned from the window, a sheepish expression on his face. "I guess I've found something else I've got to repent for. I thought I'd covered everything before my baptismal interview. Yes, I've told a few women that I loved them. It was just part of the game."

"You said you weren't good at games."

"I'm not anymore, Harriet. You're the first woman I've said that to and meant it."

"How many hearts have you broken, Kyle?"

He let out a breath of dismay. "I don't want to talk about anyone but you, Harriet. Please, give me a chance. Go out with me, and let me prove to you how sincere I am."

"I'll go out with you—but only after you date *other* LDS girls for a while. I don't think you're ready to settle down, Kyle."

"For crying out loud! You're the most perplexing woman I've ever known. I don't want to date anyone else, Harriet, and I certainly don't want *you* to date anyone else either."

"Then the answer is no, Kyle."

"You really mean it? You want me to date others?"

"Yes."

He stood up and paced back and forth. "I don't know any girls here."

"The singles ward is having a big swimming party next Friday night at Peter's house. You're invited. I'll introduce you to all the girls, and you can choose one or two or three of them to date."

"Doggone it, Harriet!"

"I think it's time to say good night, Kyle."

He followed her to the door. She smiled up at his glowering face. "Thank you for the ride home. See you at the party next Friday night."

PETER'S BATTING AVERAGE was about the same as Kyle's—zero. He had driven around, keeping Jenny captured for awhile hoping the wonderful evening would have touched a sympathetic chord toward him. At his home after the program, she had laughed at his jokes, and they all had a great time, but here alone with him, she was quiet.

He could hardly engage her in conversation until he said, "Jenny, the good you're doing with this program is far surpassing any negative influence you think you might have caused with your movies."

"I hope so, Peter. The stake president told me tonight that he wants us to do the program every month until all the wards have seen it. Then he's going to tell the other stakes about it."

"That's what my father told me. At least I'll get to see you once a month, Jenny, unless you'll go out with me between programs." She was silent. "Will you, Jenny?"

"Peter, don't ask me anymore. You know the answer."

His hands gripped the wheel. "All right," he breathed out impatiently, "I'll leave you alone, but only if you'll tell me you don't like me."

"I can't tell you that. I do like you, Peter."

"If you only like me as a brother or as a friend, and don't like me any more than that, I'll quit bothering you."

He watched her closely. She seemed to be agonizing over the answer.

Stopping under a lamplight in front of her condo, he turned off the ignition. He took her hand and kissed it, holding it tight.

"Peter, please," she begged, trying to extricate her hand.

"Why, Jenny? Why won't you go out with me? I care for you so much."

"Please take me in, Peter."

"The singles ward is having a swimming party at my house next Friday night. Will you come with Harriet?"

"I don't know."

Feeling dangerously close to defeat, Peter waited through a long silence, then stated bitterly, "Well, if you're not going to date me, you might as well go to the swimming party and get acquainted with all the other guys who want to take you out."

Chapter Twenty-Four

Peter dove into his work the following Monday, trying to take his mind off the most enigmatic female he had ever had the misfortune to meet! By afternoon, however, he admitted to himself, *enigmatic or no, I'm one fortunate man to have met Jenny and to have had the privilege of getting to know her.*

That night, he alternately prayed and paced the floor of his bedroom. He knew that Jenny was the girl for him, and when he prayed about it, he felt it even more strongly.

The next day, he fasted and went to the temple, acknowledging what he now realized was *love* for Jenny. As he asked for a *confirmation* that she was the girl he should marry, a gentle peace and a warmth spread through him from head to toe. When he asked for help in softening her heart, the wall went up. Something was wrong—but what was it?

It was afternoon when he left the temple. Instead of going back to work, he drove over to Jenny's condo and parked in the guest parking space. Why he had come here he didn't know. He just felt he needed to for some reason. Was he hoping to get a glimpse of Jenny and get her to talk with him? He shrugged his shoulders, totally puzzled.

WALLY WATTS FILLING his gas tank was a picture of gloom. His head, atop a short skinny frame, moved back and forth in a marked statement of agitation. Then he saw the girl. He gaped at her, hardly believing his eyes. It was Jeni! It was his friend Jeni Logan! She was filling her car at a pump across from him. "What's she doin' here in Phoenix?" he muttered under his breath. *Oh, yeah, there were rumors she had split the Hollywood scene*. Noting the Arizona license plate on her car, he wondered if she had moved here.

He was about to whistle at her to get her attention, but suddenly, gas was pouring out of the tank onto his shoe. "Blasted, stupid thing!" he exclaimed, blaming the pump handle as he slammed it back into its cradle. Anxious to get over to Jeni, he was about to call her name when an idea began to form in his mind. *An idea that just might save my bacon*! he thought.

He got into his car and waited for her to finish. Someone honked behind him, and motioned for him to move his car away from the pump. Swiveling his head around to give the driver his best glower, he almost missed Jeni driving off. Quickly starting the car, he recklessly pulled out of the station and followed her, leaving a thin trace of smoke where his tires had spun against the asphalt surface.

Carefully staying far enough back that she wouldn't recognize him, he memorized the make and color of her car as well as the license plate just in case he lost her. He smiled. "Wally, you're one smart dude," he commended himself. "You're going to get yourself out of trouble after all."

He followed her into the parking lot of a business and watched her go in. He parked and waited. "Gee, it's hot!" he muttered. There wasn't a hint of a breeze coming through the open windows. Finally Jeni came out, got in her car, drove to another place of business, then another and another. "What's she doin' anyway? When in the heck is she goin' home?" he blurted out. To put his plan into action, he had to find out where she lived.

It was afternoon when he followed Jenny into an expensive condominium complex. He wasn't surprised. *She's rich enough!* he thought. "Yeah, she's rich enough," he mumbled, chuckling.

Backing into the guest parking so he could watch her condo, he started working on the idea that had come to him at the station. Drumming the steering wheel with long bony fingers, he tossed several ideas around. It was then that he saw a car turn into Jeni's garage driveway. His eyes bulged in shock. It was Kyle! "What in the devil is *he* doin' here? He's supposed to be in California."

Wally watched the garage door open and close behind Kyle. His breathing turned erratic. *It'll be dang tricky with Kyle here!* Just as that thought came, almost instantly another one took its place. *No! It'll be easier!* With Kyle in the picture, the idea gained a dimension it hadn't had before. He grinned in triumph and again applauded himself aloud, "Wally, you're one smart dude." Deciding that since he couldn't put his plan into operation here, he would just have to follow her until she was alone somewhere—sometime.

PETER, STILL PARKED in the guest parking of Jenny's condominium complex, had observed the man in the red car drive in behind Jenny and back into one of the guest parking spaces. He was puzzled at the behavior of the man behind the wheel. He seemed to be watching Jenny's condo. *Strange,* Peter thought. Since the man was parked only one car away from his, he could watch him surreptitiously. He looked unkempt. His stringy, blond hair was shoulder length, elongating his already long narrow face. He noted that when Kyle drove in, the man's head lunged forward as if he were surprised.

When the man finally drove off, Peter followed him to a rundown motel. He took down his California license plate, wondering if the man was a stalker or had something more sinister in mind. His imagination was probably running away with him, but nevertheless, he decided to take off work tomorrow and watch the guy for one more day, just to be sure.

JENNY WAS EXHAUSTED. At every job she applied for, she was hired simply because she was Jeni Logan—not because they thought she was right for the job. She was sick of it. Besides that, she felt she must be getting paranoid. She thought she saw the same red car behind her several times. Was someone following her?

Kyle walked in looking disgruntled. She had asked him several times what was bothering him, but he refused to tell her. Certain she knew, she smiled. Harriet was giving him a bad time, and he didn't want her to know that his days as a 'playboy' had come home to haunt him.

THE NEXT DAY, Jenny traveled to two different libraries to go through the newspapers for a job—any job so innocuous the people there would be ignorant of her role in the movies. Feeling nervous for some reason, she watched for the car she thought was following her yesterday. Sure enough, there it was behind her. The man she glimpsed yesterday had been clean-shaven, but the man driving what looked like the same car today had a beard. *It's all coincidence. I'm just imagining things,* she thought and promptly put it out of her mind.

"Why in the blazes is Jeni goin' into libraries?" Wally muttered. "How can I pull this off in a public place?" But now, in his nervousness, he thought he saw a car following *him*! "It's just my nerves," he assured himself as he parked a few cars away from Jenny's. He had to go to the restroom. Looking around furtively, he got out and went into the library.

Just as he exited the restroom, a tall blond guy bumped into him. Trying to go around him, he stepped forward stumbling over the guy's protruding foot, propelling him forward onto the floor. Wally looked up at the guy standing over him. "Hey!" he yelled, jumping to his feet. "You tripped me!"

"Sorry. My big feet are always getting in the way. By the way, I think your beard is coming off."

Wally's hand reached up, and sure enough, it was! He whirled around and ran to the door and out.

"Peter! You tripped that man on purpose." Jenny said, coming out of nowhere.

Peter was startled. "Jenny!" Recovering quickly, he asked innocently, "What are you doing here?"

"Never mind. I saw what you did, Peter. Why did you do that?"

"Do what?"

"Trip that man."

"Do you know him?" Peter asked

"I don't know. I didn't get a good look at him. I was watching *you.*"

"Oh. Well, I better get to work," he said in an off-handed manner. "See you Friday at the swimming party." He strode rapidly away before she could interrogate him further.

Peter drove directly to the police station. There he asked to speak to Lieutenant Doyle, an old family friend. When the lieutenant, a burly red-headed Irishman, came out, they exchanged greetings. Peter explained the situation giving him the license number. Lieutenant Doyle contacted the California authorities. It wasn't long before Peter had the name of the owner.

Next, he went to Kyle's office. He stepped in and looked around. *Nice*! he thought.

A receptionist greeted him. "May I help you, sir?"

"I'd like to speak with Mr. McDuffy for a moment."

"Your name, please?"

"Peter Holmes."

She spoke through an intercom. "A Mr. Peter Holmes is here to see you."

Presently Kyle appeared. "Peter! Come on into my office."

Peter followed him. "Nice office you have here," he said, seating himself.

"Thanks. What brings you here in the middle of the day?"

His concern didn't allow for the usual amenities. "Do you know a Wally Watts?"

"Yeah. He's a two-bit actor that hung around Jenny at the studio because she was nice to him. Finally, I suggested that he leave her alone. He doesn't like me very well. How do you know him?"

Peter told him everything. Kyle frowned. "I appreciate you looking out for Jenny, Peter. You know, the guy is a little timid and bit of a nuisance, but I don't think we have anything to worry about. What you did in the library will probably scare him off."

"I hope so. Well, I guess I better get to work. See you at the swimming party."

FRIDAY EVENING, KYLE begged Jenny to go the swimming party with him.

The last thing Jenny wanted to do was go to the party and feel miserable visiting with men other than Peter. Kyle had looked so crestfallen when she refused, she changed her mind and went with him.

Wearing a cover-up, Jenny arrived with Kyle, who was carrying a bag of towels and wearing a big smile for all who introduced themselves to him. It wasn't long before Harriet took Kyle off Jenny's hands and began introducing him to the girls, noticing how each pair of eyes lit up as she did so.

"Gee, thanks for the help," Kyle whispered to Harriet after each introduction, making her laugh. In spite of it, she found herself becoming jealous over his friendliness.

He doesn't have to lay it on so thick! she thought.

Harriet left him visiting with the last girl, certain he knew what to do next. Several young men surrounded her, competing for her attention, agitating Kyle, whose eyes never wandered from her for very long.

Unaware of what his buddy, Harrie, was doing, Peter grimly brought over to Jenny every drooling male in the singles ward who hadn't met her. He introduced them, then went about visiting with anyone he could corral, trying unsuccessfully to keep his mind off Jenny.

Water games were planned, and before long, Jenny noticed Peter slip off his shirt and dive into the pool. She watched him wistfully, trying to keep her heart from skipping a few beats as she noticed his wonderful build and heard his winsome laugh.

"Hey, Jenny, let's join the water games,"one of the boys said, eager to see her in a swimming suit.

"Later maybe," she said, smiling. Finally managing to disengage herself from a group of admirers, she wandered away and found a seat in the shadows where she could just watch. After the water games, music was turned on, and a few couples began dancing.

Maribell Gunther had been waiting for just the right moment to catch Jenny alone. She pulled over a chair and sat beside her. "Hi."

"Oh, hello," Jenny replied.

"My name's Maribell."

"I'm Jenny. Nice to meet you."

"Nice party, huh?"

"Yes, it is."

"I've seen your movies, Jenny, and I hate to see you quit. You're such a good actress. But I heard you speak and sing last Saturday night and I want to tell you that if you have the courage to do what you did, the least I can do is be more careful about the movies I see."

Grateful to hear this, Jenny smiled. "Thank you for telling me that, Maribell."

"You're welcome." She cleared her throat. "I've seen you with Peter Holmes a few times and, of course, I saw that he accompanied you and Harriet last week."

Maribell seemed to want a reaction from her. *What does she want?* Jenny wondered. Since she didn't know, she remained silent and looked at her expectantly.

Finally, Maribell said, "I've known Peter for a long time."

"Oh?" was all Jenny could say.

"I ... uh, guess you've heard about Peter's reputation?"

Jenny was beginning to feel a little irritated. "No, I haven't. I ..."

"Well, I thought I ought to tell you about it after hearing you speak and learning of your high ideals and values."

"Maribell, I don't believe I want to hear about it. You see, Peter and I are just friends—and not really close friends at that."

This stumped Maribell momentarily, but since she had gone this far she was determined to finish. "You may think of Peter as only a friend, but it's obvious, he'd like to be more than a friend to *you*."

"I still don't think you ought to tell me about ..."

"When Peter was sixteen ..." Maribell began, steam-rolling ahead in spite of Jenny's protests. She continued until she had blurted out all the details, making Peter sound as contemptible as she could.

Jenny smiled and even laughed a couple of times.

"I don't think you're taking Peter's actions as seriously as you should, Jenny," Maribell stated a little indignantly.

"But he was only sixteen, Maribell."

"But the big question is—has Peter Holmes changed?"

"As I said before, Peter and I are only acquaintances, so it really doesn't matter to me. Please excuse me, Maribell, I think I need to go get something cold to drink." Jenny walked away quickly leaving a thoroughly dissatisfied Maribell behind.

Arriving at the refreshment table on the patio, she saw that the table was filled with sandwiches, potato chips, soft drinks, cakes, and cookies. Picking up a can of pop, she opened it, took a couple of swallows, then turning to leave, she stumbled over someone's foot. Strong arms, caught her. She looked up into Peter's grinning face. It was *his* foot she had stumbled over!

"Oops," she said in a small voice.

"Got any spare applications yet?"

"Just ran out again. Sorry." She tried to go, but he still held her.

"How about a sandwich to go with that drink?" he asked.

"That sounds good. Pick one out for me."

Happily surprised, he grinned. "All right! Stay right there."

While his back was turned, Jenny ran around the house to her car, got in, and drove off. Kyle would just have to find his own way home!

When Peter had finished piling Jenny's plate with everything, he turned only to find her gone. He sauntered around looking for her. Relieved, he found Kyle among a group of girls. Since Jenny and Kyle had come together, he knew Jenny must still be around. With the plate of food in hand, he walked around becoming more and more puzzled at not finding her.

"Who are you looking for, Peter?" a voice behind him asked.

Turning, he saw Maribell with a smug smile on her face.

"It looks by the expression on your face that you already know. Have you seen her?"

"Seen who?" Maribell asked, a self-satisfied smile on her face.

"Jenny McDuffy, that's who," he stated with impatience.

"Oh–h, Jenny. Wel–l–l, I believe I saw her take off while you were apparently getting her a plate of food. Surely, she couldn't be running away from *you*, Peter. No girl would ever do that, would they?"

Peter seethed with irritation. "Where did she go, Maribell?"

"I have no idea, Peter. I just saw her walking rapidly around the house to the front."

He was so annoyed with Maribell, he shoved the plate of food into her hands. "Here, you eat this!"

Maribell watched him stride out of the pool area and through the backyard. Smiling, she thought, *Maybe my little talk with Jenny did some good after all.*

Peter looked for Jenny's or Kyle's car. Kyle's wasn't around and neither was hers. "Darn that girl!" Dejected, he went back to the party and plunked himself down, wishing he could leave! He was really too old to be in a singles ward anyway! He was sick and tired of the single's scene, but try as he would, he couldn't seem to get out of it! At least for tonight he was stuck since the party was at his house.

Glumly, he considered his situation as he watched everyone else having a good time. He had been so busy watching Jenny all evening, he hadn't noticed before, but Kyle seemed to be having a great time with the girls, and Harriet was laughing and flirting with a group of guys. *What in the heck is going on with those two?* he asked himself. *Nothing seems to be working out for any of us!*

WHEN JENNY WALKED into her condo, she plopped down in the chair by the window, thinking. All the way home she went over and over the conversation with Maribell and had come to the conclusion that Maribell had a crush on Peter and wanted to sabotage any possible relationship between her and Peter. The story she told about Peter was humorous to her at first, but the more she thought about it, the more she thought about Maribell's question: "Has Peter Holmes changed?" At last, she came to the conclusion that, as far as she was concerned, he hadn't! Why else would he try to kiss her the way he did?

Tonight, she had begun to waver again as she watched Peter, but thanks to Maribell, she was able to strengthen her resolve. With it, however, a heart-wrenching sadness arose inside her, ending in a bucketful of tears.

IT WAS SOME time before Kyle realized that Jenny was nowhere around. He ran out to the front and found Jenny's car gone. "Now, how am I going to get home?" he muttered as he walked back to the dispersing party-goers. "I'll learn to bring my own car!"

Seeing Peter, he went up to him. "My sister has left me stranded. Would you mind giving me a ride home?"

"I wouldn't mind at all. I have a bone to pick with her. On second thought, I'm sure she won't let me in."

"It sounds like things didn't go well with you either, Peter," he said, sitting on a patio chair beside him.

"Looks like you had a great time, Kyle. You had girls swarming all over you."

"Yeah," he said glumly. "Harriet is determined that I meet every girl in the singles ward so I can find someone to date."

Peter smiled. "I'm not surprised."

"Do you know why she's doing this?"

"Not for sure. I just know that Harriet doesn't trust most guys' motives."

"I'm not most guys. I'm in love with her."

Peter looked at him, an expression of skepticism on his face. "Isn't that a little fast?"

"Apparently she thinks so—and she doesn't trust me either. She wants me to date other Mormon girls for a while before she'll go out with me."

"Sounds like Harrie. Are you going to?"

"I've met some cool girls tonight, but outside of Harriet, I've only found one woman I'd like to take out."

"Are you going to take her out?"

"You bet I am."

Peter's brow rose. "And you say you're in love with Harrie?"

"Hey, Peter what do you mean asking me if that's a little fast?" he asked, changing the subject. "How do you feel about my sister? Are you in love with her? If so, when did it happen with you?"

A grin spread across Peter's face. "I plead the fifth."

Chapter Twenty-Five

Monday evening, Harriet arrived home after several fruitless job interviews. Entering the kitchen from the garage, she fell onto the family room couch exhausted. Since her degree was in music, interviewing for secretarial jobs, and clerking positions in department stores only revealed her uselessness in the job market. Besides, her heart hadn't been in it. It had been somewhere else—at the swimming party Saturday night!

A tear escaped as she remembered Kyle's seemingly good time with all the girls she had introduced him to. She was right. He wasn't ready to settle down. In fact, he was downright flaky! Just as she was leaving that night, he had thanked her for introducing him to so many good-looking girls, telling her that he was going to take her advice and date. All day Sunday she had been miserable because he hadn't called, then berated herself for expecting him to.

The doorbell rang, startling her. Wiping away the tears, she walked quickly to the front door. When she opened it, her eyes widened in surprise. On the step stood Kyle, his clean-cut face strikingly good-looking in a light blue suit and tie. A wide grin split his features; his blue eyes twinkled with delight.

"Good evening, Harriet."

"Kyle! What are you doing here?"

"Hey, is that the kind of greeting I deserve? I'm going on a date with someone like you wanted me to. May I come in?"

Harriet's heart fell to the floor. She silently stepped aside for him. He promptly walked on into the living room and waited for her to seat herself. When she did, he sat down.

"So, Miss Flower, why the long face?"

"So, Mr.'Player,' why is that any of your business?"

"Oh, so I'm a 'player' now since I'm going out on a date just as you wanted me to."

"Not *since*, Kyle—always."

He grinned. "Guilty as charged. I want to thank you again for introducing me to so many cool girls Saturday night. Out of all I've met, I've chosen the only woman in the world I want to take out besides you. I'm taking her to dinner at a nice restaurant tonight. Just wanted to let you know."

"Thanks, Kyle," she replied sardonically. "I don't think I could have lived without that information."

"You're welcome. Glad to oblige," he grinned, seemingly unaware of the sarcasm.

Camille Flower stepped into the room. "Hello, Kyle," she said, smiling. "You look quite dashing tonight."

"Thank you," he said, rising. "You look mighty nice yourself, Grandma Flower."

Incensed, Harriet's head swivelled to Kyle. How dare he speak so familiarly to her grandmother? She opened her mouth to express annoyance just as Kyle stepped over to her grandmother.

Holding the crook of his arm toward her, he asked, "Shall we?"

"Yes, Kyle," she said, taking his arm and smiling up at him.

Stunned, Harriet's mouth dropped open. "What's going on here?"

"Isn't it obvious, my little cactus flower? This is the woman I chose to date."

Camille smiled at her granddaughter. "It's not every day I get to go out with a handsome young man, Harriet, so I jumped at the chance. You look tired, dear. Go find yourself something to eat, and go to bed early."

Still in a state of shock, Harriet couldn't respond. She watched them walk out the door. Stepping over to the window, she watched Kyle open the door for her grandmother, settle himself behind the wheel, and drive carefully into the street. A slow smile spread across her face, and soon tears of relief coursed down her face. She fell into a chair and laughed through the tears.

BY MONDAY EVENING, Peter's determination had reached a fever pitch. He felt he had to make one more try to change Jenny's mind. He thought about Kyle's question to him. When *had* he fallen in love with Jenny? It seemed, when he saw her at the refreshment table, that it had been almost instantaneous. Who was he to ask Kyle if his falling in love with Harrie was a little fast?

He had received his answer in the temple. Jenny was the one he was to marry. But why wasn't he getting an answer as to how he could break down the barricade Jenny had put around herself? Ironically, his prayers seemed to hit a wall when he asked for help in this area. Why? What was the Lord telling him? *Maybe He's telling me that I'm on my own with this one. If that's the case, I'll just have to figure something out myself.*

After pacing the floor of his bedroom, he shot his fist into the air. "I've got it!" *Or at least,* he thought, *I hope I do. I hope it won't backfire on me. Everything else I've tried with Jenny has!* However, the more he thought about it, the more excited he became. Instantly, his hopeful and happy nature surfaced. He smiled as the details of his plan came together in a marvelous manner. He had some work to do this week to make it come about. The first step toward his plan was to go see Jenny and bang her door down if necessary.

Grabbing his keys, he ran downstairs, waved at his mother, and strode out to the garage. Saying a prayer that he would at least get to first base with his plan tonight, he backed out of the garage and headed toward Jenny's. Upon arriving, he parked and ran to her door. Taking a couple of deep breaths to calm his erratic heart, he said another quick prayer. He pushed the bell and waited … and waited. He knocked loudly. Still no Jenny. Placing his finger on the bell, he kept it there. Finally, an exasperated Jenny opened the door.

"Peter! Will you stop ringing my bell?"

Relieved, he quickly stepped inside.

"I didn't invite you in, Peter."

"I know. I'm sorry, but I've come to plead my case, Jenny."

"That won't help, Peter, I …"

"Please, Jenny. Hear me out." He couldn't help but smile at how cute she looked with her shoulder length hair pulled back into a small ponytail.

"May I?" he asked pointing to a chair.

"I don't think I have a choice." She sat across from him. "What is it, Peter?" she asked, slightly breathless, afraid her racing heart might betray her.

"Thank you. I came to tell you that I think Maribell got indigestion from eating that plateful of food I fixed for you Saturday night, especially since she probably already had a couple."

She couldn't help smiling. "Is that pleading your case, Peter?"

"Kind of." He grinned. "I came to ask you if you would go with me to the singles ward banquet this Friday night. It's our one big event of the year where we dress up and have a special program afterward."

"You know the answer, Peter," she replied, disappointed. "I hardly think that's pleading your case either."

"It isn't. I'm saving that until after the banquet."

Jenny now realized he wasn't going to say what she longed to hear, what she *needed* to hear. She looked down at her lap and picked at her fingernail, a knot of grief twisting inside her.

Peter waited, barely breathing.

Bitterness and disappointment welled up in Jenny. *I can't let my hopes be dashed any more,* she thought. *This has to end!* Suddenly, an idea came to her—a way to stop Peter from pursuing her. She was too vulnerable; she couldn't go through this any longer. The actress in her looked up and smiled. "All right, Peter, I'll go with you."

Hardly believing his ears, he let out a deep breath of relief, then smiled. "Thank you, Jenny."

Jenny steeled herself against that infectious smile and against the painful thought of hurting him.

THE WEEK WENT by interestingly for Harriet as she watched Kyle take her grandmother out two more times, the last time on Thursday night. She waited up for them. When she had asked her grandmother why she had consented to go out with him, her grandmother only smiled and said, "I like that young man. If you don't, that's your problem."

When they walked in the door, she greeted them. "Well, did you two have a good time?"

"I did," Kyle was quick to answer. "Your grandmother is very stimulating and fun to be with."

"I had a wonderful time, Kyle. Thank you," Camille said.

"Could I speak with you a moment, Kyle?" Harriet asked.

"You bet!"

"I'll say good night to both of you," Camille said, amused, knowing her granddaughter well.

"Good night, Grandma Flower, and thanks," Kyle said, taking one of her hands in his.

When Camille left, the two seated themselves, and Harriet promptly chided Kyle. "You're certainly brash to be so familiar with my grandmother."

"I am at that. What do you want to talk to me about, my little cactus flower?"

"You win, Kyle."

"You mean you'll go out with me?"

"I have no other choice. I don't want Grandma to make a fool of herself by falling for such a 'scamp' as you—using Grandma's own vocabulary."

"How about you making a fool of *yourself* and falling for me instead?"

"Well, at least you've motivated me by asking my grandmother out."

"Hey!" Standing up, his smile as wide as Grand Canyon, he opened his arms. "Show me."

Harriet stood up and hesitantly went into them. The excitement of being in each others arms consumed them for quite a few moments. Then Kyle leaned down and tenderly kissed her. Looking into her warm brown eyes, he saw in them what he had hoped. He kissed her again—passionately. "I love you, Harriet," he said, his voice husky with emotion.

"I feel a little overwhelmed at the quickness of it all, Kyle, but I think I may be—your 'cactus flower,' after all."

Chapter Twenty-Six

Jenny immediately noticed the happiness on her brother's face when he came home from his date. Not only that, he could barely settle down, he was so excited.

No matter how many times Jenny had asked him, Kyle wouldn't tell her who he was dating. All he would tell her was that it wasn't Harriet. This had disappointed Jenny. Harriet was the kind of girl she always hoped Kyle would find, and now it looked like her brother wasn't as taken with her as she had thought.

"All right, Kyle," she said, stepping over to him, her hands on her hips, "who have you been dating? You can't bounce around like this and not tell me now, this minute."

Grinning, he took hold of both her hands. "I've been dating Grandma Flower."

Incredulous, she repeated, "Grandma … you mean Camille Flower?"

"Yeah," he grinned. "After meeting all the lovely girls Harriet introduced me to at the party, I couldn't find one I wanted to date. Since Harriet told me I had to date other LDS girls before she'd date me, the only one I found myself wanting to be with besides Harriet was her grandmother, who was gracious enough to go out with me this week."

Jenny laughed. "How utterly clever of you! How could Harriet resist you after that?"

"She didn't, sis. She told me that she may be my little cactus flower after all." He grabbed his sister and hugged her exuberantly.

"Oh, Kyle, I'm so happy for you. Where do you go from here?"

"Harriet thinks we need to get to know each other better. She feels that no decision should be made until we date awhile. But you won't hear me complain. Just being with her will satisfy me, for the time being, that is. Now, how about you, Jenny. When are you going to give in and go out with Peter? I can tell you like him—a lot."

Her smile disappeared. "I'm going out with him this Friday night to the singles ward banquet."

"Great! Harriet and I are going, too." His exuberance left as quickly as it came. "You don't look very happy about it, Jen, why?"

"Oh," she began lightly, "I guess happy isn't the word that would describe my feelings about it. I would say it's relief that maybe Friday night something will be settled once and for all."

Kyle, still puzzled, studied his sister, not quite certain what she meant by "settled." All he could see was a fierce determination, and knowing Jenny, he felt a little concerned about his friend, Peter.

ALL WEEK EVERYONE at the executive offices of Holmes Department Stores had been buzzing over the change in disposition of the vice-president of marketing. They had taken Peter Holmes' good-natured personality, his smiles, and his humor for granted, so when he changed, it left everyone feeling a little off-balance and things didn't run quite as smoothly. Now that Peter was almost his old self, everyone's spirits had lifted, especially Ed Holmes.'

In the privacy of his office Friday morning, Ed asked Peter what was happening, but Peter only said, "Don't know yet, Dad. Hope to be able to tell you more after tonight. Jenny has consented to go to the singles ward banquet."

"Great, son!" Ed exclaimed. "Your mother and I will be anxious to hear more." After Peter left, Ed leaned back in his chair and frowned. Even though Peter's spirits were up all week, apparently things weren't settled with Jenny McDuffy yet as he and Gladys had hoped. *At least,* he thought, *Gladys was happier and more hopeful over Peter, and that's always a good sign.*

PETER EYED HIMSELF in the mirror and grimaced. Once more, he tried to comb back the unruly curl. It stayed, how long would be anyone's guess. It was about as unpredictable as Jenny! As happy as he was that she had finally accepted a date with him tonight, for some reason he felt a little uneasy about it. He had asked himself why more than once and came to the conclusion that it was probably because of what he planned to do *afterward.* Just thinking about it sent his heart skittering unevenly.

Glancing at his watch, he realized it was time for him to leave. Jenny had told him she couldn't leave until 7:00. Since the banquet started at 7:00, they would be a little late, which was okay with him. He wouldn't mind walking in when everyone could see Jenny on his arm.

He ran downstairs to the family room to say good-bye to his parents. They both looked up and smiled at him.

"Oh, Peter, that suit is still my favorite. It brings out the color of your eyes and enhances your blond hair," his mother said.

"Thanks, Mom. Hope Jenny notices."

"And I hope things go well, son," his father said.

"Thanks. Both of you say a prayer for me. I'm feeling nervous as heck. See you later."

Arriving at Jenny's, Peter took several deep breaths, hoping with all his heart that everything would go as planned—that Jenny would react in the way he prayed she would, that tonight would be a new beginning for them. Striding to her porch, he rang the bell, his heart drumming against his chest. He waited on one foot, then the other. After some time had passed, he began to get slightly anxious. Was she going to stand him up? He was just about to impatiently push the bell once more when the door opened. He blinked in disbelief. Before him stood Melba Beasley! Not quite the same grotesque Melba—the makeup having been tone down somewhat—but still, definitely Melba Beasley, flowered dress and all.

"Come in, Peter. I just have to finish my makeup."

Peter couldn't move. It felt like his heart had stopped beating entirely.

"What's the matter, Peter?" she asked in the familiar nasal twang.

His mouth moved, but nothing came out.

"Oh, never mind. Stay there, and I'll be right back."

After the first initial shock, hurt and disappointment spiraled down to his gut—more intense than anything he had felt up till now. He recalled his concern earlier. Jenny accepting his date was too good to be true after all! Slowly, anger salvaged his fragile composure. *If she dares to go to the banquet looking like this, then I dare take her!* he thought bitterly.

"Melba" appeared at the door, with two dobs of blush added to her makeup, just as before. "I'm ready," she said, attempting to smile.

Peter smiled ruefully. "You look lovely, Jenny—or do I call you Melba at the banquet."

"At the banquet?" she asked, forgetting the nasal twang.

"My, but your voice has improved all of a sudden. Of course at the banquet. Isn't that where we're going?" he said taking her arm, leading her out the door and shutting it.

"B–but Peter, surely you're not going to take me looking like this."

"We have a date, remember?"

This wasn't how it was supposed to turn out! Jenny thought miserably. *I thought he would be so hurt and angry, he would never ask me out again. After all, can't he see that this is a slap in the face to him?* Swallowing back tears of frustration and unhappiness, her voice sounded more husky than usual. "This isn't how I thought you'd react, Peter. Even though you had the courage to take me out to dinner like this, I thought you'd be too embarrassed to take me to a ward function."

"You're getting cold feet?"

"Peter ..."

"We're going to the banquet, Melba." Taking her arm, he propelled her down the steps and on to the car. He opened the door for her, but she stood there stiff as a board, fuming at Peter, and distressed that things had gotten so far out of hand.

Suddenly, her anger turned to defiance. "Okay, Peter Holmes, if you have the guts to take me to the banquet looking like this, I have the guts to go." She got in, folded her arms tightly across her mid-section, her lips pursed in gritty determination.

He got in beside her and grimly started the car. Backing rapidly, he slammed on the brakes, and squealed his tires as he left the parking area. The silence was combustible. Both looked straight ahead, holding in smoldering emotions, not daring to speak for fear of igniting an explosion that neither of them wanted.

Reaching the church building, Peter quickly found a parking place. He got out, slammed the door hard, went around and opened Jenny's. Holding her head high, she stepped out and walked beside him; the trepidation on her face unrecognizable through the makeup.

They entered the building and moved toward the cultural hall doors. Just before they entered, Jenny stopped, suddenly getting cold feet about humiliating Peter—as well as herself if anyone guessed who she was.

Peter's jaw clenched with determination. Taking her hand, he pulled her along. Fiercely, she tried to extract it, but Peter only gripped it tighter. The room was decorated nicely with plants and flowers. Round tables covered with white tablecloths were filled with members of the singles ward. Dinner music was playing from a stereo, and everyone was eating and visiting.

Stopping midway, Peter glanced the tables, trying to find a place for them to sit. Only a couple of seats at a table on the far side were left. Some of the ward members who first noticed them, gasped. Others stared open-mouthed. They all knew Peter, and it was obvious that they couldn't believe their eyes.

Purposely taking the long way around to the two empty seats, Peter, still holding tightly to "Melba's" hand, smiled and greeted people as they passed, noticing that none of them were able to hide their shock. Feeling mortified for Peter, Jenny couldn't help but admire his courage, though his stubbornness was something else! This wasn't at all how she thought he would react to the most *unkind* thing she had ever done to anyone, let alone to someone as wonderful as Peter!

Peter pulled out the chair for Jenny, then seated himself. He smiled at the stupefied faces surrounding the table. "Hi, everyone. I would like you to meet my girlfriend, Melba Beasley." Two individuals found their voices and responded, after which Peter introduced Melba to each one.

"I'm glad to meet all of you," she replied with the nasal twang.

Soon, a couple of plates of food were placed before them by one of the servers from the Young Womens organization. Taken back by Melba, the girl would have dumped the contents of Peter's plate into his lap had he not righted it quickly.

A pair of eyes, at the table closest to them were gaping, stunned. Maribell Gunther couldn't eat one more bite until she got up and found out who that horribly homely girl was that Peter, of all people, had brought! Pushing back her chair, she stepped over to him. "Hi, Peter, who's your friend?"

Peter looked up and was about to say something when, Jenny quickly spoke up. "Hi. I'm Melba Beasley, Peter's girl friend."

Peter's head swivelled around to her, blinking in astonishment.

"Peter, darling," Melba said, the nasal twang more pronounced, "we're going steady now, aren't we?" She reached for his hand and gave it a squeeze.

When Peter had regained his equanimity, he grinned. "We are! In fact, Maribell, Melba and I are engaged to be married."

Maribell's gasp overrode Jenny's and all those round the table. "Y–you are?"

"We are." He smiled at the whites of her eyes and the cavern of her mouth.

"C–congratulations," she stammered. Unable to think of another thing to say, she turned and stepped back to her table.

Jenny elbowed Peter so hard in the ribs, he grunted. "What was that for, Melba darling?"

An edge to the already-grating voice, she answered, "You shouldn't have announced our engagement—*yet*."

"Oh, I know, but my excitement just got away with me, my lovely girl."

Every word that Peter and his girlfriend uttered sent another reverberation of shock around those at the table, as well as through everyone within earshot.

A few yards away, a couple was whispering to each other while closely watching Peter and his garish companion.

"You can't mean it, Kyle," Harriet whispered. "You really think that's Jenny?"

"I'm not sure, but I think so," he whispered back. "I haven't seen that particular face she's put on, but that ghastly wig looks very familiar."

Harriet laughed. "Let's go talk to them."

"Peter," Harriet said walking up to him, "we haven't had the pleasure."

"Harrie, sweetheart, nice to see you. You too, Kyle. I'd like you to meet Melba Beasley, my fiancée."

Harriet almost choked. "Your fiancée?"

"Yes, Harrie, she sure is. Melba, this is Harriet Flower and her friend Kyle McDuffy." He grinned, thoroughly enjoying Jenny's discomfort.

Jenny looked into Kyle's eyes and saw recognition. "Glad to meet you Kyle and Harriet," the adenoidal voice responded.

"Peter! You scoundrel," Kyle said loudly, "where have you been hiding this beauty?"

Heads turned at nearby tables. Necks were straining, eyes were staring, and all were silent—listening and watching in amazement and disbelief—waiting for the answer. Raising his voice a few decibels, Peter answered. "I didn't want any competition, so I've been keeping her to myself."

Choking sounds issued from the subject of their conversation as she tried to hold back an attack of giddiness. The thickly applied makeup moved around in a peculiar manner as she attempted to smile.

Struggling to keep a straight face, Kyle said, "What a beautiful smile you have, Miss Beasley."

This sent Peter and Harriet into an explosion of laughter. The others at the table smiled uneasily, certain that this must be an inside joke. Snickers and laughter from the surrounding tables compounded the commotion.

Harriet and Kyle soon scuttled back to their table, not wanting to add anymore disturbance to the nice banquet than they already had. Peter began eating his dinner as if nothing out of the ordinary had happened. Jenny nibbled at hers. When the young server began removing the empty plates, Jenny handed over her plate of half-eaten food hitting a glass of water, knocking it over.

"Oh my! I'm sorry," she said forgetting her nasal voice. Remembering, she blushed underneath the disguise. Hoping they hadn't noticed, she added the twang with an exaggerated gesture, "I'm such a klutz!"

"A beautiful one, my dear," Peter said as he helped her mop it up, then added suggestively, "I know something that will cure you of your klutziness."

Jenny giggled nervously. "Thank you, but I think it's incurable."

Before Peter could answer, a dessert was placed before them. Everyone at the table ate in silence, interrupted only by a polite question to Melba now and then about where she was from, did she like Arizona, and so on.

Immediately after the dessert, the tables were moved, and the chairs were placed in front of the stage.

"Let's go, Peter," Jenny whispered.

"No." He gripped her arm tightly, leading her to a seat.

Resisting as best she could without calling attention to herself, she refused to sit down. Peter stepped into a row of seats and pulled Jenny along. Her toe caught a chair leg and she fell forward. Peter caught her, but not in time to save his suit. Jenny stared at the smudge on his lapel and quickly felt for her nose.

"It's still there," he stated grimly, pulling out a tissue trying to wipe the stuff off.

Unaware of their audience, Peter whispered, "The cleaners are going to question me again. They had a hard time getting the last smudge off, and this is my best suit."

"I'm sorry, Peter," she said sincerely.

"Yeah, I'll bet."

The program began, but Peter was hardly aware of it; his mind was on what he had planned for this evening after the banquet. His disappointment returned. Jenny had ruined everything by masquerading as Melba Beasley! Or had she? *No. It was perfect!* He almost jumped out of his seat, he was so excited at the new thought forming in his mind.

After the closing prayer, Peter grabbed Jenny's hand and led her out of the cultural hall to the car so fast she could hardly catch her breath.

"Thank you for getting us out of there quickly," she said getting into the car.

"You're welcome," he said, bestowing on her one of his endearing smiles. Starting the car, he drove out of the parking lot toward his destination.

Jenny was contemplative. *Peter was being a terribly good sport*, she thought. She couldn't believe his bravado this evening, but he did carry it a little too far! *Engaged? How in the world was he going to explain that away to his ward members?*

It wasn't until he turned into the parking lot of the Holmes Department Store on North Central that she spoke. "I thought you were taking me home, Peter," she stated with concern.

"I will, eventually."

He parked near the entrance of the store, got out, and opened Jenny's door. She didn't move. "Why are we here, Peter? It's obvious that the store's closed. Do you have some business in there?"

"Yes, I do."

"I'll wait for you then."

"The business concerns *you*, Miss Melba Beasley."

"Take me home, Peter," she demanded.

"No way, Miss Beasley. You accepted a date with me, and this is part of the evening I've been planning all week."

Jenny remained seated. "Peter, I only agreed to go to the banquet with you, nothing else."

"You have the choice of me carrying you or you can walk."

Just the thought of Peter picking her up and carrying her in his arms accelerated her heartbeat. "Oh! Peter Holmes, I've never met such a stubborn, persistent man. I choose to walk, but it better not take long."

"I'm disappointed. I was looking forward to carrying you, but I'll take second best. Come on, my beautiful Melba Beasley." She rolled her eyes at him.

Arriving at the front door, he glanced at his watch. It was twenty minutes after the time he asked Marv to let him in. Even though Peter had a key, he didn't want to be tackled again by the big fullback, so he knocked on the door and peered in. Soon, a grinning Marv came, unlocked the door, holding it open for them. The grin disappeared when he saw the bizarre-looking young woman Peter had with him—a face he would never forget.

"Thanks, Marv. You may remember this young woman, Miss Melba Beasley?"

He nodded, mute.

"Melba darling, you remember Marv don't you?"

She nodded, amusement in her eyes.

"We'll be ready to go out again soon, so stay within yelling distance, Marv."

"Uh … sure thing, Mr. Holmes, sure thing," he muttered backing away. Quickly turning, he strode rapidly down the aisle.

Peter took hold of Jenny's hand, holding it firmly, suggesting a tighter hold if she tried to pull away. Leading her to men's clothing, he stopped at the very table where he had once watched her pick up a shirt which had fallen to the floor and place it neatly back where it belonged.

"Do you recognize this table, Jenny?"

She studied it, perplexed. "No, should I?"

"You stopped here and picked up a shirt which had fallen on the floor. I was standing a few yards away. It was the first time I had ever seen you. Of course, I only saw the back of you—your nice figure. The shock came later."

She couldn't help laughing. "You should have seen your face when I turned around. You did, however, recover your aplomb very quickly, I'll have to say."

"Thanks." Moving a pile of shirts, he lifted her and placed her in the space.

"W–what are you doing this for, Peter?"

"Because I want you to be comfortable. This particular place is very special to me because it's the first time I ever saw you." He knelt on one knee and gazed into her blue eyes. "I love you, Jenny. Will you marry me?"

The makeup covered her expression, but her eyes gave her away. They softened and a tear rolled down her cheek. *No!* She thought. *This can't be happening!* Her desire to accept warred unbearably with her disappointment in him for his lack of respect on that first date—and more than anything, his lack of *remorse* over it. She looked down, away from those compelling green eyes, and picked at her nail, unable to say a word for a full minute.

At last, she spoke softly and as kindly as she could. "I'm flattered, Peter. I wasn't expecting anything like this. I … I can't respond to your question."

He felt utterly disappointed. *But—she didn't say no!* he told himself. "All right," he said lifting her down and taking her hand. The thrill of touching her again gave him hope. "Come over here with me."

Subdued and humbled, Jenny went along without coercion. Peter led her around the costume jewelry and the perfume counter to the corner where the fine jewelry was housed. He had previously arranged for Marv to open and pull back the security gates before he came. With his hand Peter indicated for her be seated on the small lavender love seat in front of the jewelry counter. He couldn't see the expression of anguish beneath the theater veneer, and he was too nervous to notice it in her eyes.

Stepping around the counter, he pulled a key from his pocket, opened the case, and pulled out a velvet-lined tray of diamond rings. "I want you to choose one, any one you like for your engagement ring. I have already chosen one, but you choose the ring *you* like."

Tears started cascading down her cheeks. "Oh no!" she said pulling out a tissue. "I can't wipe my tears. All I'll wipe off is this horrible stuff on my face." She sniffled. "I can't even wipe my nose."

Hopeful that the tears meant something positive, Peter said, "Please, Jenny, choose one."

Peter gave her that smile of his, melting her heart. A few more tears flowed. "I can't, Peter. I didn't accept your proposal."

"I know. But, just for kicks," he persisted, "which one *would* you choose if you had?"

Sniffling, she tried to see the rings through blurry eyes. Blinking away the tears, she studied them, wondering why she was giving in to this. Slowly, she pointed to one.

"That's the one I chose!" he exclaimed. "Don't you see, Jenny? That's a sign. Try it on and see what it looks like on your hand."

She stood up. “No, Peter. Please take me home,” she said softly, but firmly.

Peter looked down and tried to swallow back the ache in his throat. This was his last-ditch effort to win her over—and it had failed!

“All right, Jenny.” He locked up the case and walked around to her. “Let’s go.” This time he didn’t attempt to take her hand, but just walked to the front door and whistled for Marv who came running.

“All through, Mr. Holmes?”

“Definitely *all through,* Marv,” he stated with grim emphasis.

Peter and Jenny walked silently to the car and were silent all the way to Jenny’s condo. On the porch, Peter’s pain-filled eyes gazed into Jenny’s for a moment before he spoke. “I love you, Jenny, but I won’t bother you anymore. Good night.” He turned and strode quickly to his car without a backward glance.

Chapter Twenty-Seven

Jenny stood before the bathroom mirror and attacked the disgusting makeup with vigorous, impatient strokes, then pulled the film of skin-like material away from her face. Still dazed and a little numb over Peter's proposal and his last remark on the doorstep, she tried not to think. When her face was all cleaned off, and the appalling wig put back into its box, she went into the living room and picked up the novel she had been trying to read to take her mind off Peter.

After reading the same paragraph about five times, she dropped the book onto the floor and stared out the window. Soon, her chest involuntarily heaved with grief. An avalanche of tears followed. This was the condition in which Kyle found her when he came home.

Kneeling down beside her chair, he took one hand and cupped it with both his. "What is it, sis?"

"Peter proposed to me tonight," she mumbled.

"He proposed to you with that terrible face you had on tonight?"

She nodded, the sobs becoming more uncontrollable. Kyle wondered if he would ever understand women, especially his sister. All he could do was hold her hand and wait. When her sobs subsided, he asked, "Why all this sadness over a proposal that you obviously want to accept?"

"B–because I turned him down."

"Then you don't love him. Is that right?"

"I don't want to think about it. I've never been in love before, Kyle."

"Think about it, Jen."

Her eyes slid away from his, thinking. "I have never felt like this about any man. I feel so miserable away from him. If this means that I'm in love with him, I guess I am."

"What are you going to do about it?"

"Nothing, Kyle, and please don't ask me why because I don't want to tell you. The only thing that comes to mind is moving far away from here so I'll never see him."

"Have you prayed about it, sis?"

"Yes."

"And?"

"And I haven't received an answer."

"Can you tell me why you dressed like you did and why you wore that homely face tonight?"

"Peter wouldn't give up on asking me out. I thought he wouldn't take me to the dinner when he saw me and that this would stop him from asking me anymore. I was wrong. He insisted I go anyway and went ahead and proposed afterward as he had planned."

Kyle stood up and gazed down at his sister. "Since you won't tell me why you turned him down, Jenny, I can't help you."

"Don't worry about it anymore, Kyle," she replied, standing up. "I'm tired. I think I'll go to bed. Good night."

PETER ENTERED THE family room and found his parents waiting up for him, eager to hear how the evening went. He sat down. His elbows on his knees, he held his head. "It's over, Mom and Dad, and I'm moving out."

Gladys and Ed looked at each other, both devastated at the news.

"What happened, Peter?" his mother asked.

Peter looked up, anguish on his face. "I asked Jenny to marry me, and she turned me down."

"She said she didn't love you?" his mother asked in disbelief.

"No, Mom. I've told her before that if she didn't care for me, I wouldn't bother her any more. She has refused to say that."

"Do you think she *might* care for you, Peter?" his dad asked slowly.

"At times it has been very obvious that she does, but her determination not to go out with me certainly doesn't bear that out. I'm worn out with the mixed signals I get from her."

"Peter, have you done something to offend her?" his dad asked cautiously.

"We've both done something to offend each other," he hedged, "but if two people love each other why should they hold on to offenses?"

"Would you like to tell us about those offenses, son?" Ed asked.

"No, Dad. It's over, and I'm moving out. It will be a long time before I even try to find anyone to date, and I don't want you and Mom to worry about me."

Ed looked at his wife questioningly. She nodded her go-ahead. "Peter, you may move out anytime you want, of course, but we would rather you stay here with us for a while."

"I'm afraid I won't be very good company, Dad."

"Nevertheless, Peter," his mother added, "we prefer you stay here for now."

"Thank you. Thanks, both of you. I don't really want to move out."

Gladys desperately wanted to keep her son talking as long as she could. "Peter, I know you've always wanted to find a girl with values like your sisters. I don't know why Jenny won't go out with you, why she turned you down, but I would like to tell you something. I have never met anyone with a stronger value system than Jenny. I don't even know if your sisters are as strong. I have never heard of any member of the Church who was an actor or an actress in the movies and who gave it up right in the middle of their popularity like she did. You're dealing with a very determined young woman."

Peter pondered this a moment. "You can say that again! I guess I can't put myself in her shoes because the movie industry isn't interesting to me. It doesn't seem like such a sacrifice to give it up."

"Maybe it wasn't such a sacrifice for Jenny either, Peter," his dad replied in a contemplative voice. "But what's so *amazing* to me is that, though not a member of the Church at the time, she didn't want to go into it in the first place because of her high morals."

Why hadn't I thought of this? Peter wondered. "You're right, Dad. That I can relate to. It *is* rather amazing."

"With this in mind, Peter, maybe you can come up with an

answer as to why Jenny is acting toward you as she is."

"I'll try, Dad, but I doubt if I'll be able to come up with anything. I've already thought it to death. Well, I guess I'll turn in. Good night, Mom and Dad. Thanks for talking with me."

The minute he entered his bedroom, Peter stepped over to the phone and called Harriet. Grateful she was home, he replied to her hello, "Harrie, I'm glad you're home. Is Kyle still there?"

"Hi, Peter. No, he isn't."

"Well, I just called to ..."

"To tell me about being engaged to Melba Beasley?" She laughed. "You've got to let me and Kyle in on all this, Peter."

"I wish *I* could find it amusing, Harrie. I called to tell you that I will no longer be able to accompany you and Jenny. You have a week to find someone else."

Her voice suddenly serious, she asked, "What's happened, Peter?"

"I would rather not discuss it. Maybe Jenny will explain it to Kyle."

"I'm sorry, Peter."

"Thanks, Harrie. See you Sunday."

Peter hung up and lay on the bed. He stared at the ceiling, numb with grief. How could he go on without Jenny in his life? *I guess I misinterpreted the answer I got in the temple concerning Jenny!* he thought. Then he shook his head. *No. I didn't misinterpret it. It was too clear. It's Jenny who isn't seeking an answer—and I can't do a darn thing about that!*

He told his dad he would think about Jenny's amazing strength of character, and how it might bring some answers as to why she was acting this way. But tonight his brain felt muddled with confusion, his heart embittered by his first experience of being seriously rejected by a woman—not just any woman, but the only woman he had ever loved! And he felt totally helpless to do anything about it—a feeling altogether foreign to him.

Chapter Twenty-eight

The first week in June moved tediously slow for Peter. His passion for life and his enthusiasm for work had diminished to such an extent it was affecting his vitality. The ideas that flowed from his unique flair for marketing came laboriously. When Dan Markham walked into his office Thursday afternoon and reminded him again that he needed an assistant, Peter was fertile ground for any suggestion.

"I've found someone I feel is just the person I need, Peter."

"Good," he responded languidly. "What's his name?"

"*Her* name is Bette Markham. She's my first cousin. She's thirty-five and never married." He shifted nervously in his seat. "Her career in the marketing field has been her life. She just arrived from Chicago leaving a lucrative job with Marshall Fields in order to live where it's warmer. She has a great resume, Peter," he added, leaning forward. "Shall I bring it in for you to look at?"

"Sounds impressive. Later, maybe, Dan."

"What's the matter, Peter? You've had all the verve of a wet sock this week."

Peter shrugged his shoulders.

"What is it they say about 'all work and no play,' Peter? I have a better idea. How about my wife and I introducing you to Bette at dinner tomorrow night at a nice restaurant?"

Peter held his palms outward. "Dan, I'm not into socializing right now."

Dan grabbed his tie and loosened it. "I promise, it will only be a business dinner, not a social event. This way I can kill two birds with one stone—take my wife out and introduce you to Bette. I haven't promised her a thing, Peter. I just told her I'd suggest you meet and talk with her before personnel interviews her."

Peter sighed with irritation. At best he could only take Dan in small doses and an evening with him sounded arduous. *However,* he thought, *it actually sounds better than a lonely evening home on a Friday night.* "All right. Where and what time?"

Dan almost bounced out of his seat with exuberance. "How about 6:30?"

"Fine. Where?"

"Well, we don't go out for dinner much. Where would you suggest?"

Automatically, almost wistfully he replied, "The Terrace Dining Room."

"Wow, that's a little over my head, Peter."

"The company will pick up the tab, Dan. No sweat."

Dan jumped to his feet. "Thanks, Peter, thanks! Shall we meet you there?"

"Yes," he replied, hoping he could excuse himself early. "See you tomorrow night."

JENNY'S UNHAPPINESS INTENSIFIED when, in the middle of the week, Harriet called to inform her that they had a new accompanist and that they needed to practice with her. *Why am I shocked over Peter choosing not to accompany us anymore?* she asked herself as she hung up the phone.

Unbearable loneliness sent her daily out of her condo to the library to look through the want ads. She desperately needed to work! Sitting home and pining for what could have been with Peter Holmes was unacceptable!

Immediately upon moving to Phoenix, she intended to send her application to the local school district for a teaching position in one of the grade schools. But when she received so much recognition as Jeni Logan at church and everywhere else, it stymied her. She certainly didn't want the parents of the grade school children recognizing her! *What kind of an example would I be to them as Jeni Logan?* she had asked herself, discovering that her short stint as a Hollywood actress had had a devastating effect upon her career!

The same problem existed when applying for any job—first the recognition, then the palavering, bowing and scraping—then all the questions. "Why are you applying for a job? Aren't you going to do any more movies? Why not?" She was weary of it all. But every time she regretted accepting a movie role, she always asked the cogent question: *If I hadn't, would I have been ready to accept the gospel when the missionaries knocked on my door?*

However grateful she was for the events which led her to the gospel, the same harrowing question remained—what was she going to do with her life? She had to keep busy doing something!

One thing she had decided to do was start accepting dates, grueling as it would be at first. She had accepted one for dinner Friday night. When he asked if she had a favorite restaurant, without thinking, she told him the Terrace Dining Room. When she had hung up, she felt chagrined. What if he can't afford that expensive restaurant?

PETER TRIED TO keep his thoughts from Jenny as they entered The Terrace Dining Room. At the table after visiting a while, Peter realized that Dan's wife, Lucille, a petite blonde, was the calm steadying force of the family. It was obvious by her attentiveness to Dan that she admired her husband and his accomplishments. This pleased Peter. His dad always said: "A good wife behind a man helps make him a better employee."

In his efforts to be cheerful and attentive to Miss Bette Markham, Peter noted that she resembled her cousin, Dan, in that she was short and had light brown short hair. She was attractive and had a witty and effervescent personality. He found himself actually laughing now and then—something he hadn't done lately. Deciding that Miss Markham would be an asset to the company if her ability matched her personality, he suggested she meet with him at his office the following Monday. If he liked her resume, he would have her meet with the head of personnel.

Unaware of a pair of anguished blue eyes watching him several tables over, Peter's evening with the Markhams extended beyond dessert. Jenny, hidden behind people at other tables, saw Peter almost immediately. He hadn't seen her, and she was determined that he wouldn't since he was apparently out on a date. *And so soon!*

she thought. But why shouldn't he date? She'd made it clear that nothing could come of their relationship, hadn't she?

From where she was sitting, she could see his profile clearly. She tried to be attentive and interested in her date, but it was difficult when she saw Peter laughing and having a good time.

Jenny managed to get through the evening without any major mishaps, just a couple of tipped over water glasses. Her date hadn't taken the accidents with the panache that Peter had, and in fact, he was more than a little embarrassed the second time.

Her misery at seeing Peter on a date having a good time provoked a decision. She had to get away—go someplace where she wouldn't encounter Peter! She seemed to run into him everywhere she went— here, the library, and at the moment, the thought of even seeing him in the halls at church seemed more than she could bear.

Chapter Twenty-Nine

Jenny's program went well, but it wasn't the same without Peter accompanying them. Jenny hadn't realized how much support she felt in his presence, and how much she *needed* it—him. She had never felt this kind of need before and recognizing it now only added to her distress. The next morning, she told Kyle she didn't feel well and that she wouldn't be going to church.

"Are you ill, Jenny?"

"I don't think it's anything but the stress of making some hard decisions about a job and what to do about my life. I feel so physically and emotionally worn out with it all, I don't believe I could smile and greet one person today."

"Sis, why don't you take me up on my offer and come and work with me?"

When Kyle had offered her a job, she had told him that she couldn't type without making mistakes, that she would ruin his books, and that she wasn't good at business investments. He hadn't argued with her because he knew it was true. "We've gone over all this, Kyle."

"Just come over and help out until you find something else."

"Thanks, Kyle, but I have to work on finding something fulfilling."

He studied her with concern. "Okay, see you after church, Jen."

After Kyle left, Jenny showered and quickly packed a small suitcase. The night before, as she lay in bed thinking, she had convinced herself that away from everyone and everything, she could think things over more clearly and make decisions more objectively. She decided to leave Kyle a note and go to Camelback Inn for a couple of days. Her intention was to take her laptop and keep herself busy looking for job opportunities—even if it meant making the painful decision of moving from Arizona, away from her brother.

PETER HAD PURPOSELY hung around the entrance of the church at the time Kyle and Jenny usually entered. He was surprised to see Kyle alone.

"Hi, Kyle. Where's Jenny?"

"She didn't feel like coming today."

"Is she's sick?"

"Not exactly. I think she's suffering from the stress of not finding a job, along with a few other things."

"I hope she feels better soon," he said, starting down the hall. "See you later, Kyle." Peter's concern over Jenny led him to the entrance nearest his car. He stopped. *Why am I here?* he thought. *I guess I was on my way to Jenny's.* He argued with himself. *I need to be in church. What can I do for her?* Nevertheless, the more he tried to convince himself otherwise, the more he felt uneasy over Jenny. He quickly stepped out the door and strode to his car.

Still puzzled over why he felt such concern, he nevertheless found himself heading toward Jenny's condo.

WALLY WATTS HAD been lying low for about two weeks. The incident in the library with that big blond guy had scared him. *What if he's one of the bookie's collectors out to get me for my gambling debt?* Frightened, he decided to keep a low profile doing odd jobs here and there to pay for his food and lodging until he could go ahead with his plan.

This morning, he decided he had been careful long enough. He hadn't seen any sign of the guy, and no one seemed to be following him. After a quick cup of coffee and a doughnut at a nearby café, he went back to the motel and put on the beard and mustache. Jeni hadn't seen him since he had let his hair grow long, so she wouldn't recognize him, at first, anyway.

Wally drove to Jenny's condo, but decided not to park in the guest parking closest to her place. He could still see her garage from the next closest one. His air conditioning had gone out, and he was beginning to sweat, not only from the heat, but from a severe case of nerves. In spite of the temperature, his hands were cold and clammy.

PETER ARRIVED AT Jenny's just in time to see her back out of her garage and drive off.

She must be going to church after all, he thought. He was about to follow her when he saw that sleazy runt, Wally, following her! "No wonder I was feeling uneasy!" he said out loud.

Jenny led them to Camelback Road, turned east a block, then turned north. *Where in the heck is she going?* Peter wondered. "*She certainly isn't going to church, that's for sure.*"

After reaching Lincoln Drive, Jenny drove to Camelback Inn and parked. Puzzled, Peter pulled aside and watched Wally park as far from the entrance as he could. Jenny parked closer and got out carrying a small suitcase. Just as she entered, Wally exited his car, furtively walked to the door and peered in, watching her.

Peter found a parking place quickly and followed Wally inside. He found him hiding behind a plant close to the check-in counter. Judging from Wally's stance and the way his ear was cocked, Peter knew Wally had overheard the room number. Jenny walked out of the lobby and down a hall. Ten minutes passed before Wally moved a muscle. During that time, Peter's heart pounded with anxiety. What would have happened to Jenny if he hadn't felt the need to check on her?

Wally looked at his watch, then casually sauntered down the same hall that Jenny had used. Peter followed. The hall intersected another hall, and luckily, Jenny's room was only two doors from the intersection. Peter quickly turned down that hall a couple of feet and listened. He heard Wally knock, then say, "Room service. We have something here for you."

Peter dashed around the corner and grabbed Wally from behind. Scared out of his wits, Wally let out a, "Aaagh!" just as Jenny opened the door.

Jenny gaped in shock. Peter shoved the door open, pushed Wally inside, and kicked the door shut.

Wally swivelled his head around to see who had accosted him and still held him by his T-shirt so tight it was almost choking him. "It's you!" he squawked.

"Yeah, it's me, you sleazy, no good ..."

"Peter!" Jenny cried, still in a state of shock, "this is the second time you've picked on this man. Why, you're three times his size!"

Wally was relieved that Jenny knew his attacker. This meant the guy hadn't been sent by his bookie after all. "Yeah! You're three times my size!" he repeated, incensed at the injustice of it all.

Peter stared at Jenny in disbelief, then let go of Wally so quickly the little man almost fell over backwards. Quickly recovering, Wally scrambled for the door, but Peter blocked him. "You aren't going anywhere, you little scum."

"Peter! Stop abusing this poor man."

"Yeah! Stop abusing me!" Wally hollered, still incensed.

Peter shook his head. All the tension and fear gone, he chuckled voicelessly, helplessly at the bizarre turn of events.

"This isn't funny, Peter," Jenny said. "Would you mind explaining how you *knew* I was here, *why* you're here, and *why* you are picking on this man?"

Ignoring her questions, Peter grabbed hold of Wally, pushed him up against the wall and felt inside his pockets, pulling out a pair of handcuffs. "What are you doing with these, Wally Watts?"

"Sssh!" he hissed, glancing nervously at Jeni. "She doesn't know who I am," he whispered.

"W–Wally? Wally Watts?" Jenny asked, stepping closer and scrutinizing him.

Peter yanked off Wally's beard and mustache.

"Ouch! Now you've ruined everything!" he wailed.

"Wally," Jenny began, her eyes boring into him. "What is going on?"

"I uh … just came to see you and this … this big bully attacked me."

Jenny looked questioningly at Peter.

"This little slouch has been following you."

"How do you know?"

"Because I've been following *him.*"

Jenny's brows twisted in confusion. "Why?"

Peter, upset over her lack of fear for her safety, felt drained. "Jenny, that is something I am not going to discuss right here and now in front of this …"

"Stop calling my friend, Wally, names, Peter."

"Yeah! Quit calling me names."

Peter pulled up a chair, placed it in front of the door, and sat down. He shook his head and his chest heaved with silent, frustrated laughter.

Jenny frowned, clearly annoyed at Peter's actions. Since it was impossible to get information from him, she turned to Wally. "Please, will you explain all this?"

"I already told you. I was comin' to see you when this big …"

"Wally! Quit calling Peter names."

"Yeah, Wally. Quit calling me names," Peter said.

"You keep out of it, Peter," Jenny said. "Now, Wally, how could you know I was coming here to Camelback Inn—unless you were following me?"

"Well, I went to your condo to see you and I saw you drive off, so …"

"How did you know where I live?"

"I saw you at a gas station. I tried to get your attention," he lied, "but you drove off too quickly, so I followed you."

Jenny's eyes narrowed with suspicion. "Is your car red, Wally?"

Wally hesitated. "I guess," then seeing her expression he quickly amended, "I mean, yeah, it is."

"How many days have you been following me?"

Wally's eyes darted back and forth between Jenny and Peter. "Uh, well you see, I was scared to stop and speak to you. You know how your brother Kyle told me to leave you alone."

Jenny thought about this a moment, then repeated the question more slowly. "How many days have you followed me? Answer me, Wally."

"Only three."

"*Three*? Why were you carrying handcuffs?" she asked. "And why the disguise?"

At last, Peter thought, *she's coming to her senses!*

Wally fidgeted, then sat down on the bed, and scowled at Jenny resentfully. "I don't have to answer that question."

Peter shot to his feet, and stood over him. "Answer her, Wally, or I'm calling the police—right now."

"Jeni, make him stop bullying me."

"Stop whining, Wally, and answer the question," Peter demanded.

"Yes. Wally, answer it," Jenny stated firmly.

"It's not fair. You two are gangin' up on me," he whimpered.

Peter grabbed his shirt and pulled him up roughly.

"All right! All right! I'll tell you. Just let go of me."

Peter shoved him back onto the bed and waited.

Putting on his most sorrowful face, Wally explained. "Jeni, I've had bad luck. The movies quit giving me bit parts, and I couldn't find a job. I thought maybe if I went to a bookie and put a little money down on a couple of NFL games, I might be lucky. As it turned out, luck was with me for awhile, then I got into debt with the bookie—big time. I couldn't pay it, and so he sent a couple of mean guys after me to collect. You don't know what they can do to you—shoot off a kneecap, break your arms and legs…" He trailed off, looking hopefully from one to the other for any signs of sympathy. Seeing none, he added more dramatics. "I had to leave the state to *protect* myself!"

"What does all that have to do with *me*, Wally?" Jenny asked, her voice growing more suspicious.

"Jeni, I know how much money you make. Uh, I was going to ask you for a loan."

"A loan?" scoffed Peter. "Why the disguise and the handcuffs then?"

"Well, if she didn't give me the loan, I was going to …" his voice becoming low, and almost inaudible, "handcuff her to something and ask her to call Kyle and tell him to send money."

I thought so! Peter said to himself. Aloud, he said, "Speak up, you pip-squeak, Jenny can't hear you."

Wally cleared his throat and squirmed around on the bed. "I … uh … I was going to tell Jeni to explain to Kyle that she wanted to make an investment on her own this time. She told me that Kyle does all her investing." He looked imploringly at Jenny. "You wouldn't have missed a measly $85,000, Jeni." As their shocked expressions greeted this announcement, he hastily added, hoping to paint a truly horrifying picture, "And it would've saved my life!"

"You owed that much?" Jenny asked, shocked.

"No. I owe $20,000, but I was going to use the rest to get out of the country and start making a decent life for myself."

"What were you going to do if Jenny refused to call Kyle?" Peter asked pointedly.

Wally paused, putting on a puzzled expression. "I guess I hadn't thought that far ahead."

"Oh, I think you thought it out," Peter said. "You were going to threaten her, weren't you?"

"Well, maybe, but," he added hastily, "I never would have hurt her."

"People who are desperate do desperate things, Wally," Peter stated. "I believe you would have hurt her. What you were planning is called extortion. I'm going to call the police." He stepped to the phone.

"Wait, Peter," Jenny said. "I've known Wally for some time, so I want to make a deal with him."

"A deal! Jenny, this man could have hurt you. And even if that weren't the case, he was planning to break the law."

Ignoring Peter, Jenny turned to the would-be extortionist. "If we let you go, Wally, will you finish high school and then go on to college?"

"Yes! Yes, I will. I promise."

"That was easy, wasn't it, Wally?" taunted Peter.

"Stay out of it, Peter," Jenny stated firmly.

"Yeah! Stay out of it, Peter," echoed Wally, moving to stay out of Peter's reach.

Once more, Peter returned to his seat at the door. "I give up," he muttered. All he could do was shake his head as he listened to the absurd deal Jenny was making with Wally.

"I'll start paying back your loan to the bookie little by little if you show me that you have gotten a job and that you are working on graduating from high school. Then, when that happens, I want you to start going to college."

"It's a deal!" exclaimed Wally. "You know, I've quit cussing and swearing, just like you wanted me to, Jeni."

"I'm glad to hear that, Wally. Now, give me the name of your bookie." Jenny handed him the little pad left on the desk and handed him a pen from her purse.

Wally wrote the bookie's name and handed it to her. "I don't have his address. I'll have to go get it at the motel and give it to you later. Thanks, Jeni. You're a real friend. After I give you the address, when will you make the first payment?"

"As soon as you enroll in high school and show me your grades."

Wally's face fell. "They may catch me and do me in before then."

"All right. I'll give you a $100 right now." Jenny knew this was an absurd amount toward Wally's large debt, but in her mind it was a test to see if he would do what he said he would do. She opened her purse and pulled out five twenties and handed them to him. "Send it to them today and go find a job that won't interfere with your schooling."

Wally jumped up. "I will, Jeni. I will. Thanks. I've gotta go back to the motel to get the address. I'll mail it tomorrow without fail."

"All right, Wally. I expect to hear from you."

"You'll hear from me, I promise," he said, hesitant to step to the door where Peter was sitting.

"Peter, will you please move away from the door so Wally can leave?"

"Sure," he said, picking up the chair and stepping away. "And leave he will—out of town with that $100."

"Peter, he promised. Don't be skeptical."

"Yeah, Peter, don't be skeptical," Wally said, grinning as he started down the hall. "Thanks, Jeni!"

Peter shut the door and gazed at Jenny in a state of disbelief. "You'll never see him again!"

"Maybe, maybe not. What I want to know, Peter, is—how come you left church, and why were you following Wally following me?"

"You know, Jenny, I'm too worn out to talk about it." He looked at his watch. "Your block of meetings is about over. I want you to go home."

She looked up at him, her face a picture of bewilderment. "But I came here to get away from running into *you,* Peter, and here you are! I can't believe it." She stepped away from him. "I needed to get away from everybody and think. I guess I'll have to actually leave town to keep away from you."

"No, you won't. Just go home, Jenny. I was scared to death over that little pip-squeak following you."

"You followed him into the library that day?"

"Yes."

"How did you know he was following me?"

"As I said, Jenny, I'm too worn out to talk about it. I just want you home safe—now. Will you check out and go?"

Jenny studied Peter's tired face, his pleading eyes. "Thank you for trying to protect me, Peter," she murmured softly.

He smiled. "You're more than welcome. Shall we go? I'm going to follow you home to make sure you get there safely."

She hesitated for so long, Peter felt his heart constrict. What would he do if she wouldn't go? What could he do?

At last she smiled. "All right, Peter."

WHEN KYLE RETURNED from church, he found Jenny gone and a note taped to his closed bedroom door. Puzzled, he pulled it off and read it.

> Dear Kyle,
>
> As you know, I'm trying to decide where I can work, what I can do with my life.
> I have to get away for a few days and think some things over. Don't worry about me. I'll be gone no longer than three days.
>
> Love,
>
> Jenny

Kyle frowned, realizing that the reason she left before he returned was so he couldn't talk her out of going off by herself. He suddenly felt angry at his parents. Jenny needed them right now, and he wanted to call and tell them off. Instead, he called Harriet and talked with her.

"I wish I could call Peter and tell him," Harriet replied. "But he told me it was definitely over between him and Jenny—still …"

"No, don't call him. Jenny wouldn't want that. Besides, what could he do? We can't tell him where she is. Frankly, Harriet, I'm feeling anxious over her, and nervous that I don't know where she went. I don't know why I'm feeling this way. In California, we each went our own way and I never worried about her."

"Did you feel this nervous when she left California?"

"No. I know why now." He chuckled. "Between you and Peter, she was in good hands."

"Speaking of hands, I'll come over and fix dinner for you and see if we can figure out where Jenny could have gone." She heard a grateful sigh over the phone.

"Thanks, my little cactus flower." Just as he hung up the phone, Jenny and Peter walked in.

Thoroughly surprised, Kyle stared at the two for a moment. "Jenny! Am I glad to see you. I just read your note, and for some reason I was worried."

"You should have been worried, Kyle. I'll let Jenny tell you all about it. I've got to go." He stepped quickly to the front door and went out.

Jenny forlornly watched him leave, wishing with all her heart she could tell him to stay.

Chapter Thirty

When Peter entered the house, he found his mother already home from church. He sat heavily onto the couch. "I've had quite a scary experience this morning, Mom."

"You have?" she asked in alarm. "Tell me."

"I'll try."

Gladys stepped to the couch and sat next to him. Gathering up what energy he had left, Peter gave her a complete account, starting at church when Jenny hadn't walked in with Kyle. He watched the expressions of fear, concern, and humor exhibit themselves on his mother's face. When he was through, he leaned back, thoroughly exhausted.

Gladys frowned in concern. "It never entered my head that something like this could happen to Jenny this far from Hollywood. Even though this Wally sounds like a bumbling, innocuous character, I believe you're right. His desperation made him dangerous."

"I hope Jenny realizes this now, but somehow I don't think she does."

"Jenny's movie career has certainly had a terrible impact on her life. I wonder, Peter, when the heavy burden of it will lessen. When will the name Jeni Logan fade from the memories of her fans?"

"I wonder that too, Mom. As long as her movies are out on video, it will continue to plague her. I wish I could protect her from it all."

Gladys studied her son, her heart aching. "It's *really* over, Peter?"

"Yes," he said knowing she meant his and Jenny's relationship.

"I want to tell you, Peter, that I'm proud of the *effort* you put forth." She smiled. "I can't call you spoiled any more. However—it was good for you to have to work for a girl, to 'slay a few dragons.' But I wanted you to succeed."

Peter put his arm around his mother and gave her a squeeze. "Thanks, Mom. I wish I knew of some more dragons to slay, but I can't think of a single one."

UPSTAIRS IN HIS room, Peter loosened his tie, sat down in his reading chair and picked up his scriptures from the lamp table. He thumbed aimlessly through the pages, feeling numb and discouraged. Putting them down, he took off his suit and put on casual clothes.

Not knowing what to do with himself, he lay down on the bed to think, but soon was sound asleep. Only a knock on the door awakened him. "Yes?" he answered sleepily.

His dad peered in. "Dinner's ready, son. Would you like to join us?"

"Sure, Dad, I'll be right there."

The meal was a silent one. Finally, his father said, "Peter, your mother told me what you've been through today."

"I thought she might."

"That was a frightening experience. I'm glad you had a feeling to go see Jenny. I hate to think what might have happened if you hadn't."

"Me too."

"What are you going to do about Jenny now, Peter?" his dad asked.

"Frankly, Dad, I'm so discouraged today, so worn out trying to reach her, I can't even think about doing anything."

As the afternoon and evening wore on, Gladys and Ed watched Peter with concern, and as Peter said good night, Ed reminded his son that discouragement was the devil's tool.

"I know, Dad, I know. But I can't seem to do anything about it tonight. I think I need to have a good night's rest and see what tomorrow brings."

MONDAY MORNING, PETER felt less numb, less discouraged, but still had no inclination to think about what more he could do to reach Jenny. Knowing what he should do, he knelt down and asked the Lord to help him find a way to ensure Jenny's safety. He then went to work and tried his best to focus totally on the business of Holmes Department Stores.

By mid-afternoon, the fear he felt yesterday over Jenny's safety returned, motivating him to find a way to protect her for the rest of her life! Like a flash, the prayer he had uttered this morning, was partially answered—the discouragement totally fled—leaving him surprisingly hopeful. He left work as quickly as possible and headed for home. He found his mother preparing dinner.

Her face lit up. "I'm so glad you're home, Peter. I feel the need to share something with you," she said, rinsing her hands off and drying them.

"Good. If you have any ideas, I could sure use them, Mom."

Gladys joined him in the family room and sat down. Peter smiled as he sat across from her. "Okay, shoot."

"I haven't told you this, Peter, because I didn't want to get your hopes up, but your dad and I have felt Jenny cared for you."

"You saw those signals, too?" he asked, his face lighting up.

"Yes. If only you knew why she's turned you down, you may find that to be the most *important* dragon to slay."

"You're probably right, Mom. But she won't even confide in Harriet or Kyle. And of course, I can't talk with her parents—so where can I go to find out?"

"I think you know *who* you can go to."

"I have, and I only come up against a wall."

"I don't have to tell you how to break down the wall, Peter."

"Maybe you do. I haven't been very successful. In fact, I had given up entirely—until yesterday when I saw the danger Jenny was in. It took that to galvanize me to try again. I *have* to try again." He stood. "I'm going upstairs to my room, Mom, and do some serious thinking and probably some serious knee-bending."

Gladys smiled, nodding encouragement to her son.

Peter took off his suit and put on casual clothes. Then as last night, he sat down and picked up his scriptures. Again, he thumbed through them, but tonight, he began reading underlined passages here and there. One in particular, Jacob 6:6 spoke to him personally.

" ... and he stretches forth his hands unto them all the day long."

"He's stretching forth His hand to answer *my* prayer," he whispered. In the past, whenever he couldn't reach the heavens, it always turned out to be his fault.

The frightening incident Sunday had humbled him. He had been *prompted* to go check on Jenny! Had he in the past felt too self-sufficient? He knew he had. Always having had success with young women, he thought he could still do it on his own. Oh, he had prayed, but was he humble enough to hear or learn what he needed to hear and learn?

Either he should be thanking the Lord instead of praying for something that had already been answered—or he needed to repent for something. This had happened on his mission many times and many times since. Logically, it didn't make sense that his prayers had drawn a blank because of the first reason. It had to be the second—needing to repent. This was almost a daily need for him, so what did this have to do with Jenny?

He got up and paced the floor wishing it was any other weekday but Monday so he could attend the temple. Not able to focus on any one thing, his thoughts were scattered. His fear over Jenny's safety yesterday was still overriding everything, forcing him to his knees.

After expressing more gratitude over Jenny's safety, he uttered, "Dear God, help me to know what I'm doing wrong, what I've done wrong ..."

When he stood up, he stepped to the window, stared out at the blue sky, and watched a couple of wispy clouds float by. His mind clearer now, he remembered something his dad had said to him about Jenny: *"Though not even a member of the Church yet, Jenny, because of her high morals, didn't want to go into the movies in the first place. That in itself is amazing to me."* Peter pondered this for some time, then he sat down and reviewed his own life.

He recalled when he turned sixteen. It was at that time he began "testing" the girls to see if any of them had set high standards for themselves. If they allowed him to kiss them, he knew they hadn't, therefore, he wouldn't date them. His sisters had made choices ahead of time and had set standards for themselves, and he wanted to date a girl like them. It wasn't until his mother talked with him about it that he realized how wrong he had been—evaluating the girls this way.

To this day, his mother's words to him at that time were indelible upon his mind:

"Peter, since you have no idea what you've done to yourself and those young girls, I'm going to try to help you understand. Remember the boxes of apples your aunt Teresa brings when she visits?" He had nodded impatiently, wondering why she was talking about apples. "Did you find a rotten apple in them now and then?"

"Yeah, so?"

"You know what a rotten apple looks like then?"

"Of course."

"Did you know that many youth in the world today are rotting before they ripen?"

He hadn't expected that shocking statement. "That sounds awful."

"It is awful. They're making choices that are ruining their lives before they've even matured. Now, let's talk about young women. Each one is like a white rosebud whose petals are just beginning to open. Slowly, the petals open as she matures, and when she is mature, one can see the pure heart of the rose."

Sixteen-year-old Peter was beginning to feel uncomfortable about where this was leading.

"What happens to a white rose petal, Peter, when you handle it?"

Peter thought carefully before answering. "It wilts and turns brown."

"Right. Do you want to marry a pure white rose or a rose whose petals have been bruised from allowing every young man she dates to kiss her and handle her?"

"You know the answer to that, Mom."

"Then why did you tarnish the white petals of all those young women you indiscriminately kissed?"

"They were just innocent kisses, Mom. I had nothing else in mind."

"I know that, Peter, but you don't want to date any of them because they let you kiss them. Do you think other boys will want to date them?"

"Sure. They don't care."

"Have you asked them?"

"No."

"What about your own white petals? Have they turned a little brown?"

By this time, Peter was beginning to feel remorse—the kind of remorse that had sent him to his knees, to the bishop's office, and finally to each girl with a heartfelt apology.

The twenty-nine-year-old Peter got up and paced the floor, wondering why *this* experience had come to his mind. He had sincerely repented of it. His thoughts turned to the present, to the manner in which he had tested girls in the ward and stake concerning movies. Had he been a little self-righteous and prideful in feeling that maybe his values were higher than theirs? Perhaps he had, even though his motive—trying to get a message over to them—was sincere. Not many young women had parents like his who taught their children to make decisions ahead of time—making it easier to resist temptation in the heat of the moment.

But what does all this have to do with my dilemma over Jenny? he asked himself. For some reason, he felt it did, but the answer eluded him. Once more, he got on his knees and pleaded for help. Rising, he thoughtfully stepped to the window and raised his eyes toward the sunlit sky, still praying in his heart. As he did so, insight, like a startling bolt of lightning, struck him. The physical shock of Jenny's punch in the stomach was nothing compared to the emotional bombshell that had just belted him. Unsteadily, he stepped back to the chair and sat down heavily.

"How could I be so stupid? So blind!" He leaned over and held his head. He groaned. "Dear God, how could I have been so dense, so oblivious? Forgive me … please forgive me."

Chapter Thirty-One

Peter held his breath as he picked up the phone to call Jenny. *She has to let me talk to her one more time,* he thought desperately. He was so nervous, his finger shook as he pushed the buttons on the phone.

"Hello," Kyle answered.

"Kyle, this is Peter. How's Jenny?"

"Hey, Peter! She kind of fell apart after you left. It finally sank in what a dangerous situation she had been in. How can I possibly thank you, Peter, for protecting her?"

Peter let out a sigh of relief. "You don't have to. I'm just grateful to hear she finally realized she *was* in danger, Kyle. She certainly didn't realize it yesterday. Are you going to be there tonight or are you going over to see Harriet?"

"Harriet is coming over here because I feel we need to be with Jenny tonight. Why?"

"Well, I'm going to try to get Jenny to let me talk with her one more time. If she says yes, can you …"

"Leave?"

"Yeah."

"I sure can, Peter. I'll go over to Harriet's instead of her coming here. We're willing to do anything to help the cause."

"Thanks, Kyle. May I speak to her?"

"You sure can."

"Hello, Peter, how are you?" Jenny's usual pleasant, husky voice sounded gray and lifeless.

"I'm fine now that you're safe. Kyle said you were doing better."

"Yes. I'm doing well, considering."

"Uh … Jenny, I have a request to make. I would like to come over and speak with you one more time."

"Peter, please don't ask. We don't get anywhere when we talk, and I don't feel up to …"

"Jenny," he interrupted, "I promise I won't ask you to reconsider or pressure you in any way. I just have to get something off my chest."

Peter waited through the unbearable silence.

"All right, Peter," she said at last. "When do you want to come?"

"Since I'm already home, it won't be long. Is that all right with you?"

"Yes. See you in a little while."

DRESSED IN CASUAL pants and shirt, Peter drove into Jenny's condominium complex and parked. Drawing in several deep breaths to calm his pounding heart, he got out and walked slowly up to the door and pushed the bell.

Jenny opened the door. Peter studied her. The slanting sun brought out the luster in her hair, but the luster in her eyes was missing. Nevertheless, she looked beautiful in the light blue cotton skirt and blouse.

She smiled wanly. "You don't have to stand on the doorstep, Peter. You may come in."

"Oh, yes. Thanks. I was just thinking about how nice you look."

"Thank you. Have a seat, Peter."

"Thank you," he said, seating himself in the chair by the window.

Curling up on the couch, Jenny sighed. "What did you want to get off your chest, Peter?" Her voice was still devoid of life—flat, listless.

How am I going to explain so she'll understand? he wondered. He hadn't had time to thoroughly think it through. He rested his forearms on his thighs, gripped his hands tightly together, and leaned toward her. "I don't know quite where to start. Give me a minute."

Her eyes were kind. "Take all the time you want. I'm not in any hurry. All I have to do is pack a suitcase later on."

"Pack a suitcase?" he asked, sitting back abruptly.

"Yes. I'm going to go back to California, the northern part, to look for a job."

Peter's heart plummeted. *She can't leave!* His first impulse was to protest, but remembering his promise to her, all he said was, "This comes as a surprise, Jenny. How does Kyle feel about it?"

"He's not happy about it, but I have to leave."

He wanted to ask why, but refrained. "Jenny, I want to tell you a few things to lead up to what I really want to say." Noting a puzzled expression come over her face, he went on. "I want to tell you about a stupid thing I did when I was sixteen."

"The time when you kissed every girl in the stake—Casanova Pete?" The missing twinkle in her eyes appeared for a moment.

His brows rose in surprise. "How did you know about that?"

"Maribell Gunther sat by me at the pool party at your house and informed me. I tried to stop her because I didn't want to talk about you, but she was determined. She has a crush on you, Peter, and she was trying to sabotage what she thought might turn into a relationship between you and me."

Peter was about to contradict her on the crush part, but as he thought back over several discussions he had had with Maribell lately, it made sense. "I had no idea she might have felt that way. If that's the case, you got quite a lurid tale about my teenage conquests then."

Jenny couldn't help but giggle. "Very lurid."

Peter smiled. "Well, I won't go into the details then. I'll just tell you the misguided reasons I did that. I have a mother who taught me and my three older sisters to make decisions ahead of time so that we'd know what to do or what not to do when temptation came our way. Well, I'm the rotten apple that fell from the tree, but my three sisters followed our parents council. They're my ideals. I wanted to date girls like my sisters. In order to find out if they were, I tested them by seeing if they'd let me kiss them. I guess Maribell filled you in with the rest."

"Yes." A smile teased her lips. "I'm afraid it wasn't a very good test, Peter. I imagine you were as charming as a sixteen-year-old as you are now. How could they resist you?"

"*You've* managed to resist me, Jenny." Her face closed, giving him an indication she still felt the same way, suppressing the hope that *still* lingered in his heart. The sudden breath he took felt painful. He went on. "I've told you how I test the girls now about the movies."

"Yes," she said quietly.

Peter swallowed back emotion. "For many years I've looked for a girl who had the ideals my sisters have—the *one* I've come to think of as a *white* rose. When I finally found her ... I ..." He couldn't go on. Placing his arms once more on his thighs, he bent his head, blinking. Unable to get hold of himself, he stood up quickly and stepped around the chair to the window, his back to her. Finally able to go on, he said, "When I found the pure white rose I was looking for, I ruined it." His voice broke. "I'm sorry, Jenny."

After a few moments, he turned and faced her. "I was so attracted to you and so upset to learn that you were Melba Beasley, I reacted in a reprehensible manner. I more than deserved that sock in the stomach." Intent on what he was trying to say, he didn't notice the tears glistening in Jenny's eyes. "Since I thought I had received my punishment for it, I was shocked that you kept turning me down. I couldn't understand it—especially since you gave off signals that you might care for me a little.

"I'm not asking you to tell me why you turned me down, but I need to tell *you* something. I was so blind, so dense, so unrepentant over the way I treated you on the doorstep after I confronted you about disguising yourself as Melba Beasley that even the Lord couldn't get through to me. I'm afraid it took your so-called friend, Wally—note, I didn't call him a name—to wake me up. My fear for your safety humbled me." He stepped closer to her. "Please, Jenny, please forgive me." It was then, through watery eyes, he saw tears rolling down Jenny's cheeks.

Jenny stood up and gazed up into his face. "You have just said the three most beautiful words in the English language, Peter. Thank you."

"Thank *you* for accepting my apology," he replied, more grateful than he could express. Not knowing what to do next without a cue from Jenny, he simply gazed at her in silence.

All Jenny could do at the moment was wonder about the woman Peter had out on a date Friday night. "I see you've started to get on with your life, Peter. I saw you out with that pretty girl at the Terrace Dining Room Friday night."

"You were there?" he asked, surprised. She nodded. "Were you with a date?" She nodded again. Apprehensive, he held his breath a moment. "Someone you're interested in?" She shook her head. Relief enveloped him like a warm cloak. "I *haven't* been able to get on with my life, Jenny. That pretty woman you saw was my marketing assistant's cousin he wanted me to meet. He wants me to consider hiring her as an assistant to him. It was purely business. I *love* you, Jenny. I've lost all enthusiasm for everything in life without you."

"Y–you do? You have?"

He nodded, his eyes brimming.

Jenny flew to him. Throwing her arms around his chest, she cried softly.

Momentarily stunned, it wasn't long before Peter wrapped his arms around her tightly, murmuring, "Jenny, my precious Jenny, don't cry."

When Jenny's tears abated, Peter tenderly asked. "Why the tears, Jenny?"

"Because … because," she began, her arms still wrapped around him, "what you apologized for was the reason I turned you down. I thought you would never understand—that you would never feel remorse for hurting me, and now that you do, I'm delirious with happiness." She let go of him and gazed into his eyes. "I love you too, Peter and I've been so miserable because I thought it was impossible for us." Her chest heaved with a spasm of breath.

"You *love* me? You really do?" he asked incredulous.

"I do, Peter. I love you."

Peter said a silent prayer of thanks and took her hands in his. His heart was so full, all he could utter was, "Oh, Jenny ... Jenny."

"I have a request," she murmured shyly.

"A request?" he asked, surprised.

"Yes. Will you take me to that wonderful Holmes Department Store after hours tonight and repeat your proposal all over again?"

"Will I ever!" He laughed and picked her up and swung her around, setting her on her feet. Breathlessly, he said, "I can't wait until tonight, Jenny. How about right now?"

"Now? With all the people around?"

"Now!" he exclaimed, his smile wide and entreating. "With all the people around."

That smile which had won Jenny's heart the moment she saw it—left her weak in the knees. "All right, Peter."

At one in their thoughts, Peter was sure that the smile on Jenny's face—the smile which crinkled her beautiful blue eyes and stopped his heart when he first saw her at the refreshment table—now, literally lit up the whole world.

HAND IN HAND, Jenny and Peter entered Holmes Department Store on North Central. Unaware of anyone else in the store, Peter led Jenny to that special table.

Once more, he made a space for her to sit. Jenny laughed when he knelt before her.

"Will you marry me, Jenny?"

Jenny, still smiling, opened up her small shoulder bag, pulled out a folded piece of paper and handed it to him.

Still on his knees, Peter took it, puzzled. Opening it, he saw it was a printed application. At the top it read: APPLICATION FOR FATHERHOOD OF THE CHILDREN OF JENNY, THE KLUTZ, McDUFFY. His joy and happiness burst out in a full, infectious laugh. "I've been waiting a long time for this application, Jenny."

"I've been waiting for a long time to give it to you, Peter Holmes."

He was astounded. "You've had this application made out for a while?"

Smiling, she nodded shyly.

His happiness still tenuous, he questioned. "This application means you're accepting my proposal?"

Jenny's eyes welled up, the tears spilling over; all the love she had held back for so long burst forth. "It does, Peter, oh it does."

Getting up off his knees, he pulled her off the table into his arms and gazed into those expressive blue eyes. His heart brimming over with joy, he bent down and tenderly caressed her lips with his, then without volition pressed them passionately into their softness. Her arms wound about his neck, melding them together in a world of ecstasy—unaware of the small audience that had gathered around them.

A large hand clasped Peter's shoulder. "Hey, mister, this is no place for that kind of stuff," announced a gruff authoritative voice.

Startled, Peter turned and stood eyeball to eyeball with Marv.

"Mr. Holmes!" He shook his head like a punch-drunk boxer. "I don't get it. What *is* this deal you have goin' with your father?" He looked down at the recipient of Peter's amorous affection, and his eyes widened in appreciation.

Peter and Jenny smiled as they watched Marv's reaction.

Marv's eyes squinted in thought. "First, you bring in this weird looking ... uh ... and now you're kissing this uh ..." He stopped, quizzically eyeing Peter who was now chuckling. "Mr. Holmes," he added, pointing to Jenny. "I like this one better."

Jenny and Peter laughed so hard, Marv scratched his head. "I give up."

"Marv, meet my fiancée, Miss Jenny McDuffy."

Marv's grin stretched across the width of his wide face. "Glad to meet you, Miss McDuffy." He turned to Peter. "Does this mean I don't have to put up with you rubbing ladies' legs and ogling all the women coming out of the dressing rooms?"

Peter laughed. "You're getting close to the edge, Marv," he warned. "It means—that you're going to miss the excitement I brought into your dull daily routine."

Marv chuckled. "I guess I will at that, Mr. Holmes."

Peter socked Marv's big shoulder. "I'll have to say, you're the biggest nuisance Holmes Department Stores has on the payroll, but since you're the best security guard on the payroll, I think you deserve a raise."

"Hey! I'll rescue all the damsels in distress on your account—anytime, Mr. Holmes. Thanks!"

Noticing the crowd around them for the first time, Peter could tell by their excitement, their whispering and pointing, that some of them had recognized Jenny as Jeni Logan. He lowered his voice. "Just disperse the crowd around us, Marv, so we can leave this department."

"I'll do that, Mr. Holmes."

Peter took hold of Jenny's hand and almost ran with her to the fine jewelry section. They sat down and anxiously scanned the trays, hoping that their ring hadn't been sold.

"It's still there, Jenny!" Peter exclaimed.

"May I help you?" the male clerk asked.

"Yes. We want a ring in that tray."

"Yes, sir." He pulled it out and placed it on the glass counter.

Peter picked up the ring and placed it tenderly on her finger. "Perfect!"

"Perfect," she said, basking in the warmth of his love.

"We'll take it," Peter said, pulling out his credit card.

The clerk took it, noticing the name. "Any relation to Mr. Ed Holmes?"

"Yes. I'm his son, Peter."

The clerk's eyes lit up. "Glad to meet you, Mr. Holmes. My name's Gary. I'm new here, but I've heard that you're great at marketing."

"Thank you, Gary. That's good to hear. And welcome to Holmes Department Store." He reached over and shook the clerk's hand.

The transaction over, Peter and Jenny left the store quickly.

IN THE CAR, Jenny gazed at the ring on her hand. "It's real,

Peter. We're really engaged!"

"We are, aren't we, Jenny?" Reaching over, he caressed her golden hair. "I have to keep touching you to confirm it. Just this morning, I thought it was hopeless—and here we are together." He leaned over and kissed her, and once more ecstacy enveloped them, fusing their hearts so profoundly, that when the kiss ended, they could only cling to one another, unable to speak for a few moments.

At last, Jenny, her eyes sparkling with happiness, clapped her hands together. "Who are we going to tell our wonderful news to first?" She immediately answered her own question. "Let's drive to your house and tell your mother first," she said fingering her ring tenderly.

"Great idea. We're going to make two people very happy. My parents love you."

"They do? I'm grateful to hear that. I'm very impressed with *them*, Peter." Wistfully, she added, "You would like *my* parents. I wish you could meet them."

"After we're married, we'll work on that, Jenny. How could they raise two such nice children and not eventually be approachable?"

When they arrived at the Holmes residence, they found that Ed's car was in the garage. "They're both home, Jenny," he stated with excitement.

They entered the family room hand in hand. His parents were so surprised they couldn't react for a moment. His mother spoke first. "Peter—Jenny!"

Peter's excitement compelled him to relate their good news without any preamble. "Mom and Dad, Jenny and I are engaged to be married."

Gladys squealed.

Ed grinned. "Does this mean we don't have to kick you out now, you'll go on your own?"

Peter laughed and pulled the application from his pocket and handed it to his dad. "That's right."

Ed and Gladys read it and laughed. Gladys rose to her feet and hugged Jenny, then hugged her son, alternately laughing and crying.

Next, Ed hugged each of them. "Congratulations to you both."

"Peter," Gladys began, "have you told Jenny about your idea to keep us from kicking you out? And then your dad's challenge?"

"No. She knows part of it, of course."

"Well, she needs to know because I have something to tell both of you afterward."

"All right," he said, his curiosity aroused. "You tell her, Mom."

Gladys nodded, smiling. After they were all seated, she related how she and Ed had told Peter he had to move out to an apartment and why. Next, she told Jenny about Peter's marketing idea and how he turned it into an absurd attempt to find a wife.

Jenny looked from Peter to his parents and back. "That's why the certificate and dinner date?"

Peter nodded, grinning.

Jenny gave a short laugh. "It *was* an absurd way to find a wife."

Peter smiled smugly. "Well—it worked, didn't it?"

Her eyes full of amusement, Jenny gazed at Peter. "Unbelievably, yes. It's incredible that I was in the store when you were there, Peter."

Ed was all smiles. "And Peter got his comeuppance when that one-in-a-million young woman turned out to be Melba Beasley."

Everyone laughed.

"Speaking of Melba," Jenny said, addressing Peter, "remember when on the way to the restaurant that night I asked you why the dinner date with you?"

"Yeah. How could I forget? Melba Beasley asked me, in a condescending tone, if I thought that going out to dinner with me was a reward for some girl."

Ed and Gladys burst into laughter.

When the fun had died down, Jenny's glowing face gazed up at Peter. "As it turned out, that date was definitely a reward for some girl—especially me."

Peter couldn't resist. He leaned over and kissed her right there in front of his parents, then said, "Thank you, my sunshine girl. But the reward is all mine."

"After that tender exchange," Gladys began, "it seems an appropriate time to tell you what I promised I would." She then related how, right after Ed had challenged Peter to find that courteous young woman, she had expressed all her concerns to him in private. "He told me that he agreed with everyone of them. I asked him, 'Why then did you challenge Peter in this ridiculous thing?' Now this is what I want you both to know: He said, 'I just had a *feeling* I should go along with it.' We've always paid attention to Peter's dad's feelings, Jenny, because they've always turned out to be inspired."

"You didn't tell me that, Dad," Peter said in quiet deference.

"I wondered if I trusted the feeling as much as your mother, Peter, because your idea was so farcical and unrealistic to begin with."

"As it turned, out," Jenny began, awe in her voice, "you *were* inspired."

"He was!" Gladys exclaimed, "and we need to celebrate. I have your favorite casserole in the oven, Peter. How about inviting Harriet and Kyle and Harriet's grandmother to join us?"

"That sounds wonderful, 'Mom,'" Jenny said.

The word, *mom*, thrilled Gladys and she murmured a quiet thanks to Jenny.

Peter stepped over to the phone and dialed Jenny's place hoping to find Kyle and Harriet. Kyle answered.

"Kyle, this is Peter."

"We've been waiting for you and Jenny. Where are you?"

"We're over at my place. Mom wanted me to invite both of you and Harrie's grandmother to dinner tonight."

Kyle was silent for a moment. "Why? Something special going on?"

"Come and find out."

THE "ENGAGEMENT" PARTY, as Jenny and Peter would always refer to it, was memorable. Kyle's happiness over his sister coming to her senses, and Harriet and Camille's happiness for Peter and Jenny added to the joy Ed and Gladys felt.

After an enjoyable meal, they all gathered in the family room. Peter, his arm around Jenny, was just getting comfortable when Jenny, her eyes twinkling with mischief, asked him to tell the group about the day he tried to reward her for being a courteous customer. "I think we need to tell them what happened when I asked the clerk to call for Marv, the security guard. Remember the bad time Marv gave you when you asked him to tell me who you were?"

"I would certainly like to hear about that," Gladys said. "Peter told us very little."

Some of Peter's agreeableness waned. "Let's skip that part."

Ignoring Peter's statement, Ed suggested he tell about the tackle.

Jenny's eyes alight with curiosity, she exclaimed, "Yes! And, Peter," she added, grinning, "I am very curious about what Marv meant when he said, 'Does this mean I don't have to put up with you rubbing ladies' legs?'"

"Hey, Peter," Kyle interjected, grinning, "this sounds interesting. What actually goes on in the Holmes Department Stores? Come on, tell us all."

Harriet, though having heard it all before, was anxious to hear it again, especially since she hadn't told Kyle any of it. "Yes, tell every detail, Peter."

All agreed enthusiastically—all except Peter whose tan had turned a deeper color. "All right. I'll humiliate myself for everyone's entertainment."

And so he did.

SIX WEEKS LATER, Peter and Jenny were married in the Mesa Temple, and as hoped, Jenny's klutziness disappeared with the birth of their first child ten months later, a son they named Peter Edwin Holmes III.

Little Eddie, as he was called, was loved and fawned over by his aunts, uncles, and cousins on his father's side, and by his uncle Kyle and aunt Harriet on his mother's side. His grandparents from

California soon relented and joined the grandparents in Arizona in spoiling him with love and attention.

And so, Peter and Jenny lived happily ever after—almost, that is, between the ups and downs that life brings with a family of six—three boys and three girls.

Epilogue

The mystery of Peter Holmes' homely fiancée, Melba Beasley, who mysteriously disappeared and was never heard of again, remains unsolved to this day. It would now and then come to the lips of Maribell Gunther and other alumni of the singles ward as they recalled that infamous banquet, and the outrageous shenanigans of "Casanova Pete."